THE SURGICAL VICTIM
Franklin Delano Pitts, a sixteen-year-old black basketball player, admitted to the hospital for simple surgery and released as a corpse . . .

THE MEDICAL MURDERER
Joe Thatcher, a hopelessly incompetent, alcoholic doctor, who performed countless unnecessary operations before making his fatal mistake . . .

THE INSURANCE COVER-UP
A frightening conspiracy of deadly silence involving forged records, attempted blackmail, bribery, prejudice, and bloody violence . . .

AND THE LEGAL CRUSADER
Yancey Marshall, a small-time lawyer faced with the biggest challenge of his career—to take on the whole medical establishment in a no-tactics-barred battle to save the unsuspecting people of Pine Hill, Georgia, from a cure that could kill them . . .

Malpractice

"Strong stuff here . . . to keep readers scared and entertained"

—*Kirkus Reviews*

The Best in Fiction From SIGNET

Malpractice

a novel by

JOHN R. FEEGEL

A SIGNET BOOK
NEW AMERICAN LIBRARY
TIMES MIRROR

The chapter at the end of this book is from *Not a Stranger*, by
John R. Feegel, an NAL BOOK to be published in 1983.

SIGNET TRADEMARK REG. U.S. PAT. OFF. AND FOREIGN COUNTRIES
REGISTERED TRADEMARK—MARCA REGISTRADA
HECHO EN CHICAGO, U.S.A.

SIGNET, SIGNET CLASSICS, MENTOR, PLUME, MERIDIAN AND NAL
BOOKS are published by The New American Library, Inc.,
1633 Broadway, New York, New York 10019

First Signet Printing, October, 1982

1 2 3 4 5 6 7 8 9

PRINTED IN THE UNITED STATES OF AMERICA

PUBLISHER'S NOTE

To small-town doctors and small-town lawyers and the people they selflessly serve.

Chapter 1

THERE were two gas stations left in Pine Hill, Georgia. Three, if you counted the self-service pump at the convenience store. There were also a pharmacy, a two-story department store (the upper level had been closed for years), and a sixty-four-bed hospital. The medical staff at the hospital consisted of three GPs with full privileges and seven women hired as nurses, although only one was an RN.

The courthouse was located on the village square behind the Confederate monument and displayed a cracking, silver-painted dome and random pigeon droppings. The courthouse, constructed of red brick, enclosed a rotunda accessible only from the second floor. In the lobby a plaque exhorted the town's dwindling population to remember the struggle between the states, but not many of them still gave a damn. Even Sherman had bypassed the town in his incendiary march through Atlanta to the sea.

At one time, logging had been the major industry, and for a while, gold mining until a bigger strike near Dahlonega shut down the thin vein. In later years, there was little or nothing to support the twenty-five hundred or so who persistently called Pine Hill home and refused to move on. They scratched meager existences from the begrudging rocky soil and studied each other twice weekly at religious services offered by similar protestant sects now fragmented beyond all hope of survival.

The highway to Chattanooga had also bypassed Pine Hill, sealing its fate forever and immortalizing the governor in whose term it had been built. Older residents (there were hardly any others) vilified his name and blamed him for the failure of their children to return from the regional high school, some twenty-three miles away.

For better or for worse Pine Hill had remained the county seat, clinging desperately to the courthouse as its only identification. Most of the people in the county preferred to live nearer the new business district, the high school, and the hated governor's highway, and, therefore, so did the lawyers.

Yancey Marshall, the exception, had returned to Pine Hill after law school in Atlanta and opened an office. This choice had made him at once the best, the worst, and the only lawyer in town, and at twenty-nine years old he accepted all three roles with surprising grace.

While the courthouse was highly regarded by the townspeople, lawyers in general were not. In fact, few of the citiezns found any need for formal legal services, preferring to settle their infrequent disputes in private. "As far as I'm concerned," one of them had said, "a good handshake is better'n a piece of paper any day." It was, they said, the decent Christian way to get things done.

Yancey Marshall, who preferred red-and-black checkered outer shirts, midcalf boots, and seasonal hunting to the practice of law, quietly agreed. "For me," he had remarked in law school, "criminal law is just a racial fight between those that have and those that don't, and torts is nothing more than a public display of poor manners between folks who forgot how to forgive each other." He also found the U.S. Constitution an interesting document to study but confusing, inconsistent, and not often applicable in his part of Georgia. "The law," Yancey said, "would do well to stick to recording deeds and providing a place for folks to file their wills."

Mr. Marshall had opened his office over the drugstore. The rent was cheap and Ray Bexley, the pharmacist, had sweetened the deal by carpeting the outer office and painting the back stairs that served as a private entrance. The carpet had been salvaged from a Primitive Baptist Church that closed after its pastor admitted to an affair with a woman, not his wife. Bexley had wisely remarked that none of the scandal had rubbed off on the carpet, although three stained areas made Yancey wonder whenever the sunlight hit them. Yancey Marshall was not married, and quietly refused to classify intercourse between consenting adults as anything but their own business. Meager fantasies, but enough to brighten an afternoon, came to him whenever he thought of Heb Cogley's furtive sexual efforts with Mrs. Denton somewhere inside the PBC out in the valley. The Reverend Cogley had been a sinewy wisp of a man and Ella Denton a corpulent carboholic whose abdominal wrinkles were probably indistinguishable from her vaginal recesses.

Mr. Marshall, as the townspeople called him in deference to his legal training, had saved his textbooks from law school, displaying all twelve of them on a plain shelf behind his desk. With the courthouse across the street, there was no need to buy the appellate volumes. An LEAA grant to the sheriff's office had provided a full set of Southern 2d *Reporters,* and that was good enough for Yancey Marshall, visiting judges, and the sheriff, who, by the way, could not read. This singular lack of talent had not prevented Thad Gallow from serving well as sheriff for more than twenty years. He could, after all, draw his name, and had common sense enough to keep several literate deputies on staff at all times.

It was a gray, overcast September day, threatening a flake or two of early snow on the mountain west of town but still comfortable in front of the courthouse. The Texaco station had closed early because its proprietor's cows had escaped their pasture and were reported marching on Atlanta single file, along the county road. The incident had provided a laugh for the daily inhabitants of the square and then an equal number of volunteers to round the herd up once the joke had been enjoyed. Their departure had left the square silent and almost lifeless, except for two squirrels on the lawn and Eula Pitts.

There were not many blacks living in Ridge County, making Eula Pitts's appearance on the street immediately identifiable, although there was no one there to see her. She looked older than her thirty-four years and walked slightly bent over, a pose adopted from her mother and her mother's mother in a concerted effort to remain inconspicuous and thereby trouble-free.

Josh Pitts had been her second marriage. Her first husband had been killed in a ditch cave-in when the new storm drain was being laid. The first marriage had been childless, but she and Josh had produced a tall boy and a fat stupid girl who, by the age of fifteen, had miscarried twice. Dr. Thatcher had tied her tubes after the last one but never told the girl or her mother. "Something's got to be done," he remarked to his colleague Dr. Brownlea. "Leave 'em be and they'll breed everyone else right out of town." There was, of course, no argument on that point from Brownlea.

Eula did not notice that the courthouse square was empty. She seemed worried or preoccupied, not an unusual frame of mind for her. With Josh's hit-or-miss employment with the county's street maintenance crew, and her own poorly paid position as the housekeeper at the motel, there was just never enough money to keep her from worries and preoccupations. "They's hardly enough time to work, eat, sleep, and pray," she told her children. "Even then, you has to keep right after all of them things to get 'em done properly."

Her son, Franklin Delano, had been somewhat of an exception to the family rule. He had grown tall, lean, and interested in the world around him. Eula knew his curiosities would one day lead him to Atlanta and probably into trouble, but still she hoped she would find a way to send him to Morehouse College after high school. He had been the only one in the family to start high school and she hoped he would become a preacher. That *would* be nice, she had mentioned to Josh, but she wasn't going to get her heart set on it, just in case Franklin wanted to do something else. Now something else would be all right, but a preacher would be perfect!

Franklin had avoided all serious discussion concerning his intended career. For the time being his best talent was displayed on the high school basketball floor and his personal dreams ran as high as the Atlanta Hawks. He never spoke openly about pro basketball, of course, not even to Josh, but he knew an athletic scholarship was a better ticket out of Pine Hill than anything his folks could provide for him. He was the only black boy on the team, but this was not a racial gesture. It was because he was deadly from the corner.

Eula's mind was on that boy as she trudged up Main Street and turned in behind the drugstore. She had seen the signs pointing to the back stairs many times before, of course, but a lawyer's office was just not one of those places in Pine Hill where a sensible black woman goes to visit, unless she has important business to discuss.

This cool, gray September day Eula Pitts had very important business to discuss.

Chapter 2

RIDGE County Hospital had been built in 1947, but extensive renovations in the early seventies, using Hill-Burton funds, had obscured the original floor plan. In the early days, there had been a separate facility for black patients. This had been a converted two-story house and was less than inadequate. Even then surgery on blacks had been performed at the county hospital, followed by a hurried transfer to the "other" facility to avoid integrated floor care. Nursing skills "over there" had been poor and the rate of postoperative complications enormous. Ironically, the infection rate was lower. At that time the doctors had attributed this to hardy black stock and natural immunity, but modern hospital epidemiologists and nosocomial experts would have recognized that postoperatively the black patients were left alone. White patients' wounds were frequently inspected, redressed, and thereby infected. However small this consolation, the separate and hardly equal facilities were forced to come together shortly after Mrs. Brown decided to sue the Topeka Board of Education. Failure to integrate by the late sixties would have meant a loss of precious federal funds for the renovation. Even in a place as remote as Pine Hill, outside money had a way of speaking clearly.

Doctors Brownlea, Thatcher, and Kern were the only physicians who had remained after the new hospital opened in Dahlonega. Not that there had been a mass exodus. In fact, the staff had never been more than five MDs at any one time, and that counted old Dr. Thompson who went blind and retired just before he died. Brownlea, at sixty-two, was acknowledged as senior by the other two. He had graduated in the lower third of his class at the Medical College of Georgia, and after a one-year general internship in Augusta, had settled in Pine Hill. He considered himself a family physician long before it had become a specialty, and in his later years, had given up surgery and obstetrics. In his day he had removed his share of tonsils, appendixes, and the occasional gall bladder when, as he put it, the operating room was "less complicated." But when Joseph Thatcher arrived, Brownlea bowed to his superior training, better experience, and "modern" methods. At least the methods had been modern at that time, some twenty years ago. Thatcher was an Emory graduate with two years' training in surgery at Grady Memorial. He was fifteen years younger than Brownlea and five under Charlie Kern. The townspeople said Thatcher was a pretty good surgeon when he wasn't drinking, but Joe knew that wasn't really true. That's why he drank.

Charlie Kern did his best to remain uninvolved. He could never remember a time when he did not feel inadequate and scared. He was frightened at military school as a boy, intimidated as an undergraduate at Chapel Hill, and petrified at medical school in Virginia. For Dr. Kern, Pine Hill was more than an isolated small town in northern Georgia. It was a refuge.

While the doctors maintained separate offices, they often shared responsibilities for patient care in the hospital, Thatcher deferring to Brownlea in medicine, Brownlea to Thatcher in surgical cases, and Kern to both of them in everything.

Surgery, obstetrics, and the more complicated medical patients were housed on the upper floor of the two-story building. Simple medicine and the five beds designated as pediatrics were downstairs. The arrangement didn't totally please the inspector from the Joint Commission on Hospital Accreditation, but little improvement could be hoped for, given the isolation of the town and the fact that none of the three doctors gave a rap for AMA approval anyway. Warnings from the commission were ignored and only lip service was paid to proposed improvements at the brief annual staff meetings. The three doctors were confident the patients were satisfied and if any of them weren't, they were free to go elsewhere, or at least so it was said.

Cal Brownlea paused at the nursing station on the second floor, reached over the counter, and helped himself to a cigarette from Mary Atkins's half-filled pack. She called them Pell Mells while Cal stuck to a more literal pronunciation. She flashed her eyebrows knowingly, but did not comment on the doctor's newest violation of his own resolution to quit.

"Mrs. Carrington's urine is showing a trace of sugar by dipstick," Mrs. Atkins reported flatly. She was in her early forties and was one of the LPNs. When she had first been moved to the floor station, she felt nervous and unqualified, but these fears had faded after none of her obvious inadequacies were mentioned by the medical staff. She was somehow better than the incompetent RN she had replaced, and occasionally slept with Dr. Thatcher when he got drunk and felt lonely. Their relationship had never ripened into a true affair, and had lately become only a memory for both of them, but it was enough to insure her position.

"You adjusted her insulin?" Brownlea asked, sorting through the short stack of charts in front of him. He held the cigarette in the corner of his mouth so that his eye escaped the smoke as he read.

"I followed the schedule."

"She'll straighten out. But keep an eye on her." He dropped the first chart on the counter, its metal clipboard clattering loudly.

"And the Beasley girl?" the nurse asked. She knew she had to get all her questions in while Brownlea was there in front of her. Once he returned to his office, she would have a slim chance of getting through by telephone.

"What about her?" The chart he was reading was not the Beasley girl's.

"She wants to quit breast-feeding and put the baby on formula."

"Good. It'll be easier for all of us. Tell her it will make her breasts look better when she's older."

Nurse Atkins had breast-fed both of her babies and her breasts still looked good enough. "Can I put her on hormones to shut off her milk?"

"I already did. Right after the delivery." Brownlea looked at the nurse and winked. "I knew she'd see it my way." He had made it to the sixth chart, scanning rapidly and making an occasional entry on the order sheet.

"Is there anything special?" she asked.

"I want a blood count on old Jack Peacock."

"Stat?"

"Tomorrow. If he's still alive. We've run his lab bill up far enough. He'll never pay it anyway."

"What about his leg? What did the pathologist say?" There was no real concern in the nurse's voice.

"What can he say? It was gangrene. We all smelled it. He'll send back some long-worded report from Dahlonega, but it will be gangrene just the same."

"You want me to phone it to you when they bring it over?" Atkins reached for the charts with the new orders and began to leaf through them. Brownlea's orders were often confusing and never quite legible.

"I'll catch up with it later. I'll sign it out in the record room." Everyone knew that might take weeks. Brownlea's stack of incomplete charts was taller than anyone else's, but not by much. It often took him weeks to plow through his incompletes, searching his fading memory to add missing progress notes or other information so that the charts could be filed. The record librarian had given up trying to get any of the doctors to conform to the rules. Charts had to be completed within twenty-four hours of discharge. Everyone knew that. It was only during the few days preceding inspection by the Joint Commission that there was a flurry of activity in the chart room and even then many of the belated entries were fiction or rapidly designed ambiguity to get the job done.

"Did Dr. Thatcher look in on Elmer Ferguson?" Brownlea asked, pausing at his last chart.

Nurse Atkins gave a feeble shrug. "I put your request for consultation in his box two days ago, but . . ."

Brownlea nodded knowingly. "Well, he'll come around. I saw him last night and he didn't look too bad."

Atkins knew that when applied to Thatcher the diagnosis of "not too bad" was frequently terrible. She knew that better than any of the others. One night she had found Dr. Thatcher collapsed in his own vomit on the floor of the examining room and had put him to bed in the isolation ward to sleep it off. On that night he had been on rounds, or so he had thought. At least he had not tried to operate, Atkins had acknowledged philosophically. On other nights he had not been as prudent.

Brownlea wore green golf slacks and a yellow sports shirt, opened at the neck. His black-and-white saddle shoes did not match the outfit, but for Pine Hill it was high fashion.

"I'll stop downstairs at the other station, if you want to catch me," Brownlea said, turning from the desk.

"Yes, Doctor," she said. She watched him walk away, his step seeming heavier than before. "Oh, Dr. Brownlea," she called. "Is there any word on the Pitts boy?"

He paused to glare at the nurse without speaking. Then, trapped by her question, he shook his head and said, "No. Nothing yet. But they done finished his autopsy."

The nurse nodded as if she understood, but there was no way that she could, and both of them knew it. Autopsy reports were seldom shown to floor nurses—or anyone else for that matter.

Chapter 3

I N Dahlonega things were a little better. The hospital there was two and a half times larger and the medical staff a lot younger. They watched each other as much as they did their patients, and problems were seldom ignored. William B. Markham had become the first pathologist to practice exclusively at Dahlonega. At first he had been concerned about practicing alone, but the slow, even pace of the small hospital had eventually reassured him. After his fifth year of solo practice, he had come to enjoy life in a small town. Not as small as Pine Hill, by any means, but a far cry from the frantic pace he had escaped in Atlanta.

Markham was a transplanted northerner. Raised in Massachusetts, he had gone to medical school in Boston. Milder winters and the reputation of the pathology residency at Emory had lured him south, and after nine years, he no longer had thoughts about going back. He had married a lab tech from Emory and she had jumped for joy when, in the last year of his training, he told her they were looking for a pathologist in Dahlonega. She had come from a small town south of Macon, and nothing sounded better than the chance to get out of Atlanta.

Pathology services in Dahlonega had been provided by a group from Gainesville, Georgia, before Markham took the job. The administrator had always felt the hospital could provide enough business to support a full-time pathologist, but the Gainesville group had discouraged that kind of thinking. They even tried to recruit Markham after he had accepted the job. Markham had seen the group as an extension of the bureaucracy he had left in Atlanta and had decided to go it alone. That had meant little or no help from Gainesville and two full years without a day off. In the end he had worked out a vacation schedule with a pathologist from Atlanta, and sent his problem slides to Emory for consultation. In time the Gainesville group had come to respect him as a north country colleague, but only for the purpose of agreeing on uniform fees for lab procedures.

Markham was tall, lean, and prematurely gray. His slow gait and his hesitant speech gave him a superficial resemblance to a southerner, but this was quickly dispelled by his careful attention to detail. He became annoyed whenever things in the lab were not completed on time and was openly intolerant of inaccuracy. Lab techs found him hard to work for at first, mistaking his professional demeanor for repressed anger. Later, when they got to know him, they found Billy Markham an almost infallible leader, loyal to their causes whenever a personnel dispute arose with the administration.

The hospital in Pine Hill had sought pathology coverage from Dahlonega shortly after Markham's arrival. Everyone knew Pine Hill would never be able to afford its own pathologist, and Dahlonega was a lot closer than Gainesville. The loss of Pine Hill did not make the Gainesville pathologists any happier with Markham, but the two administrators had been pleased. Markham gave Pine Hill quicker service on surgical reports, and his inexperience had provided both administrators with an early opportunity to cheat him on fees. After a while Billy figured it out and the fees had been raised, but for a while, it was a windfall for Pine Hill. Some of the windfall had, of course, found its way very quietly into the pockets of the Dahlonega administrator, where it was carefully hidden.

"I ought to get over here at least once a week," Markham had announced to the administrator at Pine Hill. "You need that much for quality control and to keep the girls in the lab in line."

"Can't afford once a week," Hamp Jessup, the administrator, had replied. "We'll have to make do with once a month."

Billy knew this would not be enough but it was better than the Gainesville group had provided and it fulfilled the minimum for the JCAH. Markham also knew the Pine Hill doctors weren't too interested in his newer diagnostic tests anyway. All they wanted from him was to read the surgical slides, do the infrequent autopsies, and to legitimize the lab by wallpapering the place with his hard-earned certificates. Under medicare he could legally supervise three hospital laboratories, and more than anything else, Pine Hill needed his credentials.

Days before, the courier service had arrived with the routine surgical specimens from Pine Hill. Markham had arranged the little plastic pots of formalin and tissue in front of his cutting board like soldiers on parade. He had read the labels on the pots carefully since he knew that no one at Pine Hill paid much attention to accuracy or patient names. One of the containers had read, "Pitts boy—appendix—Thatcher." As he opened it, Markham had been pleased to see that they had at least correctly identified the organ. Inside the pot there was an appendix, slightly curled on itself and hardened by the formaldehyde.

Markham's job was to describe the specimens removed at surgery and then to cut them for microscopic sections. The surgeon would of course describe the specimen in his report of the operation, but an independent examination by the pathologist served as a basic cross check. With specimens that were grossly normal the microscopic studies were often unnecessary, but by doing both examinations, the hospital and the pathologist were able to bill for two procedures. Since Blue Cross and medicare allowed two payments, neither Markham nor the administrators made any attempt to change it.

He had adjusted the microphone on his tape recorder with a wet gloved hand to drone, "The specimen is received in formalin and consists of a vermiform appendix measuring six by point five centimeters. The surface is smooth, gray, and shiny. The vascular pattern appears normal." He had then placed the organ on his cork board and made several quick slices across it. "On sectioning," he had continued, "the wall is uniform in appearance and the lumen contains soft brown feces."

Later, under his microscope, Markham saw a normal mucosal pattern with no inflammatory infiltrate into the wall. His diagnosis was "vermiform appendix, no diagnostic features."

"Score one more normal appendix for Joe Thatcher," he had mumbled out loud as he replaced the slide in the tray next to his microscope. For this exercise in futility the hospital would demand thirty-five dollars from the patient or his insurance company, and Markham would extract his percentage. This kind of game did not cure any rare diseases or advance medical science, but it did keep the pathology department and the hospital solvent. In addition it fulfilled the requirement of the Joint Commission that all tissue removed at surgery be examined by a pathologist and a report added to the patient's chart. The JCAH hoped that would slow down substandard surgeons, but everyone knew the regulation was useless.

For Pine Hill the normal reports had no corrective effect. How could they? With a cooperative staff of three, who was left to complain when normal tissue was removed? But the mockery went on, Markham supplying the routine reports, occasionally critical, and the Pine Hill staff ignoring them, protective of each other. But the job got done. So far he had never reported false pathological findings on a Pine Hill specimen, and no one had asked him to. The arrangement had become comfortable.

Now Markham sat at his desk reviewing his autopsy notes of Franklin Delano Pitts. The body had come to him as a surprise. In fact, the slide on his normal appendix had not even dried enough to be filed.

"This is the unembalmed, well-developed body of a Negro male, appearing approximately his stated age of sixteen," he had written on his clipboard. "Black" had not yet become popular in that part of Georgia. Thatcher had an even more offensive name for them and made no effort to hide it.

Markham employed this opening jargon out of habit. In fact, Franklin Delno was larger and taller than the average sixteen-year-old in Pine Hill, but his basketball stature was not an important autopsy observation. The report would carry his height and weight if anyone cared. Without doubt, Markham's major finding would overshadow these statistics, if he left it in the autopsy report. The Pitts boy's case was the first time in his career the pathologist had ever considered a deletion. His job was to tell the whole truth, but this time he was not happy with the task. He had written the preliminary report in longhand, not to insure attention to detail as he had done when he was a resident, but to keep the findings from his secretary. The secretaries normally didn't comprehend many of the pathological terms, but even in Dahlonega they could understand plain English.

He continued to read silently to himself, making an occasional irrelevant correction and wearing an uncharacteristic frown. He had not noticed the clock and was equally oblivious to the opening and closing of his office door as his wife entered.

"Hi, Billy," she drawled happily. She wore a light dress that tantalized by a glimpse of her underthings every male she passed. The scent of her favorite perfume swirled around the room, announcing her arrival simultaneously with her greeting. It was sweeter and cheaper than Billy preferred, but more acceptable to the other doctors' wives. Pathologists' wives were not supposed to compete.

"Oh, hi, Carrie," Markham said, glancing up from his report and then at his watch. "That time already?"

"Uh-huh," she purred, leaning over the desk to accept his little kiss. "Unless you want to have lunch in the hospital cafeteria."

"Black-eyed peas, greasy pork chops, and rice with gravy?" he asked. "Spare me."

"You might get the same tonight," she said.

"What's tonight?"

"Brownleas. Did you forget?"

Markham sighed deeply. "I think I wanted to. He's a pain in the ass."

"He's worse. He's also *very* boring. I've heard about his duck hunting a hundred times." She bent her neck slightly to glance at the papers on her husband's desk without really caring. "Can you stop for lunch?"

"Yeah. Why not?" he said, snatching away the handwritten yellow sheets and locking them in his top desk drawer.

"The atomic bomb?" she asked.

"Something like that," he said, grabbing his jacket. "Where to? The Wagon Wheel?"

"Whatever you say. How many choices do we have in Big D?" She looked at him as he twisted his tweed jacket off the back of the chair and squirmed into it. He was upset and she could tell.

"I want two bourbon old-fashioneds and one of Bernie's little steaks, charred black," he announced.

"You must have had a hell of a morning."

"It could have been worse," he said. He paused to look at his wife through heavy eyes.

Carrie put herself between the door and her husband. She slid her arms around his waist under his jacket and held her face tightly to his chest. The pleasant smell of her morning shampoo drifted up to him and for a moment, they were in bed together. Markham held her tightly and looked straight ahead.

"Tell me what it is," she said softly.

"Not yet. I have a couple of things to sort out first."

Chapter 4

E U L A Pitts was out of breath at the top of the stairs to Yancey Marshall's office. When she worked her dust mop over at the hotel, she assumed a slow pace that would last her all day, but stairs were another matter. The Mountain View Motel was a single-story structure with twenty-two rooms and no bar. It was halfway between Pine Hill and Dahlonega and had seen better days. It was still cheap, but it was too conspicuous for local guests and a little too remote for travelers. Actually, it had a respectable view of the mountains, and business picked up a little in the fall when people came up from Atlanta to see the leaves change.

The sign on the office door said, "Yancey Marshall, Attorney at Law." Eula carefully avoided touching it when she knocked. She knew someone would have to clean it if it got smudged. In fact, Yancey would have had to polish his own sign, if it were to be polished at all, but he didn't give a damn.

Her gentle knock did not make much noise, but the door, already slightly ajar, began to swing open, slowly. Eula paused on the wide, top step, waiting for someone to say "Come in" or whatever, but no one spoke. The outer office, suitable for a receptionist, was empty, except for a fat, worn leather chair and a lifeless schoolhouse clock on the wall. She listened carefully for a few moments, wondering if there really was a lawyer at the top of the stairs as the sign had promised. Eula Pitts was not one to barge in before she was clearly invited. Being a maid at a small-town motel had taught her that much. "When a man takes a room, Eula," the motel proprietor had lectured her on the day of her grateful employment, "he has a right to do whatever he wants in there, so we *never* walk in on him unannounced." Eula understood that rule and lived by it. She accepted the fact that a man might take off his clothes to make love to his wife—although, Josh never did that—but she saw no reason for a man to leave the light on while he was doing it or to walk around stark naked, not even to the bathroom.

"Hallo?" she sang, breaking the word in the middle like a hymn. She had waited long enough and was beginning to get cold feet. She wasn't sure what one was supposed to say to a lawyer. She knew how to say howdy-do to the doctors and how not to speak at all to the judge and how to answer questions quickly for the deputy sheriff, but lawyers were still a mystery.

There was a clacking sound from the inner office that Eula could not identify. She stepped into the reception area and stood with her back to the open door.

"Mr. Marshall?" she called, a little louder. The clacking noise stopped.

"Is there someone there?" Yancey Marshall asked loudly.

"Yessuh. Eula Pitts is he'yuh, Mr. Marshall." She turned and closed the door quietly. The reception area was poorly lighted and the window was half covered by a thick green drape that needed cleaning.

Yancey appeared in the doorway between the two offices with a shotgun in his hands.

"Lord Almighty," Eula said softly.

"Come in, come in," Yancey said, lowering the shotgun. His hands were oily and the office had a metallic smell that painfully reminded Eula of her son's bicycle repairs on the back porch. "What's the name again?" Yancey asked, laying the shotgun across a low stack of law books on his desk.

"Eula Pitts." She pronounced Pitts in more than one syllable. She glanced uncomfortably around the sparsely furnished office and then stared at the gun on the desk.

"Mrs? Pitts?" Marshall asked. He came around again and positioned a small straight wooden chair for the woman, leaving an oily hand print on the back of it. "Pardon the mess, Eula. I'm trying to get the cobwebs out of my shotgun before the season starts."

"Oh," she said, somewhat relieved. She had never realized shotguns accumulated cobwebs in the off season, but then she accepted the fact she knew nothing about guns.

"What can I do for you?" he asked, wiping his hands on a rag.

"It's about my boy, Franklin," she said, hesitating.

"Is he in jail?" Marshall sat down behind the desk wearily and put one foot up on the corner.

"No suh. . . . He's dead." She paused and swallowed hard.

Marshall's foot fell from the corner of the desk. He looked at the black woman's emotionless face. The entire history of the South was there, but it hid her pain. The lawyer allowed a moment to solemnize the announcement.

"An accident?" he asked.

She shook her head. "Uh-uh. He took sick. I carried him on over to the doctor and they put him in the hospital."

"Pine Hill?" Marshall asked needlessly. He knew "the hospital" could mean only Pine Hill when Eula Pitts said it. The hospital would have had a name if she meant anywhere else.

"Uh-huh. He come down with belly pains and cascadin'. It went on for a couple of days before I carried him to Dr. Brownlea." For Eula and all other rural southern blacks cascading meant vomiting.

Marshall nodded. The choice of physician was also obvious. Most of them went to Brownlea, even after he closed the separate entrance to conform with the new civil rights regulations.

"Did Dr. Brownlea find out what was ailin' him, Eula?"

"He told me it was his appendix. We figured he knew best." She adjusted herself in the chair but found no comfort. Her face had started to shine with perspiration now and she fidgeted with the strap on her handbag. She wore a faded dress and brown cotton stockings that made her legs look slightly gray. Her shoes were worn and cracked along the sides where the leather and her corns had finally stopped fighting each other, years before.

"How old was your boy, Eula?" Yancey asked compassionately.

"He were sixteen. Played basketball with the high school."

Marshall acknowleged the accomplishment with a respectful nod.

"They kept him in the hospital for a day or so and tole me they had to do some tests."

"And?"

"Dr. Thatcher come in and said he had to operate."

"On his appendix?"

"Uh-huh. He done took them out. 'Course he 'splained how the appendix was all rotten, and tole me not to worry."

Marshall had begun to make notes on a yellow pad, but as yet, he wasn't sure why. "Go on, Eula. What happened next?"

The woman showed her palms helplessly. They were pink and sweaty. "After the operation, he got better for a couple of days, but then the pain come back real bad. The doctors, they come and looked in on him, but he got the fever. They tole me he's going to be all right, but he commenced to lookin' worse and worse. They they put them needles in his arms and his leg. He didn't even know me by then." Her voice broke with a small sob.

"He was delirious?"

"Ravin' and shoutin', that's what he was, Mr. Marshall, and I . . ." The story became too much for her. She lowered her head to hide the lonely tear that ran down her cheek. She brushed it aside with her hand and wiped her nose with her thumb before she found the strength to continue.

"Josh—that's my man—he come up to see him on the last night. He don't like no hospitals, but he got to worryin' when I told him how bad Franklin was lookin'. And when Josh seed him and heard him talkin' out of his head like that, he broke down and cried. Then he got mad."

"What did he do?"

"Josh started yellin' at the nurses and sayin' all kinds of bad stuff about the hospital and the doctors. They called the sheriff and a deputy come."

"Josh got arrested."

"No. They just put him out and tole him not to come back no more. He stayed in the truck. But they let me stay in the room with Franklin. Right to the end."

"When did Franklin die, Eula?"

"That same night. He never did get no better. After a while, he stopped yellin' and got awful quiet. I thought maybe he was going to sleep at last, but after a while, the nurse come in to check him. She carried a shot to give him, but when she seed how quiet he was layin', she listened to his heart with them things you put in your ears. And then she looked up at me. She didn't say *nothin'*. But I could tell from the look on her face. My Franklin was gone." She was crying openly now and accepted Yancey's handkerchief even though it wasn't clean.

"Did she—call anybody or do anything?" Yancey asked softly.

"She run out of the room yellin' and carryin' on somethin' terrible. And then a lot of people come into the room. They put a mask with a balloon on it over Franklin's face and started in bangin' on Franklin's chest like they was fixin' to beat him to death!"

"They were just trying to save him, Eula. They're supposed to do that."

"Oh, yessuh. I knows that now," she said, recovering a little. "They come over to me and made me go out in the hall so I couldn't see what they was up to. They brung in some more stuff to stick in his arm. I know, 'cuz I seed the needles." Her reddened eyes became very wide. "After a while, they all come out of the room and the nurse tole me . . . Franklin was dead."

"Did they let you see him then?" The lawyer's tone had softened until his questions came almost in a whisper.

"Uh-huh. They had him all cleaned up and he was covered with a new sheet and all the arm tubes was gone. He looked sorta peaceful, if you knows what I mean."

Yancey nodded slowly. "Did they let Josh come up and see him?"

"No suh!" she said indignantly. "They said Josh might never be let back in the hospital again, 'count of the trouble he made. They told me to go out to the truck and tell him while they got the papers ready."

The mention of papers got the lawyer's attention immediately. "What papers, Eula?"

"For the ortopsy."

"Oh." Marshall paused for a moment, searching the woman's story for a legal problem. So far, she hadn't given him much to work with. He assumed she would get around to the hospital bill. Most patients didn't realize how expensive medical care had become.

"You signed the permit for the autopsy?" he asked encouragingly.

"I didn't want to at first, but the nurse say they might find something in Franklin's body that might could help somebody else."

"Pine Hill. The great teaching hospital," Yancey said cynically.

"Suh?"

"Nothin', Eula. You go right ahead. Tell me the whole story." And get to the damned problem, he added mentally. He glanced at his watch and then at the shotgun. Some of the oil had dripped onto the cover of the law book, causing a dark spot in the middle of the title. His movements were deliberately slow and nonthreatening as he moved the gun off the desk and into the corner behind the desk. He rubbed the oil spot with the rag, making it worse.

"That's goin' to need some Texize on it, Mr. Marshall," Eula said professionally. "Nothin' else is goin' to cut through that oil."

"Thank you, Eula," Marshall said, moving the book to a shelf behind him. "It's an old book, anyway."

"Uh-huh. But that's why I come to see you."

"Me?" He was still thinking about the oil spot.

"You bein' a lawyer and all. I thought maybe you could call them or somethin' and maybe they'd tell you."

"Tell me what, Eula?"

"About why Franklin died and what-all they found out when they done the ortopsy."

A frown appeared on the lawyer's brow. "You mean they haven't told you the cause of death?"

"They ain't tole me or Josh *nothin'*. And I call them just 'bout every day. Sometimes I talks with the nurse and once I got to talk with Dr. Brownlea."

"What did he tell you?"

"He said they wasn't done with the tests they have to do in the ortopsy and even after they was, it would be up to Dr. Thatcher to tell me about it."

"Did you call Dr. Thatcher's office?"

"A couple of times, but they always say he's over at the hospital or busy with a patient."

"He's a busy man, Eula." Yancey wanted to add, and frequently drunk, but bit his tongue.

"Yessuh. I knows that. And I knows he done the best he could, but I jes has to *know*."

"The autopsy was done in Dahlonega?"

"Yessuh. The funeral home carried him over there the same night. Mr. Jackson said he'd have to wait till the ortopsy was over before he could start in on the preparations, but he done a real nice job on Franklin."

"Well, then, Eula, let me see," Yancey said, adjusting himself in his chair and reviewing his notes. "You want me to see if I can find out when they might have the autopsy report ready and then let you know what they found out. Is that right?"

"Yessuh. I'd sure appreciate it if you could do that for me. It ain't like I'm tryin' to cause no trouble, but I jes *got* to know."

"I understand, Eula," Yancey said, standing up, telegraphing a signal that the conference was over. He didn't need black clients hanging around the office. "I'll do what I can. You just give me a couple of days, and I'll see what I can do."

Eula got the message and stood up. "Thank you, Mr. Marshall. I'll tell my Josh you was awful kind. Awful

kind." She wiped her nose on the handkerchief once more
and gave it back to the lawyer.

"A couple of days, Eula. And mind them steps now."

"Yessuh. Thank you, Mr. Marshall. You *is* awful
kind."

The lawyer watched the woman leave the office. If she
had been a white woman, he would have escorted her to
the door and helped her mind the steps.

Resuming his seat, Marshall picked up the shotgun,
opened and closed the action loudly, and sighted at the
ceiling, unconcerned.

Chapter 5

CAL Brownlea's house was old but by no means antebellum. It had been built on a hill overlooking both the valley and the road to Dahlonega with enough gingerbread to qualify it as neo-ugly. There were fourteen rooms on three floors, connected by schizoid hallways and narrow stairs. The floors creaked appropriately and after air conditioning was installed, only a few of the big windows opened, giving the place a faint but permanent mildew smell, like Cal's favorite shoes.

Eunice Brownlea's taste in furniture varied between occasional antiques to horrible examples of glass and chrome skillfully forced on her by a homosexual interior decorator in Atlanta. Except for the den and the master bedroom, Cal had no interest in the furnishings, thereby abandoning her to her own devices, or lack of them.

Dr. and Mrs. Brownlea (she *always* referred to Cal as "the Doctor") couldn't keep a housekeeper. They could afford one, of course, but no one other than "the Doctor" could tolerate Eunice's sloppy living habits for more than a few months. They were presently between housekeepers, making the party a little more difficult than usual. Without Truman's help, the evening would have been a complete disaster. Truman, gardener, chauffeur, handyman, and, when decked out in a clean red coat, bartender, had been with the Brownleas for years. He was oblivious to Mrs. Brownlea's housekeeping and preferred his little apartment over the garage to the cabin he would have been otherwise able to afford in the black section of town.

It was to be a backyard affair, with a mountain of barbecued ribs, a washtub of canned beer, an open bar featuring Jack Daniels, and a long table of salads, corn bread, corn on the cob, apple fritters, and salty snacks to encourage drinking. Truman had filled and distributed Eunice's smoky tiki lights on seven-foot steel poles and was ready to light them at dusk. She got them by mail from some place in New York with an Oriental-sounding name and thought they added charm to the backyard. The charm could be debated, but there was no question they added smoke and the smell of kerosene. Cal said it kept away the mosquitos, but the moths they attracted made up for them.

The doctor had promised his wife he would be home early to help, but, as usual, by six o'clock he hadn't appeared.

"You got enough ice out there, Truman?" Eunice shrieked from her bedroom window. Hers was one that opened. "They'll want that beer good and cold. You hear?"

"Yes, ma'am. They's plenty of ice. I seed to that early," he shouted without looking up. Eunice was not unknown to appear in the bedroom window half dressed and Truman knew it wouldn't do him any good to be caught looking at her. The fact that he was in his late sixties and she was ugly did not change things. At least not in Pine Hill, Georgia.

"You mind the time now," she added. "I want you cleaned up and into that red coat before anybody arrives." Cal Brownlea had admired the Negro waiters with soft polite manners and red coats at the faculty parties in Augusta when he was a medical student. As a result, there had never been a party at the Brownleas without a serving man of color, dressed in red.

As dusk approached there was no doubt that Truman had done a good job. Every light in the house was on, the doors were wide open, and the tiki torches were belching flames right on schedule. As expected, the first guests were the hospital administrator and his wife. They arrived shortly before Dr. Brownlea and were loudly admiring

Eunice's latest acquisition, a grotesque orange chair, when he drove in.

"I just *love* tangerine as an accent color for this room," Eunice cooed. The gay decorator had known it as orange, but recognized he'd have an easier time telling it to Mrs. Brownlea if he called it tangerine.

"It's *lovely*, Eunice," Wing Jessup whooped. She had been christened Wingate by her mother, who hoped an unusual first name would attract a socially prominent husband for her after Wesleyan College. The scheme didn't work. Wing had managed to marry the perfectly uninspiring Hampton Jessup, whose father had hoped two last names would lead him into law or medicine. Instead, Hamp had taken an assistant administrator's position with a nursing home in Tennessee after he got out of the army, and had survived with only on-the-job training. Later, he atoned for his failure to attend the University of Georgia by taking courses at one of the junior colleges and by learning to agree with every doctor on the staff.

Wing Jessup was a distant cousin to Cal Brownlea, and when Pine Hill Hospital needed an administrator, she had chosen Hampton for the position. Eunice thought Hamp was an excellent choice, too, and that was that. Not that he had been a poor administrator. Hamp got the job done, avoided all disputes with patients, and stayed out of sight.

"Truman!" Brownlea bellowed from the upstairs bathroom. "You bring me a black Jack Daniels on ice and fetch one for Mr. Jessup, too." He lowered his voice and added, "I suppose he's ready, by now."

"Evenin', Cal," Hamp shouted back. "We're admirin' the new orange chair."

"Tangerine, dear," Wing said, smiling at Eunice.

"I'll be down directly," Brownlea yelled. "What chair?"

No one was required to answer the question. The doctor would forget about the orange chair from the very first moment he failed to notice it.

Truman came in from the back porch with the drinks. He presented Jessup with a Jack Daniels swaddled in a moist paper napkin. "Something for you, ladies?" he asked.

"Not quite yet," Eunice said, fully aware that Wing was dying for another drink. She couldn't have left home without at least one.

"Yes, ma'am. Excuse me, ma'am. Evenin', Mr. Jessup. Mrs. Jessup," Trruman supplied, all in a string. "I'll just see to the doctor." He enjoyed playing the university club bartender, the glass skillfully balanced off center on the silver tray, defying gravity.

He paused at the bathroom door. The steam from the shower poured into the bedroom like fumes from a volcano. There was a warm, moist smell of deodorant soap that he identified with the doctor's bathroom. Truman's smelled of ivory soap and the Lysol he used to clean it every week, but he liked that better than Irish Spring.

" 'Scuse me, Doctor. Yo' Jack Daniels?"

"Bring it in here, Truman," Brownlea shouted over the roar of the shower. He threw the curtain back and held out a wet hand for the drink. His face was soapy from shampoo and he kept his eyes shut tightly. Truman put the drink in the doctor's hand with all the skill of an OR nurse passing a delicate instrument. Brownlea wiped his mouth with his other hand and took a long pull on the drink, his first of the day.

Truman admired his boss as a doctor and as a man. Over the years he had accepted every opportunity to see which of them was growing older faster. There in the shower he saw the doctor's pot belly and his shriveled penis peeking out from his graying pubic hair. So far the two men were about even.

"Heaven," Brownlea announced, handing the glass, three quarters empty to the servant. He let the water run across his head and face before he opened his eyes.

"Truman, you old son-of-a-bitch, you look good in that red coat."

"Yassah," the man said, smiling widely.

"You could work at the dean's house in Augusta."

"Yeassah!"

"Now—let's get something straight." Brownlea reached

over and shut off the faucets simultaneously. "Dr. Thatcher's comin' tonight and I want you to keep an eye on him. Clear?"

"Well, Doctor, you knows Ah'm goin' to try, but . . ."

"Look, I'm not askin' you to shut him off or nothin', but slow him down. Water his drinks. And for Christ's sake, don't let him walk around with a bottle."

"Ah'm goin' to see to him, Dr. Brownlea. You just watch. It won't be like last New Year's."

Brownlea paused for a moment, recalling Thatcher's performance. He motioned for a towel and accepted it from Truman without comment. "Let's hope not," he sighed.

"Dr. Thatcher's a fine man," Truman said. His place was not to criticize.

Brownlea was still lost in the recollection of Thatcher throwing up in the driveway and blowing a party horn at the same time. "Huh? Yeah. You're right, Truman. Dr. Thatcher's a fine man. And a good doctor, too."

"Yassah." He offered the rest of the Daniels to his boss.

"But we want to do the right thing tonight, Truman. There's going to be a few others with us. I mean it's not just the doctors and wives."

"We got plenty of everythin'," Truman said, confidently. "The missus, she done seed to that."

"The missus. Shit, Truman, you don't fool me." He put his hand on the black man's shoulder and squeezed it firmly. He sipped his drink and smiled at the servant. Alone in the bathroom, one of them naked and one in his best red coat, they could afford to be friends. "You did it all, just like always, and I appreciate it."

"Thank you, suh. Ah does what Ah can."

The moment lasted a fraction of a second too long, stiffening Brownlea. He took his hand from Truman's shoulder, finished his drink and gave up the glass.

"See if anybody needs anything, will you?"

"Yassah. And Ah'll tell them you'll be along directly."

A few hours later the backyard was filled with people

eating, drinking, laughing, and talking louder than when they had arrived. Truman had arranged for a friend's sons to assist him, not in red coats, of course, but in clean white shirts, with long sleeves and black bow ties. The deal was that Dr. Brownlea would pay each of them whatever Truman felt was fair, and his final judgment was never passed until the party was over and the yard cleaned up.

There was no music at the party because Dr. Brownlea had never found time to listen. This, among other unproductive human pastimes, was unworthy of the doctor's attention. He not only believed that, but he said so, publicly.

The lack of music inhibited the parties at first, forcing people to talk and to listen regardless of how boring the conversation began. But later in the evening, after a few drinks, the talkers did not have to shout over a band and could attack each other's arguments with rare insight and alcoholic logic that would safely disappear by morning.

Truman had erected the bar along one side of the redwood shed used for landscaping tools. It was a pretty little building, built especially for the doctor by a grateful carpenter who was short on cash. Brownlea had successfully treated the carpenter's wife at home for infectious hepatitis and the carpenter had tried to repay him. Between the three of them, only Brownlea knew there was no effective treatment for hepatitis and that admission to the hospital would only create an isolation problem for the nurses. The carpenter and his wife had interpreted the home treatment as a special consideration, but Brownlea had figured she might as well die in her own bed as anywhere else. Her survival surprised the doctor, who was smart enough not to tell the carpenter. As a result, the carpenter built him a lovely shed.

The bar was sturdy enough to support Joe Thatcher as well as the bottles. By then he had had several drinks and showed it. He seldom smiled when he was sober. His wife, Marilyn, was at his side, watching and protecting him as usual, and trying to follow the mayor's argument about planting rose bushes at the Confederate memorial on the green. The mayor, Harry Long, was also the town's only dry cleaner and knew nothing about roses. He had wisely decided the rose bush project could be better handled by the Women's Club. Winning Marilyn Thatcher's support, he realized, would go a long way toward success for the idea, and for Pine Hill there were few other civic projects worth proposing.

"I think American beauties would be best," Harry said. "Don't you?"

"And you could come by once a week and feed them horse shit," Thatcher suggested.

"American beauties are so common," Marilyn said, ignoring her husband's remark.

"Well, I'll leave the choice up to you ladies," Harry said. He looked across the lawn for another group to join. He had wasted enough time on Dr. Thatcher anyway. "Excuse me," he said, "I need to talk to Reverend Caldwell for a moment." He smiled at Mrs. Thatcher and faded into the crowd, recognizing that her husband was approaching the blood alcohol level where his strained humor gave way to insults. The mayor had had enough of that at the New Year's party.

"C'mon, Joe," Marilyn said, "let's see what Cal's up to." She knew it was time to pry her husband from the bar.

"Ducks," Thatcher slurred. "He's telling them about shooting those goddamned ducks again. I'll bet my ass on it." He stuck his glass in front of Truman without looking and waited until it was refilled with Daniels before responding to his wife's tug on the sleeve.

Cal stood in a small circle of men, playing host. The conversation was light and a small burst of laughter greeted the Thatchers as they joined.

"That's not a sailor, it's a monkey," Cal said, repeating the punch line. The group laughed again.

"Bad stories or can a girl join in?" Marilyn asked. She still held her husband by the sleeve, tolerant of his slight stagger.

"Just an old joke, Marilyn," Brownlea said. "You

know Billy Markham and Yancey Marshall." His tone implied she did. It was obvious he was repeating her name for their benefit. Even in small towns men were capable of forgetting the first names of their colleagues.

"Sure she does," Thatcher broke in. "Markham here used to be a doctor. Before he went into pathology."

The group gave a small laugh.

"And Yancey is our local Clarence Darrow," the surgeon continued. He offered his hand around quickly, spilling a little of his drink.

"How are you doing, Dr. Thatcher?" the lawyer asked. "Mrs. Thatcher? Enjoying the party?"

"It's just wonderful. One of your best, Cal," she said.

"We'll have to get Cal over to Dahlonega to show us how to put on a party like this," the pathologist offered. He shook hands with Marilyn Thatcher and remembered how sensitive her mouth always looked. She was at least fifteen years younger than her husband and Markham wondered how she put up with him. Her father had been stationed at Fort MacPherson in Atlanta when she enrolled at Georgia State. She met Joe Thatcher at a dance and by the time her father was reassigned to an army post in Kansas, the doctor had asked her to marry him. Compared to Kansas and her folks, he had looked like a prize.

"You get enough to eat, Joe?" Brownlea asked. He hoped a full stomach would somehow slow down the surgeon's alcohol absorption.

"Ducks," Thatcher slurred. "I thought we'd be feasting on your goddamned ducks again." He smiled to show he was trying to be funny.

"Next time," Brownlea explained. "I've got a freezer full of them." He was instantly reminded of a story. "Did I ever tell you folks about the time we set up our blinds just south of Charleston and—"

"Pathologists think they know everything," Thatcher announced loudly. He smiled again, missing his mouth with his glass.

"It just seems like that, Joe," Yancey Marshall supplied. "It's because they get the last look." The lawyer glanced at the pathologist to see if Thatcher had offended him. Apparently, he hadn't.

"You got a last look at one of mine this week, right Billy?" Thatcher asked.

Markham took a sip on his scotch and water and nodded. He glanced at Dr. Brownlea over the rim of his glass, making momentary eye contact.

"Dr. Thatcher had an unfortunate loss last week," Brownlea announced for Marshall's benefit.

"Who?" Marilyn asked. It was clear that no one had discussed a tragic loss with her.

"Oh, I operated on a nigger boy last week and he didn't make it," her husband said flatly. "Win some, lose some."

Marilyn looked at her husband for a moment. She hated to find out about his problems from others. In their early years, he shared things with her long before others found out, but that was a thing of the past.

"He did everything he could to save him, Marilyn," Cal supplied. "The boy had appendicitis. Too far gone, I guess."

Markham swallowed half of his drink in a loud gulp that started him coughing. His spasm pulled the attention off Thatcher as Brownlea thumped the pathologist on the back.

"We don't need any café coronaries at one of my parties," Cal said jovially.

"At least not with so many doctors around," Yancey added.

"Tell me what you found at the post before you choke to death," Thatcher slurred.

"Oh, I don't think this is the time or the place for that kind of thing," Markham said, regaining his breath.

"Why the hell not?" Thatcher persisted.

The pathologist hesitated for a moment longer than it seemed appropriate.

"He's probably not finished with the slides, Joe," Brownlea suggested. He glanced at Yancey and then at Markham. "Where's Carrie, anyway? I haven't seen her since you arrived."

"The mayor is trying to get her to plant some roses," Markham said, welcoming the change of subject.

"Well he's certainly cut the tissue by now," Thatcher said. He had finished his Jack Daniels and was shaking the ice in the bottom of his glass. "Ain't that right, Billy?"

Trapped, the pathologist nodded his head. "I'll get the report out to you this week." It was his turn to glance at Yancey Marshall. The lawyer seemed to be inspecting something floating in his drink.

"Harry's going to get us all involved in his rose bushes, if we don't watch him," Marilyn said lightly.

"Where does he want them planted?" Yancey asked. He pulled a speck to the rim of his glass with his index finger.

"By the monument," she said. "If you were married, he'd have your wife out there, too."

"That damned appendix was stuffed way down behind the caecum," Thatcher said. "Had one hell of a time getting it out."

"Joe, your glass is empty," Brownlea announced. "Let's get Truman to pour you a fresh one." He reached across the group and took the weaving surgeon by the shoulder. Brownlea knew someone was going to have to do something. It looked like Thatcher was going to stay on the Pitts case until he got an answer or fell down, whichever came first.

"Yeah, Cal," Thatcher said. "That's a damned good idea. I think Truman waters my drinks when I'm not watching him. Maybe you ought to straighten him out."

"I'll mention it to him, Joe," Cal said, steering the surgeon toward the bar.

Thatcher nodded appreciatively and started away with his colleague, but then stopped abruptly to face the group again. "You could at least tell me what you found. You've had the case for two weeks, for Christ's sake." His red eyes glared at the pathologist.

"Tomorrow," Markham said.

"No, goddammit. Now!" Thatcher shouted. "You fuckin' pathologists are all alike!"

"Joe!" Marilyn said.

"No, I mean it. You give one of these bastards a speci-men from surgery and they fuck around with it and fuck around with it, takin' their own sweet time gettin' back to you with a report. It's even worse with a whole autopsy." Brownlea's hand was on his shoulder again but Thatcher shrugged it off angrily.

"C'mon, Joe," Brownlea said.

But Thatcher was warmed up now. "Spend all their time in the goddamned lab, looking through that micro-scope! And even then half of them don't know what the fuck they're doing."

Marilyn was embarrassed for Billy Markham. She knew how hard he had worked to bring the labs at the two hos-pitals up to date. She also knew how belligerent Joe could get when he was drunk.

"I've seen the appendix, Dr. Thatcher," Markham said rather formally.

"Well, we need the rest of it on the goddamned chart," Thatcher snapped. "Do you suppose you could con-descend to getting down off your ivory tower horse and tell me what you found? I mean, I'm only a lowly sur-geon, but . . ."

Markham looked at Marilyn Thatcher for a moment and then at her husband. He had evidently had enough. "The autopsy on Franklin Pitts, *Doctor*, is still under study."

"Goddammit!" Thatcher said, his eyes narrowing to slits.

"Joe—" Cal Brownlea interrupted. "Let's get a drink." He spun the surgeon around and pushed him toward the bar.

There was a long period of silence before Markham an-nounced, "I think I'd better be going. I've got a lot of work to do in the morning." He reached out for Marilyn's hand and shook it gently. "We'll get a chance to talk later in the week."

"It was good seeing you, Billy," Yancey said. He held out his hand waiting for the pathologist to let go of Mari-lyn's. He wanted to ask a few more questions about the Pitts case, but he knew this wasn't the time.

"Right, Yancey. Drop over some time and we'll find an afternoon for a round of golf."

"I'd like that," Yancey said. "I'll give you a call." He didn't play golf, but that really didn't matter. Markham didn't either.

Chapter 6

IN the car Carrie said, "That was rude, Billy." She sat with her arms folded, trying to ignore how fast he was driving.

"What was rude?"

"To leave all of a sudden like that. I didn't even get a chance to say good night to Eunice."

"She'll never notice." The car squealed around a turn and leaped over a little bridge, brushing Carrie's hair against the headboard.

"Billy! For heaven's sake! Whoever got to you at the party is still back there. You don't have to kill us both just 'cuz you're mad about something."

Her logic seemed inescapable. Markham took his foot off the accelerator and eased the car to fifty. As usual, there was almost no other traffic on the road to Dahlonega.

"I just get pissed off when I think of that drunk operating on people," Markham said through his teeth.

"Who? Thatcher?"

"Something's got to be done."

"Marilyn said he was laying off the stuff," Carrie said. It was the unwritten female mutual-defense pact again.

"When did she say that?"

"Oh. I don't know, a couple of weeks ago. We were at the tennis courts and . . ."

"Well, I hope you saw him tonight. He's going to outdo last New Year's Eve."

"Was that the night he screamed and yelled about all the blacks on welfare?"

"And the Catholics in government and the Jews owning

newspapers and the Arabs buying up the banks in Atlanta . . ."

"Maybe he needs help," Carrie suggested softly. She turned to face her husband and watched his face light up with each street light as they entered Dahlonega. "I mean more professional help than he gets from Cal or Charlie Kern or Marilyn. By the way, where was Charlie tonight?"

"He hates parties. I think they scare him. But you're right about Joe Thatcher. He does need help. But Marilyn will be the last to admit it."

"Why, for God's sake?" she touched his arm as he made a left off of the highway and onto Lafayette.

"Because she'd have to admit to herself she's married to a drunk. It's easier for her to ignore the problem."

"But the whole town knows," Carrie said.

"Sure they know. But everybody covers up for him. Even me."

"You? I thought you were mad at him. Isn't that why we left the party?" She glanced at the houses going by on Lafayette Street. She wasn't sure why they were on it. Their house was on the other side of town.

"I was, but I'm not now. He started in on pathologists again and I guess it got to me."

"Why do you have to defend the whole specialty?"

"Funny y'know? When Thatcher's sober, he thinks pathologists are the best friends surgeons ever had. One day at a conference he said without a pathologist to make the diagnosis he wouldn't know a benign lump in the breast from an infiltrating carcinoma." Markham managed a little smile on that recollection.

'Can't they tell, Billy? I mean, *really*. Can't the surgeons recognize which lumps are cancer and which ones are okay before they send it down to you?"

"Some think they can, but the smart ones know they can't. And without my microscope neither can I." He made a sharp turn off Lafayette onto Clairmont.

"Where are we going?" Carrie asked casually.

"I want to stop at the hospital for a while."

"Well I'm coming in. Sitting out there in that parking lot gives me the willies."

"When did I ever make you sit in the parking lot?"

"You didn't. But all the same, I'd get the willies if I sat out there."

"Women," Markham muttered just loud enough to be heard. He pulled the car into the doctors' driveway and opened the gate with his plastic card. The wooden arm went up, held the salute long enough to admit the car, and closed behind him. Every time the gate went up, Markham remembered an orthopod who opened it one morning, drove in, stopped short, and caught the chief of staff's Cadillac with the wooden arm. It had been a custom to scoot two cars through on one card in the morning, but the orthopod, grinning from ear to ear, simply pointed to the little sign that said, "Admit one car per card" and drove on.

Markham opened the side door quietly.

"Why do hospitals always seem spooky to me late at night?" Carrie whispered in the darkened hallway.

"Because everything seems spooky to you at night." He reached for her without turning and touched her lightly on the neck and Carrie emitted a shriek of surprise and feigned terror. Markham quickly opened a door into a pleasant, well-lighted hospital corridor, catching Carrie with an inappropriately horrified expression on her face. There was a grin on his.

The corridor led first to the lab and at that time of night, it was empty. A familiar trinkle of glasswear in the back corner of chemistry told Markham his night tech was busy.

"Hello, Hooper!" Markham shouted without pausing at the door to chemistry. It was polite to let the techs know when the boss was around. One of the staff physicians had come in the side door at three A.M. once and found a lab tech and the X-ray tech going at it in the blood bank donor chair. The doctor bubbled excitedly when he told Markham about it later, but the pathologist had said since the doctor didn't order any tests, it was none of his business. Administrative decisions like that endeared Billy to his lab staff despite his inflexible policy on technical accuracy.

"Evenin', Doctor," Hooper acknowledged, without coming out of chemistry. Markham did not have to explain his late-night visit. It was none of Hooper's business, and they both knew it.

Markham unlocked the door to his office, patted his wife on her fanny as she entered, and switched on the light. She slumped immediately into the big black leather chair in front of his desk and slipped her shoes off her heels. "Are we going to be here long?" she asked wearily.

"Just a few minutes," Markham said, going around to the other side of the desk. "I just want to read something again."

Carrie was used to her husband's sudden nocturnal impulses. The ones that were not directed at her, through her nightgown, usually resulted in his getting up, switching on a light, looking something up in a textbook or medical journal, and then returning to bed without comment. She assumed all pathologists did the same, but was afraid to ask other wives, in case she was wrong.

He unlocked the middle drawer of his desk and took out a yellow pad.

"Your state of the union address?" Carrie smirked, noticing his serious expression.

"Maybe." He hunched over the pages, his forehead cradled in his left hand. "This is the first draft of my autopsy report on the Pitts boy."

"The who?" she asked without concern.

"A kid named Franklin Pitts. One of Joe Thatcher's patients."

Carrie threw her eyes toward the ceiling. "Are you still on Joe Thatcher? Let it go. He got drunk at the party and threw you a couple of remarks. So what? Think of Marilyn. She gets them all the time."

Markham nodded without looking up. "Yeah, Carrie, I know. But *you* said he needed help. And I am going to give him some. Right where he needs it most." The pathologist took a cheap ballpoint from the expensive desk holder and began to scratch out some of the autopsy diagnoses, writing new ones furiously.

"Don't you dictate those reports anymore?" Carrie asked.

"Not . . . this . . . one," Markham said, talking and writing at the same time. "I . . . thought . . . it . . . was . . . too . . . hot . . . to . . . handle."

"Until tonight. Until Joe Thatcher pissed you off." She paused to watch him in motion. He was working with an intensity she seldom witnessed. "Billy—you're not going to put something in that autopsy report to hurt Joe Thatcher, are you? I mean, even if you're mad at him, that's not the way to—"

"I'm just going to cut out the lies and tell it like it is," he said without looking up.

"Billy," she said a little softer. "You never lied about anything."

"Well, maybe I just didn't tell the *whole* truth. It's the same thing."

"Sometimes it is, sometimes it isn't, Billy. A person can't be expected to tell the whole truth about everything every time."

"It's expected when that's his job, Carrie." He stopped writing and picked up the top sheet, reviewing it rapidly.

"Well, just because you found something at the autopsy doesn't mean you have to tell everybody in town."

Markham looked above the report and into his wife's eyes. She seemed a little more defensive than he would have expected. "Carrie. Do you remember when we were in residency?"

"Yes, but—"

"And do you remember how exciting it was to discover something about a case that not even the chief of surgery knew?"

"That was residency," Carrie argued. "You were younger and less . . . less . . . well, less responsible."

"Responsible? Is it part of my responsibility to cover for inadequate medical care and negligent surgeons? When did I take on *that* responsibility?"

"That's not what I meant," she said. "I mean, you've

got a good job now and you're on the staff of two hospitals. And we've acquired friends. It's not the same as residency."

"Only a resident can afford the truth. Is that it?"

"No! That's not it and you know it. Stop twisting my words." She was getting more emotional and began to be angry with herself. Every time she started a discussion she promised herself she would remain cool and aloof like Billy, but she usually failed.

"You don't even know how Franklin Pitts died, and you're already sticking up for Joe Thatcher."

"I guess that's because I know Joe Thatcher. And I know Marilyn. I don't know anybody named Pitts."

Markham stood up and turned around to face the window for a moment. He wasn't sure why they were fighting. He wasn't even sure *if* they were fighting. He knew Carrie was right. Over the years his attitude had changed. He had softened and become more comfortable in his own position and his own possessions. What *had* happened to the tiger from residency? Where was the thrill he used to get from the academic arguments over meaningless diagnoses and procedures?

He turned from the window not knowing how long he had looked out into the darkened parking lot. He almost spoke when he saw that Carrie was reading the autopsy report. Her face tightened from being puzzled to being upset.

"I don't believe it," she said, looking up from the paper at last.

"You don't want to believe it."

"Either way." Carrie glanced at the front sheet again and sighed deeply. "Poor Marilyn," she said.

"Marilyn? Poor Joe, that's what you mean. He's the one with his ass in the crack."

"You think he'll get sued?"

"Sued?" Markham snapped. "He ought to be hanged." He grabbed the yellow sheets from Carrie and began to read aloud. "Just listen to this: 'Peritonitis, massive, due to gangrene of the caecum, due to compression by surgical device.' " He paused to look at Carrie. "Do you know what that means?"

"I'm not sure," she admitted.

"He left a goddamned clamp on the stump of that kid's appendix! And the appendix was normal!" Markham pulled his desk drawer open and reached inside, extracting a stainless steel clamp marked with an autopsy tag. He waved it over his head like a prize captured in battle.

Carrie seemed stunned. "Left a clamp? Inside?"

Markham nodded sadly. He lowered the prize and stared at it.

"But you didn't say that, did you?" she asked. "I mean, your report says—"

" '. . . compression by surgical device,' " he read aloud. "You're right, Carrie. That's a lot more than my first Mickey Mouse report, but it's still not enough."

"What happens next?"

Markham shrugged. "I send the report to Thatcher and a copy for the administrator with one for the kid's chart."

"Why does Hamp get one?"

"To worry about. The administrator should get a copy of every screw-up. After all, he's the hospital boss."

Carrie nodded comfortably. "And who tells the mother?"

Markham wrinkled his nose, trying to choose between theory and practice. "Ideally, Joe Thatcher should call her in and explain the whole thing to her."

"Ideally."

"Uh-huh. But if you want my bet, I'll say he'll sit on it, and wait for the shit to hit the fan."

Carrie gave her husband a worried look. She had never been able to conceal her concern when it involved him. "When it does hit the fan," she said, "try not to track it all over *our* house."

Chapter 7

YANCEY Marshall could have been content with a two-bedroom trailer parked somewhere along a cold mountain stream. He needed only to sense the presence of nature immediately outside his door and the opportunity to piss on the ground anytime he felt like it. But the collapse of a Florida builder's empire had given him an opportunity he couldn't pass up. The builder's dream of the second homes in the Georgia mountains had folded shortly after the completion of a network of narrow shelf roads and the construction of a model A-frame perched on a bull-dozed clearing halfway up Wildcat Mountain. The bankruptcy had been swift and Marshall's credit, although thin, was sufficient for the local bank. With a nominal down payment, Yancey had acquired the A-frame, negotiated for a long string of power poles, and had moved in. To date there were still no neighbors, the remainder of the development remaining hopelessly entangled in a legal quagmire and investors in five states. The litigation had done nothing toward maintaining the roads from Pine Hill to his eagle's nest, but in time, Yancey had come to appreciate the potholes as silent sentinels, ensuring his privacy.

The exchange between Markham and Thatcher at Brownlea's party had aroused the lawyer's curiosity about the Pitts boy. Where Eula's story had been unsuccessful in captivating Yancey's imagination, Markham's remarks and Brownlea's silence had succeeded. It was clear, however, that a frontal attack would be hopeless. Yancey would have to approach the problem tangentially.

It was almost dusk as he stacked the charcoal briquets

on top of the electric device he preferred to the smelly liquid Gulf oil produced. The thing reminded him of a poorly designed branding iron, but he could plug it in and walk away from it, confident the Weber cooker would be ready when he was. He carefully replaced the briquets that insisted on rolling off the pyramid, the soot blackening his hands and nails, and returned to the kitchen sink, his fingers spread widely as if contaminated by a rare disease.

Inside, at the counter next to the sink, Donna Strickland displayed not only her great talent in making a tossed salad, but one of the firmest asses in the county. Yancey stole up behind her and made a sudden threatening gesture toward her blond hair with his sooty hands.

"Don't you dare!" she shrieked, her terror unconvincing.

"I'm Vidal Sassoon," he announced.

"And you'll be wearing a bowl of salad if you put even one of your black hands on me."

"Racist." He held his hands in the air and kissed her on the neck from behind. "You smell better than the salad," he mumbled.

"It's either the garlic or my Chantilly." She paused at the salad making and leaned her mouth toward his. After a moment for both of them she asked, "When will the fire be ready?"

"Twenty minutes."

"Good. You can make us both margaritas." She pulled away from him and resumed the tossing.

"Where did you put the chart?" he asked, cleaning his hands at the sink.

"It's in my overnight bag by the bedroom door. I'll get it for you if you like."

"It's okay. I'll find it. You want salt on your margarita or not?" His words trailed off as he walked toward the stairs to the bedroom in the loft, snapping the water from his hands.

"I don't care," she shouted after him, "but make them on the rocks."

He was back in a moment, the hospital chart of

Franklin Delano Pitts cradled gently in his damp hands. "Is this the original or a copy?"

"A photocopy, dummy. Give me a little credit. Wouldn't I look great smuggling an original out of the hospital and then having Jessup discover it was gone?"

"Well, Jesus, Donna, you're the goddamned medical records librarian. Who'd care if you took a chart home?" He had already begun to read the history page.

"Nobody is supposed to take a chart out," she said, wiping her hands on a dish towel. "Especially to let a lawyer read."

"I can get you an authorization from the kid's mother. But right now I just don't want to raise any eyebrows. Y'know what I mean."

"Uh-huh. Besides, it'll take a couple of weeks before Thatcher finished his notes and signs it, anyway."

"A couple of weeks! That long?"

"You mean that fast. Sometimes Thatcher doesn't get around to his old charts for months. Where's my margarita?" She snatched the chart from his hands and hid it playfully behind her back.

Yancey got out the tequila and the triple sec, inspecting the liqueur carefully to see if he had enough. "Then why do you give him only a couple of weeks with this one?"

" 'Cuz, I heard Brownlea tell him today to finish the damn thing before there was trouble."

Marshall dropped ice cubes into the glasses and rummaged in the bottom of the refrigerator for limes. "What trouble?" he asked casually.

"I figured you knew the answer to that one. If you're willing to cook me a steak and share your mountain penthouse for the night just to read some kid's medical record, there's got to be trouble somewhere."

"Why, Donna, how you talk! You know I don't do malpractice."

"You've got something more on your mind than tequila and sex," she said. She took a glass and waited expectantly for him to finish making the cocktails.

He spoke slowly and carefully, as if to improve his aim

in pouring the drinks. "Eula Pitts came into the office last week and told me the kid died after his appendectomy."

"Uh-huh. Like I said, 'trouble.' "

"Well, hell, I don't know that yet. Every mother's got to be bent out of shape when her sixteen-year-old dies in the hospital. That doesn't mean something went wrong."

"It doesn't sound like the Nobel Prize for medicine, either." She let him guide her into the main room toward the fireplace.

"I didn't think much of it until Brownlea's party," he said, putting the shaker on the rustic coffee table.

"*I* wasn't invited," she said flatly. She was twenty-eight and divorced. She had moved to Pine Hill from Savannah after her marriage broke up, looking for a place to feel sorry for herself and mind her own business. She had never received any formal training in medical records, but when the older librarian had suddenly died of breast cancer, she had applied for the job. Lack of formal training was not much of a handicap in Pine Hill.

"I could have taken you, but you would have hated it." He moved closer to her and put his arm around her waist.

"No. I meant I wasn't invited by Brownlea." She yielded to the pressure on her waist and looked at Yancey. "If you start fooling around now, I'll never get to eat that steak."

"Would that be so bad?"

"If you're as hungry as I am, it would be." She carefully balanced her drink in the air as she kissed him.

"You taste better now than you will after the garlic," he murmured.

"I'll tell you what," she said, pulling away slowly. "You read the hospital chart and I'll season the steak."

Marshall considered the urges growing inside himself and then nodded slowly. "Use a lot of salt."

Donna took her drink to the kitchen and began to rummage through the cabinets for the seasonings. "What happened at the Brownleas?"

"Nothing much. Thatcher and Markham almost had a fight over this case, but Thatcher was drunk."

"What's new?" she said.

"How's this chart set up?" he asked, slumping into a chair with his pages and his drink.

"The usual way. Front sheet, discharge summary, history, physical exam, progress notes, and the nurses' notes. But I don't think it's all there." She began to sprinkle pepper on the sirloin.

"Why not all there?"

"Because it's Thatcher's."

Yancey flipped through the pages trying to make sense out of the document. Not many lawyers were able to read hospital charts without help from a friendly physician. Most doctors were reluctant to go over another physician's chart with a lawyer, thinking that any help they offered would be used to sue a colleague. Better-informed doctors knew an adequate explanation was frequently sufficient to satisfy a lawyer's curiosity and put a potential lawsuit to rest before it got filed.

"Thatcher wrote the history and physical," he announced.

"Uh-huh. Where's the garlic?"

"Use the powdered stuff in the little jar next to the salt. He says the Pitts boy complained of stomach cramps and vomiting for several days before admission. Is that what you usually get with appendicitis?"

"How would I know? I'm only the records librarian, not a diagnostician."

"Yeah, but you read a lot of these."

"File. Not read. How much of this powdered garlic should I put on?"

"A lot. And put it on both sides. The charcoal will burn most of it off." His suggestion made him go to the charcoal cooker, remove the electric branding iron, and spread out the coals. "Let's give the fire a little while to settle down. It's still too hot." He brought the chart to the kitchen and continued to read it as he sipped on his margarita.

"At least Thatcher's operative report is on the chart," he said, holding a page in the air.

"That's unusual."

"Isn't he supposed to dictate it at the end of the operation?"

"He's supposed to do a lot of things, but he doesn't."

"Then, I wonder why . . ." he mumbled, losing himself in the technical description of the surgery.

"Maybe he smelled trouble coming," she suggested. She stood back, admiring the steak and sniffing her hands. "I'll stink of garlic for a week."

"Tell everybody you're Italian," Yancey said, still reading. "Even I can figure out some of this stuff. Thatcher's report says he incised the skin and separated the muscle layers. That means he cut into the kid's belly. See? I'm already a medical genius."

"I think you need another margarita." Donna retrieved the shaker from the coffee table and refiled both their glasses.

"And listen to this! The appendix was located in a retrocecal position, freed up by blunt dissection and found to be markedly inflamed. The mesoappendix was cross clamped before and the vessels cauterized. The lower third of the appendix was covered with purulent material while the middle third was swollen to a near bursting point.' "

"Sounds bad to me."

"Why?"

"Well purulent means pus. I guess the appendix really had to come out."

Yancey frowned at her explanation and began to flip through the rest of the chart. "Where do they put the pathologist's report?"

"It's usually the next page."

"The next page is the anesthesia record."

"Okay. Then it's the page after that." Donna leaned over his shoulder to help. "That's funny," she said, "it's out of place."

"Maybe you moved it when you made the copies."

"Maybe."

"Acute gangrenous purulent appendicitis. Seems a bit overstated."

"Hell, I don't know. That's the way those pathologists talk. You ought to read the crap they put in an autopsy." She pressed her cheek against his, spilling a little of her drink on the chart.

"That goes for Dr. Markham, too?"

"Sure. But at least he's usually up to date."

Yancey looked surprised. "That autopsy goes on the chart?"

"Normally. It would be the last three or four pages." She took the chart from Yancey's hands and turned to the end.

"I'll bet you another margarita it's not there," he said.

"You win," she agreed, tossing the chart on the table. "I'll check on it in the morning."

"Donna," he said softly, taking one of her hands. "I don't want anybody to know I'm interested in this chart."

"Why? It's my job," she explained. "If I don't hound them, they never get their charts up to date."

"Don't sweat it. That autopsy report will read just like the rest of this shit."

"I'll make you a deal," she purred. "I'll trust you to cook the steak and you trust me to get you the rest of the reports."

"Is that all it will cost me?" he asked, pulling her into his lap.

"Let's call it your kitchen down payment." She kissed him on the lips and he understood what the payment in full would be.

Chapter 8

HAMP Jessup knew the administrator in a small hospital should not have too plush an office, and kept his furnishings simple. The board of directors had gone along with the walnut paneling, the floor-length drapes, and the imitation Oriental carpets. After all, Hamp had argued, the administrator's office had to look prosperous. He had chosen a plain sofa, a couple of inexpensive upholstered chairs from Penney's in Atlanta, and a heavy mahogany desk Wing had picked out. She had also selected a couple of Currier and Ives prints for the walls and five or six leatherbound books for the bookcase in the corner. One of the prints portrayed the harvesting of a Christmas tree in the 1800s somewhere in New England, but Wing didn't think it looked out of place on a wall in Pine Hill, Georgia. Hamp never fully appreciated the scene anyway. The pictures covered part of the wall, and that was good enough for him.

Jessup sat behind the desk, rereading the autopsy report on Franklin Delano Pitts. Most of the pathological jargon was Greek to him, but the first diagnosis was painfully clear.

"Dr. Brownlea is here," his secretary, Mrs. Maxwell, said flatly over the intercom. Mrs. Maxwell was almost seventy and held her job at the pleasure of the board. Evidently, over the years she had pleased them because she had been there forever. At first Jessup had thought he should have the right to select his own secretary, but when he realized Mrs. Maxwell was the pipeline to the chairman of the board, he accepted his fate and kept from her everything he didn't want the board to know. When necessary, Wing would type a letter for him at home, adding to his conspiracy. Later, if the letter got good results, he'd file the correspondence in the office. Since Mrs. Maxwell never remembered anything beyond a few weeks, the method had worked out well.

Dr. Brownlea came through the door without waiting for Jessup's reply. As usual, he was in a hurry. "It's eleven o'clock, Hamp. What the hell is all this about?"

"Sit down, Dr. Brownlea," Hamp said, half rising. "I kind of hoped Dr. Thatcher would be with you."

"He's coming. I saw him upstairs. He had to change out of his greens."

"He was operating this morning?"

"Uh-huh. A hernia." Brownlea collapsed into one of the chairs in front of the desk and ran his fingers through his hair, making it worse. "You said you had something important to talk about."

"I do." He slid the hospital chart, but not the autopsy report, across his desk toward the doctor. "It's the Pitts case."

"Oh, yeah," Brownlea said, picking up the chart and fumbling for his glasses. "Too bad about that one. It was a shame to lose him. Gangrenous appendix, as I recall."

"Well, that's partly what I needed to talk to you about." Jessup paused to give Brownlea a chance to look over the chart.

"Yes. Says so right here," Brownlea said, thumping his finger on a page. " 'Acute appendicitis, gangrenous.' " He continued to read the page, moving his head up and down to keep the print in his bifocals.

"What page is that, Dr. Brownlea?" Jessup asked, apparently seeking simple information.

"The surgical pathology report."

"Signed by Dr. Markham, right?"

Brownlea glanced at the bottom of the page. "William B. Markham, M.D.," he announced. "Who did you expect would sign it? Donovan, from the Mayo Clinic?"

Jessup allowed a small laugh to acknowledge Brownlea's joke. "No, Dr. Markham is still our pathologist, as far as I know."

"Well, then," Brownlea said, closing the record. "What's the problem?"

Jessup paused and assumed his somewhat perplexed look. It served him well for conversations with doctors. It wasn't proper for him to know anything medical before a doctor had offered an explanation, even if the point was obvious. "I had hoped Dr. Thatcher would join—"

As if by cue, Thatcher opened the door as Maxwell announced him over the intercom. "Mornin'," he drawled.

"We was just talkin' about you, Joe," Brownlea said cordially. "Were your ears burnin'?" Thatcher's ears were normal, but his eyes, as usual, were red.

"Good morning, Dr. Thatcher," Jessup said, half bobbing from his chair. The administrator expected all nonmedical personnel to get up when a doctor entered the room.

"Betty Singleton's stitches look okay to me," the surgeon said, passing along a recent observation to Brownlea. "I took a couple of them out." He moved the other chair a foot or two away from the administrator's desk and sat down, groping in his shirt pocket for a cigarette.

Brownlea nodded, acknowledging the Singleton report. There was no need to explain further to Jessup. It was just doctor talk. Jessup was used to that. Thatcher lit his cigarette, masking his sweet alcoholic breath. He blew a puff of smoke and shook the match furiously, as if to prevent a forest fire. "Now, what the hell is all this about? I got patients to see."

"It's about the Pitts boy," Jessup said. "Dr. Brownlea's got the chart."

Thatcher continued to look straight at the administrator. "I know the case," he said. He took an enormous drag on his cigarette, inhaled half, and held it long enough to make Jessup wince.

"Have you read the autopsy report?" the administrator asked.

"I think I got a copy, but I haven't actually read it," Thatcher said cautiously.

"I got mine yesterday," Jessup said. "I thought we ought to talk about it."

"I haven't seen it either, Hamp," Brownlea said. He handed the hospital chart to Thatcher and accepted a thinner document from Jessup. Thatcher slipped a finger into the chart and glanced at a page as Brownlea began to scan the autopsy report.

After a moment of quiet reading in which Jessup studied the doctor's face, waiting for that instant of recognition, Brownlea emitted a long, almost inaudible sound. "Jesus H. Christ," he said. His eyes rose above the report and looked at Thatcher. The surgeon was grinding his cigarette butt into the administrator's unused ashtray with a heavy twisting motion of his thumb.

"Pulmonary embolus, I'll bet," Thatcher said. He was wearing a dark blue polyester suit as usual. His tie was stuffed in the right pocket of his jacket and his starched white shirt was unbuttoned at the neck. Marilyn did his shirts herself. The laundry was never quite able to please him.

"Not this time," Brownlea said, flipping the autopsy report to page two.

"Okay, then, sickle cell crisis," Thatcher offered. He glanced at Jessup, but the administrator was staring at the top of his desk. "I don't think those quick tests the lab does for sickle cell are all they're cracked up to be. You get a kid that looks healthy enough and bang!—right out of the blue, he goes into a damned sickle cell crisis and you lose him. Comes without warning." Thatcher snapped his fingers but the snap was weak.

"Markham found a clamp, Joe," Brownlea said, scanning the last page. He folded the pages on to the staple and handed the report to the surgeon.

Thatcher glanced at the report and went immediately to the description of the abdominal dissection on the chart. "This can't be right. The instrument and sponge counts were correct."

"They're always correct," Jessup said softly, still looking at his desk. "Nobody closes with an incorrect instrument count."

"Yeah, but I—" Thatcher said, still reading.

"Let's face it," Jessup said, "we've got a problem."

Brownlea squinted at the administrator, thinking. "Who knows about all this so far, Hamp?"

Jessup used his fingers to count them off. "You, me, Joe, and Markham. That is, if Markham hasn't shot his mouth off over in Dahlonega."

"He's a pretty good man," Brownlea said. "He wouldn't do that."

Jessup shrugged. "Anyway you look at it, the fat's in the fire, seems to me." He looked at Thatcher. The surgeon looked almost ill as he fumbled for another cigarette.

"We just might be able to yank it out of the fire," Brownlea suggested. Thatcher turned to face his colleague, his interest growing.

"I don't think I follow you," Jessup said.

"Well, let's just look at what we got here. Joe screwed up and left a clamp in this kid."

"The nurse is responsible for the instrument count," Thatcher said.

"Shut up, Joe, and listen to me," Brownlea snapped.

The surgeon obeyed instantly like a whipped dog.

"Markham finds the clamp and puts it in his autopsy report," Brownlea continued. "Now, if he has followed his usual routine, he kept a copy in Dahlonega, sent one to the records room here, gave you one, and mailed one to Joe at his office. Right?" The surgeon and the administrator nodded in agreement.

"Mine came in this morning," Jessup said.

"Did Mrs. Maxwell see it?" Brownlea asked.

"I doubt it. It was in a manila envelope. She slit it open, but I doubt she read it. There was a lot of other correspondence for her to take care of." Jessup displayed the envelope to support his theory.

"Okay," Brownlea said. "That leaves us with the record room copy. What about the Strickland woman?"

"She probably stuck her copy in my box without looking at it," Thatcher said.

"Why, Dr. Thatcher?" Jessup asked.

"Because the chart hasn't been finalized. It's still in my stack, waiting for a couple of progress notes."

"Dammit, Joe," Brownlea said, ignoring Jessup for a moment. "I told you to finish that chart right after the boy died. A death case shouldn't sit around unfinished. It don't look good."

"Well, I meant to, but I just didn't get around to it. Besides, I wanted to see what Markham's report said."

"To write a progress note, Joe?" Jessup asked, forgetting his subservient role.

"I've got more important things to do than all that paper work, Hamp," Thatcher whined.

"Well, let's skip all that for now," Brownlea said. "If we waste too much time, we'll miss our chance."

"To do what?" Jessup asked, cautiously.

"To, shall we say, 'safeguard' this report from prying eyes?" Brownlea said.

"Uh-huh," Jessup said without commitment.

"Look at it this way," Brownlea continued. "Joe here ain't going to run over and tell the boy's mammy about the damned clamp, and she's not going to come in beggin' to read the chart."

"She'll want *some* kind of an answer," Jessup said. "Maybe she'll go out and get a lawyer."

"Eula Pitts?" Brownlea said, smirking. "Who's she going to get in Pine Hill? Yancey Marshall? He don't do malpractice. Hell, he don't do much of anything, if you ask me."

"How 'bout one of them hot-shot black lawyers from Atlanta?" Thatcher asked.

"Takes money, Joe," Brownlea said. "She can't afford to hire anybody like that."

"Lawyers take malpractice cases on contingency," Jessup said. "Something like forty percent for them if they win, with the other sixty percent going to the family."

"Still, no nigger lawyer from Atlanta's going to waste his time with a case like this one unless he *knows* something went wrong," Brownlea offered confidently. "And if there ain't no autopsy report on the chart, nobody's going to know nothin'."

"I could tell Eula the boy threw a pulmonary embolus," Thatcher suggested.

"Something like that," Brownlea agreed. "What do you think, Hamp? Worth a try?"

Jessup thought for a moment, wrestling with the scenario. It had good and bad points. Finally, he sighed heavily. "What about Dr. Markham?"

"You can take care of him, Hamp. And I'll help you," Brownlea said. "Markham's got a soft touch here. He comes over only once in a blue moon. He gets a cut of every damn lab test we order. We send him all the surgical specimens. Think about it. How much did he make out of this hospital last year?"

Jessup calculated the figures in his mind. "Oh, I don't know exactly. Fifty? Maybe sixty grand."

Thatcher emitted a low whistle. He had not realized pathologists did that well.

"And with Dahlonega?" Brownlea persisted.

"Probably a hundred and a half total. Maybe more," Jessup said.

"Well?" Thatcher blurted. "Can't we line them up, too?"

"Dahlonega? Hell, they're not going to go along with anything like this. They've got too much to lose," Jessup said.

"The hell they won't," Brownlea said. "They need us just like we need them. If we close down, that's sixty or seventy patients they'll have to take in. They've got enough on their hands already. All you got to do is have a friendly little chat with the administrator over there and . . ."

"And tell Ray Dingle we're going to lift the autopsy off a chart and threaten our pathologist with the loss of his job if he won't go along with us? He's been administrator over there for too long to go along with that kind of horseshit!" Jessup looked more alarmed than when he started this meeting.

"Hamp," Brownlea cautioned softly. "There are ways

and there are ways. We don't tell Dingle everything. We just let him know we're not totally satisfied with Markham's services and that we've got to get together to lean on him a little bit."

"Markham won't sit still for that," Thatcher said.

"You leave Markham to me," Brownlea said. "I'll make him think there's something being discussed concerning his contract at Pine Hill and let him know I can smooth it over if he'll cooperate a little."

"By not filing the autopsy report?" Thatcher asked.

"That's a little too much to expect of the man, Joe," Brownlea said, smiling slyly.

"But you're not going to tell him what Joe tells Eula Pitts," Jessup said.

"Not a word," Brownlea purred. "And Eula Pitts ain't never going to go over to Dahlonega to talk to a pathologist." He made pathologist sound like the governor.

After a moment the administrator said, "It just might work."

"If we get to Donna Strickland," Thatcher said.

"No!" Brownlea protested. "She's not to know anything about this. Hamp will just go down there and ask for her copy of the autopsy. She hasn't filed it yet. It's not here in the chart."

"We'll all walk down to records," Thatcher announced.

"No, Dr. Thatcher," Jessup said calmly. "Dr. Brownlea's right. I've got to do it. If we all go, it will look bad."

"You pick up her copy and stick it in your locked file," Brownlea said, extending his hands to show how simple it all would be.

The administrator stood up, came around to the front of the desk and shook hands with both doctors. "This has got to die *here*," he reminded them, harvesting the nods.

"Okay," Jessup cautioned as they gathered near the door. "Let me throw some sand in the air for Mrs. Maxwell." He opened the door quickly and stepped back, letting the doctors precede him. "Thank you for coming, Dr. Brownlea, Dr. Thatcher," he said loudly. "I'll see that your ideas about new prescription forms are discussed at the next board meeting. It sounds like we might save a few dollars and improve patient care at the same time." He beamed approvingly.

Mrs. Maxwell looked up from her typewriter and assumed her pleasant, respectful pose.

"Improving patient care is what it's all about, Mr. Jessup," Brownlea said stiffly. "Now, Dr. Thatcher, let's have a look at that patient of yours upstairs."

Jessup watched them leave before he turned to Mrs. Maxwell. "Page me if you need me. I'll be in purchasing." He was already into the hallway before she responded with a nod.

The record room was adjacent to the staff medical library, such as it was. With a medical staff of three, none of whom were readers, books were superfluous. The room served as a conference area, but earned its title by displaying a few outdated textbooks and a few bound volumes of old professional journals donated by Brownlea.

To get there, Jessup had to pass by the staff dining room. Employees and visitors were invited to eat there, sharing the same food the dietician overcooked for the patients. The tasteless food was inexpensive and best described by the ultimate condemnation, "wholesome." Restaurants around the world achieve some degree of success by advertising their food as exotic, delicately spiced, foreign, or even downright strange, but none could survive on a claim of "wholesome."

Jessup paused in the doorway, scanning the tables and exchanging small greetings with employees as they passed. The eleven-thirty group was still there. Donna Strickland was seated in the far corner, chatting with a nurses' aide and picking at her salad. Jessup did not let his eyes meet hers as he quietly surveyed the room. Satisfied she was busy, he moved down the corridor, being careful not to hurry.

As expected, there was no one in the medical records room. Jessup looked at the shelves of records filed side by side according to patient number. He had no doubts of Donna's efficiency. Since she had come to work at the hospital, charts were arranged logically and easier to find. The Joint Commission inspector had given Donna high grades for her methods even though many of the charts were incomplete. Jessup knew what bothered the man from the JCAH. In the corner, on three small desks, there were stacks of charts waiting to be completed and signed. When the Pitts problem blew over, Jessup vowed to himself, he'd have to get after Brownlea and Thatcher again. Kern's stack was too short to bother with. So was his patient load.

The administrator moved quickly to Miss Strickland's desk. She was an organized person, but working alone, she couldn't be expected to be perfectly up to date. With a little luck, Jessup said to himself, she hasn't gone through the morning mail. His own mail had come at ten and he was first on the delivery list.

There were nine pieces of mail in her in-box. Jessup quickly recognized Dr. Markham's return address and grabbed the envelope, identical to the one he had received. He nervously tore it open and glanced inside. Then, on her scratch pad he wrote, "Donna—I came by for the autopsy report on patient F. D. Pitts. I need it for conference. I'll send it back later with the chart. H. Jessup." The note, he reasoned, would keep her from calling Markham's office. Sooner or later, her compulsive filing would drive her to request the report from Jessup, but by then, a lot of water would have gone over the dam.

Chapter 9

B Y ten-thirty that evening Yancey and Donna had already eaten dinner and made love. For both reasons, they needed rest. Yancey was stretched out, slightly chilled from the early fall breeze flowing across his naked and still moist body through the half-opened window in the loft bedroom. Donna, less of a pioneer, huddled next to him under the sheet for warmth and her own need to be close. There was an old war movie on the television and Donna played little optic games with herself, opening and closing one eye at a time and trapping Robert Taylor in the hair of Yancey's chest. Her ear pressed against his chest, she tried to tell from the rhythm of his breathing if he was asleep. Sometimes, right after his orgasm, it was hard to tell because he went into a few minutes of silent peace, closing his eyes, refusing to be touched. She knew if she allowed him those precious moments he'd be back, his appetite renewed. Then she could reap the benefit and be there to satisfy him.

"I don't understand it," he said softly and without warning.

"It's about the army fighting and invading France," she said, neither of them moving as they spoke. Inside his voice boomed in her ear like a radio being played too loud in the next hotel room.

"No. I mean Thatcher's case. Why would he pick a fight with Markham about the autopsy report being late?"

"He was drunk. A lot of people pick fights when they're drunk." She ran her finger through his chest hair and made little circles that sort of tickled and sort of annoyed, but not enough for him to complain.

"Yeah, but Markham's surgical report said the kid's appendix was gangrenous, just like Thatcher's operative note said it was. So what was there to get so pissed off about at Brownlea's party?"

"Surgeons are always a little afraid of pathologists," Donna suggested. "They never know what the final diagnosis is going to be."

"Uh-huh." Yancey rolled up onto one elbow and switched on the bedside light. He picked up Markham's surgical report and reread it again.

"Maybe you ought to feel lucky," she said, half sitting up and adjusting her hair. The light from the bed lamp fell across her breasts unevenly like a David Chan photo in *Playboy*.

"Why?" he asked, still reading.

"Because now you can explain the case to the boy's mother and be done with it. It's not your kind of case, anyway."

"That's for damned sure. But I don't have to do much explaining to his mother. She called the office this afternoon and told *me* the cause of death." He put the report down and glanced up at the army, still slogging through the mud.

"*She* told *you*? How'd she do that?"

"Eula said Thatcher called her at the motel and wanted to see her. She said she didn't have a car and he settled for a phone call. She said he sounded awful nice and wanted to tell her what they found at the autopsy."

"I wish to hell Jessup hadn't taken my copy of the autopsy," Donna said. "I would have brought that, too."

"It doesn't look like we need it. Thatcher told Eula the boy died of a pulmonary embolus." He paused to look at Donna to see if she understood. "Y'know. A blood clot in the lung?"

"Yeah, I know. But what does that mean to the case?"

Yancey shrugged and rolled over to face her. Her breasts pushed against his chest and he ran his hand down her spine to where her butt began to form. "What case?" he mumbled into her hair. "The kid had appendicitis, Thatcher took it out, and he died of a blood clot in the lung. So what?"

Donna moved her hand along his thigh and came to rest in his pubic hair. She liked his pubic hair. It was curly and soft. "They should have told her that sooner. Then she wouldn't have bothered you."

"You're bothering me," he said, biting her ear.

"You want me to stop?"

"Uh-huh. In about an hour."

"Brag, brag, brag," she purred.

They became aroused again more quickly than either of them expected. Maybe they owed it to Robert Taylor and the war. It was hard to be distracted by an old invasion.

She felt him growing beside her, an awareness becoming an insistence. He kissed her on the lips and she responded with a renewed hunger that spurred him on. He rolled her gently onto her back and paused above her for just a moment to appreciate how beautiful she was before gliding into her again, effortlessly, with controlled eagerness that promised he would last a long, satisfying time.

After this one, he did fall asleep, but not for long. When he awoke, the army had been conquered by "NBC News" from Atlanta. Both Robert Taylor and Donna were gone. He had no idea where to look for Taylor, but the open bedroom door to the second-floor porch told him where Donna was. He scooped the blanket from the floor and wrapped it around himself against the chilled mountain air.

Donna was leaning against the redwood railing, slowly smoking a light menthol cigarette when he came onto the porch.

"Looking for night creatures?" he asked.

She turned from her deep search into the moonlit woods and smiled at him in his blanket. "I didn't know you were an Indian."

"I am when you've got my bathrobe," he said, coming close to her.

"Isn't it a perfect night?" she asked. She looked at the woods again as if to prove it.

"Every night's beautiful up here. I don't know why anybody wants to live any place else."

"Probably to avoid the potholes in that damned road of yours."

"They keep the tourists in town, where they belong," he said. "How long you been standing out here?" He stood behind her, holding the blanket with one hand and the curve of her buttocks in the other.

"About fifteen minutes. You were asleep or wherever you are, afterward, and I just got to thinking."

"About what?"

"About Jessup and that autopsy report." She puffed again on her cigarette.

"You really *are* crazy. You screw for an hour—"

"Twenty minutes," she corrected.

"—Whatever. And then you leap out of a nice warm bed to stand out here in the moonlight. Anybody else would be remembering their favorite song, but you come out here to think about an autopsy report."

"I don't remember Jessup ever doing that before, Yancey."

"Doing what?"

"Taking an autopsy report from my desk."

"He's probably just nervous. Everytime you pick up the paper some doctor's getting sued. So when a sixteen-year-old boy croaks in the hospital, the administrator has a right to be a little uptight."

"You're probably right. He'll give it back next week and I'll run you a copy, if you want."

"Not for me. I've seen just about all I want of that case. I'll leave all that medical malpractice to those guys in Atlanta, or Florida. I'm not cut out for that kind of stuff."

"Neither is Pine Hill."

"It's just as well. We don't need things to change, up here in the mountains."

"Well, there's one thing that changed and I don't have any answer for it," Donna said, absently.

"What's that," he asked, hooking his chin over her right shoulder.

"The pathology report on the appendix. They used script type and indented paragraphs."

"I'm sure it's very professional looking," he mumbled, unconcerned.

"It is if you like that kind of type and spacing. Frankly, I prefer plain old elite and block. Like they use now."

"Like who uses now?" He still wasn't interested.

"Markham. And Dahlonega. They haven't used script for a couple of years." She finished her cigarette and turned to hand the butt to him. "Prevent forest fires," she chimed.

Yancey took the cigarette and dropped it into a coffee can in the corner he used for fishing. "You mean, that report looks different than the usual stuff Markham turns out?"

"Hell, yes, it's different. It's even different from the other surgical pathology reports that came over this week. I don't want to bet on it, but I haven't seen them use that typewriter since Markham's old secretary quit.

"You mean, got run off by Carrie." Yancey let the blanket fall to the porch deck and grabbed Donna by the hand. "C'mon inside." He pulled her into the bedroom and stood by the little table lamp examining the report. "That's the cutest thing I've seen in a hell of a while," he said.

"It certainly is," she said, looking at his penis, shrunken by the cold night air.

"Look at this." He held the paper beneath the lamp. "This is a goddamn photocopy."

"Of course it's a photocopy. I made it this morning."

"No, I mean it's a photocopy of a photocopy." He held the report so that she could inspect it closely. "Look at the shadows around the name and date."

"And that's not all," she added. "Look at the transcriber's notation at the bottom of the page."

" 'WBM:tm,' " he read.

" 'tm' is Markham's old secretary. His new one is 'pd.' "

Yancey turned toward Donna and hugged her, waving

the report in the air behind her head. "This report is as phoney as Thatcher is!"

Donna slid her bathrobe open so that she was naked and warm against him once more. "No wonder Jessup took the chart and the autopsy report. I'll ask him to give me a copy tomorrow."

"No, don't do that, Donna. It will put him on alert. If the report on the appendix is a fake, I'll want to sneak up on them from their blind side." He began to shiver slightly in the cold air. She pulled him tighter against her body.

"Have you got anything left?" she asked softly.

"That will depend on you." Still kissing, he slipped off the robe and eased her onto the bed.

Chapter 10

T H E following morning Yancey pulled his red pickup truck into the hospital parking lot and left it unlocked. The absence of theft was among the few benefits of living in Pine Hill. He had not called ahead. He presumed Hamp Jessup would be in his office by nine every morning, worrying if not working. Since it already was ten, Yancey knew his chances of catching the administrator without warning were fairly good.

He walked through the little lobby with authority, passing the two aged pink ladies at the information desk with only a nod. As expected, they did not challenge him. A terrorist could have driven a tank through the lobby before these semisenile volunteers would ask why. Security was not their problem.

Yancey took the well-marked route to Jessup's office and paused at the door for a moment before entering.

"Well, hello there, Mr. Marshall," Mrs. Maxwell chirped. "What brings you up here to our little hospital?"

"Mornin', Miz Maxwell," Yancey drawled, glancing around the empty room. "I need to talk to Hamp for a minute or two. Old accident case." He knew Mrs. Marshall would continue to pry until she got some kind of an answer. At her age an absurd reply would do where secrecy would not.

"Well, you picked a good time, Mr. Marshall. He's in there having his second cup and reading the paper." She smiled pleasantly, confident she had been both honest and forthright.

Yancey would have accepted a less personal description of the hospital administrator's activities. For Hamp's sake,

67

he was glad the man wasn't in the toilet. Mrs. Maxwell would have probably disclosed that as well.

She pushed the intercom and blurted, "Yancey Marshall is out here to see you, Mr. Jessup. Shall I tell him you're in?" Yancey started to smile, but he kept a serious face when he realized the woman was sincere.

"Send him right in," Hamp said quickly.

She motioned toward the door. "Make him give you some of that coffee," she said, winking. "It's a fresh pot."

"Thank you, Mrs. Maxwell," Yancey said, bobbing a bit, "that's mighty kind of you." He opened the door to the administrator's office and caught Jessup putting on his shoes.

"Come in, come in, Yancey," Jessup said. "It's good to see you. Have some coffee?" He motioned toward the upholstered guest chair. Hamp's jacket was draped over the back of his desk chair and the Atlanta *Constitution* covered his desk, opened to the crossword puzzle. A few horizontals had been filled in, scratched out, and filled in again.

"Thank you, Hamp. Just cream in mine."

"It's fresh. Mrs. Maxwell just—"

"—She told me, Hamp. A new pot." Yancey accepted the cup carefully, grasping it near the rim with a thumb and forefinger. Jessup had not offered a saucer, and his own pudgy finger filled the handle. Hamp would, of course, not offend the rural heritage they shared by offering a napkin. Only Yankees and city folk used such things.

"A social call, Yancey?" Jessup asked, settling into his own chair and sliding his desk book over the crossword puzzle.

"More or less, I suspect."

"Always good to see you."

"Likewise, Hamp. Still I like to stay out of hospitals as much as I can. There's a funny smell about 'em." He blew on his coffee and shifted the hot cup to his other hand. Yancey wore his green-and-black checkered shirt, khaki pants, and old smooth mocassins. The shirt was his favorite, a secret gift from Donna Strickland. He would have been embarrassed to let any real southerners know it came from L. L. Bean's in Freeport, Maine.

"That was some party old Cal threw the other night," Hamp said, still sifting and filling, waiting for Yancey to drop a clue. No lawyer had time to pay a social visit on a hospital administrator.

"Uh-huh. He sure puts on a spread."

"Seemed like everybody had a good time."

"Especially Dr. Thatcher," Yancey said softly.

Hamp tightened slightly at the mention of Thatcher's name but then recovered his plastic-pleasant expression. "He can sure put it away when he's in the mood." He shook his head as if to express his sad concern but it didn't look real.

"Outdid his own New Year's," Yancey acknowledged.

"We all wish he'd cut down on that stuff, Yancey. I know it must worry Marilyn. I just don't know why a body would carry on like that. And him a doctor, too."

Yancey nodded to concur with the administrator's wisdom. The statement and the agreement were both expected and meaningless. "That's good coffee, Hamp," the lawyer began. "But what I really came up here to talk with you about was the Pitts boy." He watched Jessup's face for any signs of alarm but was careful not to stare.

"The Pitts boy?" Jessup said carefully. He frowned slightly to sharpen his memory. "Seems like he was the boy that died. They operated on him, didn't they?"

"Uh-huh. Appendicitis." He sipped the surface of his coffee and looked away from the administrator. He had studied the man long enough for the moment. "Eula— that's the boy's mama—come in to see me a while after he died and wanted to settle his insurance."

"Insurance? He had some insurance?" Hamp seemed delighted to hear it.

"Oh, not much, you understand, but enough to pay the burial costs, with a little left over."

Hamp knew about the debit policies the black people liked to buy. Twenty-five cents or so a week, with payment at the front door of the house, in cash. He also knew the hospital's insurance problems were handled by the business office. No one sent a lawyer to clear up a debit policy.

"Well, you know we're always happy to help these folks out, whenever we can," Hamp lied, smiling.

"Oh, I know that, Hamp. That's why I come up here to see you directly. I tried goin' through one of your clerks, but they say there's a snag somewheres."

"A snag? Like what?" Jessup began to fidget with the edge of his desk book.

"Well, like the cause of death. I understand it's not on the chart yet."

"It's not? 'Course, I don't know much about that part of the business. Yancey. They pay me to administer and all I do is administer." He offered an unconvincing smile.

"I called the lady in your record room. What's her name again?"

"Strickland. Donna Strickland," Jessup supplied.

"Yeah, Strickland. I called her and asked for the cause of death. Just so I could fill out the insurance form for Eula, you understand, but she said the autopsy report wasn't back yet. Is that so?"

Hamp offered a large shrug. "Hell, I couldn't know off hand, Yancey. But I can surer 'n hell find out for you. Is that all you need to know about the boy?"

"Yeah. That's about it, Hamp. I got to put somethin' down on that form or the insurance company won't pay up."

"That's the African-American Abraham Lincoln twenty-five cents a week Mutual?" Jessup quipped.

"Somethin' like that, Hamp. You know how they are."

Jessup nodded knowingly. Both of them knew who "they" always were.

"I'll tell you what, Yancey," Hamp said, getting up from his desk. "You give me a couple of hours this mornin' to straighten a few things out, and I'll look into that little matter for you. If we've got the autopsy report back, I'll get Miss Strickland to give you a call and tell you what-all it says." He moved around to Yancey's side of the desk and held out his hand. The problem apparently solved, the meeting was being closed.

"That'll be just fine, Hamp. Anything will do. Just enough to fill out the form." Yancey put his cup on the low table and shook Jessup's hand.

"And if we ain't got the autopsy report back yet, I'll call up Dr. Markham and jump all over him." Jessup smiled again to show he was really harmless.

"Well, I guess Billy's got his hands full, what with both hospitals runnin' near full. You are 'bout full, aren't you, Hamp?"

"Just about. I ain't seen the census yet this mornin' but they was lookin' for an empty bed late yesterday."

"Sorry to bother you, Hamp."

"No trouble at all, Yancey. I'm glad you came to see me. I needed a break from all the other problems they give me around here."

Yancey released the administrator's hand and glanced at the newspaper on the desk, opened to the crossword puzzle. He wanted to ask Jessup for a four-letter word for intercourse, but decided to quit while he was ahead.

Without another word, each of them headed for a telephone. Yancey found his on an unoccupied table outside the cafeteria. He dialed 223 and waited for a familiar voice to answer.

"He bought it, honey. Now just keep your eyes open and let me know what he does." Yancey kept his voice low even though there was no one else around.

"I'll lay you odds he doesn't come near the record room," Donna said.

"You're probably right, but if he does, just play dumb. I laid it on him just like we planned."

"Will I see you tonight?" she asked.

"Let's see how it goes. I'll call you later at home."

"Be careful, Yancey."

"You too, honey." He quietly put the phone on the cradle and made his way to the front door. "Good mornin', ladies," he said to the pink volunteers in the lobby. "My nephew is receiving excellent care." The pink ladies beamed at each other appreciatively, convinced their efforts were the only things that made the hospital run smoothly. Everything else was secondary.

In the administrator's office another set of numbers were dialed. Jessup waited impatiently as a phone rang in the surgical dressing room. "Joe? I'm glad I caught you. This is Hamp."

"Yeah. What's up, Hamp? I got a hernia waitin' on me in the OR." Thatcher's voice was thick and slow, as it usually was in the morning.

"Listen. Are you alone?"

"Yeah, I'm alone. Who'd you think watches me change into my greens, the scrub nurse?"

"Joe, Yancey Marshall was here."

Thatcher hesitated for a moment. "What the hell does *he* want?"

"He was asking about the Pitts kid."

"Christ. What did you tell him?"

"He said it was about the kid's insurance. He needs a cause of death."

"Is that all?" Thatcher glanced nervously around the empty dressing room.

"I think so. But he asked about the autopsy report."

"God, Hamp. You didn't show it to him, did you?"

"No, I told him we didn't get it from Markham yet."

"Shit, he'll call Billy before the day is over, Hamp. And Billy will tell him what he found."

"I'm not so sure, Joe. He didn't sound all that interested. I mean, there can't be all that much money involved in a nigger policy."

"Yeah, but that means he's already talked to Eula. And I told her the kid died of a pulmonary embolus."

Jessup chewed his lower lip for a moment to think it over. "She probably couldn't explain that to Yancey. Shit, she couldn't even say the words. He'll want more than that."

"Then let me handle it," Thatcher said.

"Handle it? Handle it how, Joe?" Jessup did not picture Thatcher as the town's smoothest diplomat.

"Leave it to me, Hamp. I'll see that he gets my copy of the autopsy report."

"But—"

"It's the only way, Hamp. Trust me. I know it will work."

"If it don't, he'll have us cold, Joe."

"Maybe so, but you must make sure nobody gets to your copy. What about the one Billy sent to the record room?"

"I got it in my locked file," Hamp purred.

"And the Strickland woman? What about her?"

"Yancey said he called her for a copy, but she didn't have one. I got it out of her mail before she opened it."

"Didn't Yancey go with her for a while?" Thatcher sounded mildly curious.

"A long time ago, Joe. Hell, he couldn't even remember her name this morning."

"God. I hope you're right. 'Cuz if she saw the report, I could look real bad."

Jessup hesitated. "You want to change your mind?"

"No way, Hamp. I'm going to tell him what he wants to know and that'll be the end of it."

"You going to tell Brownlea and Kern?"

"I'll tell Cal, but I don't think we should bother Charlie with any of this, Hamp."

"I think maybe you're right."

"Hamp, I've got to go do that hernia. I'll call you later."

"You're playing with fire, Joe."

"Dynamite, Hamp. Dynamite."

Jessup heard the phone go dead in his ear. Thatcher had managed to come through in the clinches before. Maybe he could do it again, Jessup thought. For the moment there didn't seem to be any alternative. Jessup put the phone down and pushed the intercom.

"Yes, Mr. Jessup?"

"Mrs. Maxwell. Call Ray Dingle and tell him I want to meet him for lunch in Dahlonega. We need to work out some details on our X-ray fees." Jessup didn't wait for a reply. He walked to his private file drawer and made sure it was locked. He knew he had the only key.

Chapter 11

AT exactly five P.M. Marilyn Thatcher entered Yancey's inner office and collapsed onto the worn leather couch. "I don't know *when* I've *ever* had a day like this one, Yancey Marshall. All this runnin' around, makin' copies. You'd think it was the Supreme Court of the whole United States!"

"You didn't have to make a special trip, Marilyn. Joe could have just dropped the report in the mail." Yancey sat on the corner of his desk, holding the manila envelope.

"Well, you know Joe. When he says get something done, he means get it done." She fanned herself with her hand and emitted a theatrical gasp.

"It was nice of him to let me have his copy, like this." He undid the clasp but did not open the envelope. There was no need to look too anxious.

"Joe said to make you a copy of the Pitts boy's report and get it on over to you. He said that ought to clear up your problem." Marilyn slipped off her shoes and curled her feet toward each other. It was as if she had walked a hundred miles.

"What problem?" Yancey asked absently. He studied the woman as she toyed with one shoe with her foot. No one could accuse Marilyn of failing to stay in shape. She was trim and tight and tanned, the way she thought a tennis player should look. There were no deep lines in her face to indicate the grief Joe Thatcher's drinking had given her. In their earlier years she had joined him, but there was no way she could keep up. After a while it was quit or drown and she wasn't ready to sink. She couldn't

74

get Joe to quit. It was hopeless to try. A psychiatrist in Atlanta had once told her she married Joe because her father had been an alcoholic and she needed to be mistreated by another one. She wanted to believe that was just foolishness, but she was never able to openly discuss it with her mother, either.

"Joe said something about the boy's insurance?" she asked.

"Yeah, well, it's not worth much, Marilyn. Just some details. You know how it is." He tossed the envelope on the desk and offered her a smile. For a moment she did not respond. There was a twinge of anxiety around her soft blue eyes that almost melted before it caught his attention.

"Yancey," she whined, "when are you going to let some woman make an honest man of you?"

"Who have you got in mind, Marilyn?"

"Oh, hell, I don't know. But livin' all alone up there on that mountain. It must get kind of spooky."

"It's closer to heaven," he sighed.

"I'll bet it's a mess, too. A man can't look after himself. Never has been able to."

"I get along. Besides, who could stand me for more than a day or so?"

Marilyn thought for a moment, or at least looked like she did. "What about that cute little medical records librarian. What's her name, again?"

Yancey paused and looked puzzled. It could be that Marilyn is really concerned about his spartan bachelor existence, he thought, but it's more likely she's on a fishing expedition. He pouted and frowned as long as he dared and then said, "Donna Strickland."

"Donna Strickland!" Marilyn agreed triumphantly. "I recollect you used to be kind of sweet on her. Ain't that so, Yancey?"

"Uh-huh. A while back."

"Who're you seein' now?" she asked devilishly, enjoying the question.

Yancey leaned toward Thatcher's wife and cupped his

hand around his mouth. The world's darkest secret was about to be disclosed. "Can you keep it just between us?"

"Won't breathe it to a livin' soul."

Evidently, Yancey thought to himself, that excludes her husband. "I keep an Indian woman tied up in the shed behind the A-frame."

Marilyn reached up and drew his face closer. "Is it going to be bad, Yancey?" she asked softly.

"I—" he began. Trouble showed in her eyes, but it rested there, almost at home, no longer able to quickly disturb her. Trouble now only evoked her weary, practiced response. It was like old shoes that still pinched the little toes, but not as much as when they were new.

"When Joe's in trouble, I can tell," she sighed. "It's not just 'insurance,' is it, Yancey?" She held her hands still and firm on the back of his neck.

"Eula Pitts wants to know what happened, Marilyn." Half bent over, his back was beginning to complain. He took her face in his hands, her lips parting slightly.

"Eula Pitts isn't worth it," she said just before she leaned into his kiss. She pulled him gently onto the couch.

"Is Joe?" he asked, sliding off her mouth and onto her cheek.

"He's all I've got, Yancey," she purred.

"Is he all you want?" He felt her breasts against him, mature and heavy. She slid one if her hands off his neck and onto his thigh.

"Sometimes I need a lot more." She squeezed him gently.

Yancey moved back slowly, placing his hand on hers, making her stop. He got up quickly before she could change her caress into a clumsy right hook. "Tell Joe it won't work, Marilyn."

"Joe didn't send me to you, Yancey," she yelled. "I came because I wanted to be with you. But you're too stupid to see it." Tears filled her eyes but her anger wouldn't let them fall.

"Dammit, Marilyn, I don't want to be involved in this case either. You know what I think about Eula Pitts and her whole damned tribe, but I'm stuck with it." He walked behind his desk, groping for that professional wall that lawyers and doctors instinctively build for security.

"Joe's done a lot for this town, Yancey," she said, softening.

The lawyer nodded, his arms folding across his chest.

"He's operated on them when he's been up all night on some accident case, he's looked after them when they didn't have a dime to offer. Hell, you know who he is, Yancey. He's a good man."

"He's a drunk and he's dangerous, Marilyn."

"And he's loud and offensive and all those things, Yancey, but you're not going to help by suing him." Her anger gone for a moment, a tear began to streak her makeup.

"What makes you think I'm going to sue him?" he asked. It was a probe, but a gentle one.

"Because he's worried sick about it and that means it's more than some stupid insurance problem."

"Marilyn, you're his wife and I'm not going to ask you what you know about the case. It wouldn't be fair."

"Fair? What's fair, for God's sake? Was it fair to make him chief of surgery in some godforsaken little town where he had to handle everything by himself? Was it fair of Cal and Charlie to carry him along like they did all these years, knowing he needs help? Where can he go now? What can he do if you come down on him like a ton of bricks?"

"Are you sure it's him, Marilyn? Are you really worried about Joe Thatcher the surgeon, or are you thinking about Marilyn, the doctor's wife and the country club and the big house and the—"

"—You're a son-of-a-bitch, Yancey Marshall. You're going to take on this case for one old nigger woman and throw Joe Thatcher to the wolves." Her anger was rising again.

"How about one nigger boy?" he asked.

"How about the thousand nigger boys he's helped? Don't they count?"

"Sure they count, Marilyn. They all count. And so do

all the other folks he's helped. But what can I do? I've got my job just like he's got his." The lawyer showed his palms helplessly.

"This ain't your job, Yancey, and you damned well know it. You never took on a case like this before. You've been happy here in Pine Hill just like the rest of us. You've got your easy practice and your cabin up there on the mountain. You can look after your hunting and your fishing just like you always have. This case isn't you."

"Maybe none of it's me, Marilyn. When I came back here I thought I wanted to be a lawyer, but they didn't need one. Not really. They needed somebody to show them how to fill out forms and where to file wills at the courthouse, but they didn't need *me*."

"But you needed them, Yancey. Just like you need all of us, even now. And you're going to lose them all if you pick on Joe."

"If I win."

"Even if you lose. All you're going to prove is something everybody already knows. That Joe's not perfect. That he makes mistakes. That everything doesn't always come out exactly like we planned. But the people in this town know that. They never thought they were living next to the Mayo Clinic. They could go to Atlanta if they want better. But they don't. They're no different than anybody else, Yancey. They want to stay home and they want to believe in their own little town. They don't want you or anybody else to tear it apart and prove it's really nowhere."

"You could say the same about me," he muttered.

"You want me to, Yancey? You want me to tell you you're a pokey little lawyer in a pokey little town? You're not down there in Atlanta fighting for indigent criminals. You're not locking horns with corporation lawyers from New York. You're down home, Yancey, can't you see that? Pine Hill is you, just like it's Cal Brownlea and Hamp Jessup and—"

"—and Joe Thatcher?"

"Yes, goddammit, and Joe Thatcher. Whatever you

want to say about him, he's not worth throwing to Eula Pitts or a half a hundred like her."

"He's got insurance," Yancey offered softly.

"Sure he's got insurance. But it won't be some asshole from Hartford on trial. It'll be Joe Thatcher, and everybody in town will know it." She picked up her handbag, knowing it was time to get out of there. She wasn't sure if she had convinced Yancey of anything, but she knew he wouldn't admit it to her anyway.

"Is that what's really bothering you, Marilyn? That the whole town would know if he got sued?"

"Yancey, the people in Pine Hill love Joe Thatcher, whatever he is. You just remember that. You may throw a lot of sand in the air, and some of it may get into people's eyes for a little while, but in the end, they're still going to love Joe Thatcher. They need him."

"I can't argue with that, Marilyn."

"And they're going to be your jury," she purred. She leaned over the desk and offered him a small but obvious kiss which he accepted without emotion. "I've got to go, Yancey. You think about what I said."

"I'll have to, Marilyn." He came around the desk to escort her to the door. "And you tell Joe I'm not mad at him, you hear?"

"Uh-huh. He'll understand. You find time to come by to have a drink with us, Yancey Marshall," she chimed. "There's more to do around here than just draw up deeds and look for trout." She slipped her arm around his waist and gave him a promising squeeze.

"You mind them steps goin' down, now," he drawled.

Marilyn kissed him quickly on the lips and picked her way down the stairs, confident that he was watching the swing of her fairly trim buttocks. From the entrance landing above, he studied each of her theatrically careful steps and smiled gently. Suddenly, the smile faded and was replaced by a worried frown, as he recalled Eula Pitts clumping down the same steps.

His eyes followed her to her aging Mercedes coupe. Joe had bought it for her after one of his binges. The one she had called the last straw and had threatened to leave him.

Thatcher had begged like a helpless little boy and she had said no and no and no, but had finally settled for a new car. It had been flashy when it had arrived from Atlanta, but by now everyone had gotten used to it and the clack of its diesel. So many servicemen had been to Europe for a year or two that the sound of German cars and the names of foreign beers no longer suggested Yankees from New York when heard in Pine Hill. Lifelong locals, of course, still clung to pickups and Budweiser for identity and stability. The stability they could still associate with Red Man in the cheek and fading Wallace stickers on the bumper.

She paused as she got into the car to look up at him and wave temptingly. He waved back and wondered if she really would have laid him on the leather couch. A half an hour later, as he sprawled across it, reading the autopsy report again, he wondered if he would have let her.

Chapter 12

A week later some of the cooler air that had begun to color the leaves above Dahlonega whistled along Marietta Street in Atlanta, reminding everyone downtown that summer was gone at last. It was a good feeling. Atlanta summers were a little too hot, although cooler than New York or Chicago, but fall was almost heaven. Now there could be wool skirts and expensive sweaters from Lenox Square and football at Georgia Tech. The drinking crowd was back from "the Lake" and southern summer excuses for avoiding overdue work were shelved for another year, along with memories of the Braves and concerts in Piedmont Park.

Southern Casualty was almost an institution on Marietta along with the Federal Reserve, the row of banks and that johnny-come-lately, the Omni. Southland now occupied nine floors at the Atlanta National Bank Building. In 1937, when they had just moved in to the first small office complex on the fifth floor, they had been humble tenants, promptly paying on the fifteenth but privately worrying about coming up with it for the following month. They wrote policies on just about anything in those days, and business had been good. So good, in fact, that now, while no one except Southern stockholders knew it, the insurance company owned the building and the bank was the tenant.

The founders of Southern Casualty had made their money on cheap labor in western North Carolina. Eventually, they had exercised unusually good judgment by recognizing that textiles and furniture in the Carolinas would face hard times and by publishing their names as

Wallace and Bone when they switched to the insurance business in Atlanta. Their real names, Wallinsky and Bunczkowski, would have made them as welcome in Atlanta in the thirties as Al Smith or Franklin Roosevelt. But by staying out of the way and hiring a roving band of "good ole boys" to peddle policies for them they had become as southern as okra. By the time they could afford life-sized oil portraits in the corporate board room, Southern had captured most of the larger accounts and had become synonymous with fiscal conservatism; a tribute to the ghosts of Wallace and Bone. Executives were now graduates of Emory, Vanderbilt, or Duke, but salesmen were invariably recruited from the University of Georgia, rebel yell, red shirts, sour mash, and all.

Medical malpractice coverage and hospital liability policies had not contributed much to the company's success until the later years. In the early days it was unnecessary and therefore unsaleable. In the middle years it had become fashionable but remained dirt cheap since there were no suits. Later, when California and Florida juries began to hand out six-and-seven-figure judgments, medical liability became a hot item. All of the doctors wanted coverage and hospitals stood in line to be interviewed, although Georgia juries turned a deaf ear to plaintiffs. As a result Southern Casualty sold policies like snake oil, confident there would be no big awards to worry about. The men in the board room were happier than pigs in shit (or so they said) and knew—they just *knew*—it couldn't get better. But it did. Argonaut and St. Paul and a few of the bigger boys got stung by a few astronomical judgments following anesthetic accidents and surgical bungling and worry swept the industry. As if they weren't enough, the insurance industry's bad investments failed almost simultaneously, and panic replaced the worry. To solve the problem, the liability giants got together and sold the medical community a piece of goods that sent doctors and hospital administrators scurrying around in little groups in search of security, a quart of scotch, God, and a warm tit. The cover story was no less than sheer genius. They told the doctors there was a national malpractice "crisis." It relied on two factors for success. First of all, large jury awards in doctor suits was news. The papers ate it up. Second, and more important, they knew that doctors as businessmen were assholes. Doctors were willing to lose money on almost anything provided the scheme promised a quick payoff and they didn't have to do anything personally. Doctors had lots of money but no time.

Using this master plan, the liability insurers doubled and tripled their rates for malpractice insurance and convinced the doctors it was all the plaintiffs' lawyers' fault. Big awards, they said, cost money. Big losses made the premiums cost more. A hell of a lot more. As much as twenty thousand dollars a year for a typical neurosurgeon who had never been sued. Some of the medical societies balked and formed their own cooperatives, Argonaut decided to quit the malpractice trade altogether, and a few doctors went naked, choosing to carry no insurance at all. But most of the medics went along with the hoax and paid through the nose.

At Southern Casualty the whole mess was manna from heaven. They had written almost all the malpractice coverage in Georgia, and while an occasional suit appeared in the courts, most of them were decided in favor of the doctor. The few cases that held for the plaintiff awarded peanuts, and the second rule of the scheme proved itself again. Doctors were still assholes. Southern announced there was a Georgia malpractice crisis, pointed to big cases in California, and doubled their rates. The profits from the move were enough to make an Arab choke. In fact, several Arabs were quick to make buy-out offers for several insurance companies.

The get-rich-quick scheme at Southern had been master-minded by Bobby Lee Thorpe, Emory, Class of 1952. In appreciation for the windfall, Bobby Lee had rewarded himself with a lavish redecoration of his office, a raise in salary, a vacation in Cozumel, and an unconscionable bonus. As head of the medical malpractice division, he knew he deserved it and as vice president he knew they could afford it.

Thorpe's office was on the eighth floor. At nine-thirty,

his private, two-man elevator from the executive parking
deck opened opposite the office fireplace, emitted one
man, and slid silently back together again, becoming a
bookcase. Bobby liked to make it to his desk and review
the calls on his phone pad before the rest of the staff descended upon him. "You got to get the jump on 'em," he
reminded his sales staff whenever he got the chance. The
little private elevator was his jump on them.

Thorpe was a lean, tanned, handball-playing six-feet-
one. At forty-eight, he could still outtalk, outsell, out-
think, and outrun almost everyone else on his staff. A few
years earlier, he could also legitimately claim to outdrink
them, too, but he quit all that one day when he realized
gin and tonics had cost him a new car and two marriages.
He married Debbie Ashbury at college when he was
drunk, and divorced her three years later when she was
drunk. Her family had all the money in the world so the
divorce didn't cost him much. She didn't care. Neither did
he. There were no kids. Another day he had missed a
curve in the mountains after a sales meeting. Of course he
had been drinking ("What's a sales meeting without an
open bar?") and took out a row of fence posts and some
weekender's mailbox. He totaled the new Fiat but somehow wasn't killed. Connections between Southern Casualty investigators and the nose-bleed county sheriff's office
took care of the details and that was that. One marriage
and one car down the tube.

He was sober the day he gave matrimony another try,
but wasn't very often while it lasted. Melinda had been
twenty when he met, dated, bedded, and then married
her. The whole courtship lasted only three and a half
weeks. Thorpe was thirty-nine then and up for the vice
presidency. He knew he had to show something more
than his legendary ability to grab the cutest, tightest asses
in town before anyone else on his staff had even said,
"How-do?" The run for VP slot had caused him to
consider (just for a moment, of course) dropping the
chase for Melinda and concentrating on sales. As a compromise he ran after all of these things a little harder. At
full drive Thorpe was a tiger with a hemorrhoid. Melinda

surrendered gracefully, if only by consenting to marriage, to get a full night's sleep. One of his malpractice salesmen had a heart attack trying to reach the quota Thorpe had set, but by the end of the year, Bobby Lee was the VP and married. The marriage lasted a couple of busy, boozy years before Melinda had had enough.

As vice president Thorpe could have delegated his job as chief of the malpractice section to someone else, but he loved sales too much to let go. He had built the section from a nothing part of the company to a high-yield division that also provided the rest of the program with hot prospects, to wit doctors. Viscerally aware of the Peter Principle, he knew he wasn't a great vice president. He also knew he was one hell of a malpractice defense man, and for him that was more important.

Looking backward through three sober years, he knew he could have kept Melinda if he had tried, and no longer saw her departure as a personal defeat. He classified his change in life-style without her as "management reorganization" and offered no further explanations. Actually, no one asked.

Thorpe poured himself a cup from the Mr. Coffee near the big dictionary on the stand and stood behind his desk, reviewing call slips. An invitation to lunch "sometime" from a hospital administrator in Newnan could wait. (All "sometime" invitations could wait.) A reminder that the negligence section meeting was coming up in a few weeks—good for Mrs. Dillard, she knew how to nudge him toward completing his report. Carol Simpett called— said it was personal. Carol is back in town. Might be worth a try later in the week; great legs. Attorney Montgomery from Florida: got a good settlement offer on the case against his surgeon and the local blood bank; wants to talk about limits. If he wants to raise the limit, the offer can't be too hot; still, Montgomery's a damned good lawyer.

Thorpe continued to sift through the first third of his call slips, all left over from the previous afternoon. He liked to leave the office with a clean desk, but the day before had been perfect for racquetball, or so this aggressive neurosurgeon had thought. Thorpe's group had saved the neuro from a malpractice suit a year or so before despite the fact the doctor had been negligent as hell, and Bobby Lee had given in to his demand to play all afternoon. Bobby Lee liked to hear from the guy, but only once a month.

Thorpe frowned over the next call slip and blew the steam from his coffee on it. Britches at Lenox Square said his jacket was ready. What jacket? He hadn't bought a jacket from Britches. Too expensive. Had to be a mistake. He reached for the intercom lever without looking.

"Mrs. Dillard?"

"Yes, sir. Good morning, Mr. Thorpe," she replied evenly. She glanced at the clock. He was right on schedule.

"This call from Britches. I don't recall. . . . Could you come in here for a moment?"

She knew a call from Britches would catch his eye. When he had been drinking, he would have assumed he bought a jacket three sheets to the wind and accepted it. But not lately.

Mrs. Dillard came into the office without further reply. She knew he had hung up on her anyway. Thorpe was like that. He never entertained the slightest thought an employee would not instantly obey.

"Good morning, Dixie," he said after she had closed the door. She was sixty-two but full of piss and vinegar. Bobby Lee often told her so. He was also the only one who could call her Dixie in public. Her real name was Sara, but she hated that more than Dixie. There was no Mr. Dillard anymore. He had died of a heart attack exactly one month after retiring from the Atlanta police department. Dixie had already predicted retirement was going to kill him. Bobby Lee was a little amazed when she was proved right so quickly, but she seemed to take it well enough. Three days off for the funeral and back in, bright and early on Monday. That was just about what everybody expected from Dixie.

"Mornin', Bobby Lee," she sang. Mrs. Dillard had been with him for years and years and comfortably called him by his first two names whenever they were alone. But always the first two, never just Bobby.

He waved the Britches slip in the air. "What's this all about?"

"Lord, I surely don't know, Bobby Lee. I figured you saw something you liked and—"

"Not this time. Call them and tell them they've got the wrong Thorpe."

"Okay." She glanced at the coffeepot and the desk in one sweep. Everything seemed to be in order.

"I wonder what it looked like?" he said, picking through the rest of the calls.

"Tweed."

"Tweed? How do you know?"

"Why not? You don't look good in tweeds, so it might as well be something I don't like, if you're not going to take it."

"But I didn't buy it, Dixie."

"That's why it's a tweed," she said, adjusting the little calendar on his desk. Dixie always adjusted, never fussed. Her hair was all gray now and she had picked up twenty pounds since Ben died, but she stood tall and confident.

"Uh-huh. What's the worst thing I should know about today?" He finished his coffee and went to the little table for a refill.

"Things seem pretty quiet. Sister Josephine-Marie called from St. Joe's in Tampa and wanted to know when their contract would be ready. She said the new wing would be open soon and—"

"—and she's getting nervous about being bagged before she can use the new beds to make a buck."

"It's a pretty big policy, Bobby Lee."

"Have Jenkins call the dear sister."

"Jenkins is in Savannah. Besides . . ."

"Besides what?"

"Oh, nothing. It's just that I think Sister Josephine is kinda sweet on you. She won't talk to anyone else around here."

"Why, Dixie, how you talk!" he scolded playfully. "Sister Jo is a nun!"

"Uh-huh. And so was the assistant principal at the Catholic school in Decatur. Who'd she run off with?" Dixie squinted to remember every detail.

"An insurance salesman," Thorpe sighed. "All right, I'll call Tampa this afternoon. What else do we have?"

"Could you find time to talk to Jack Pierce?"

"What's across his ass?"

"The usual. You know how he is. The newest problem is the biggest problem. He calls me every five minutes."

"Goddamn worry wart." Thorpe had reached the last of his call-back slips.

"He's young," Dixie said. Her tone implied she had known Bobby Lee during his younger, more impulsive days.

"Put him on the list for later."

"That's why he keeps calling. He's got to drive down to Macon. That new OB/GYN group wants coverage."

Thorpe squinted for a moment.

"You assigned him to it, Bobby Lee. You told him it would be good experience for him. Want me to cancel?"

Thorpe shook his head. "Naw. Let him go to Macon. Let's see what he brings back. Dr. Tinsley down there is a tough cookie. Locking horns with him will put some hair on Jack's chest."

"At the expense of what's left on his head," Dixie added. "Want me to call him?"

"Yeah, Yeah," Thorpe said hastily. "Get him over here and let's see what's on his mind.

Mrs. Dillard used his desk phone to make the call. "Now you be easy on him, Bobby Lee," she said when she had finished. "He's going to be all right one of these days if you'll just give him a chance."

"I'll give him a swift kick in the ass," Thorpe said playfully. "That's what he needs."

"Be sweet," Dixie said as a knock sounded on the door.

"Come in, Jack," Thorpe said, sitting down behind his big desk to gain the advantage. "Thank you, Mrs. Dillard." Dixie was already leaving the room. She knew where not to be and when.

"Mornin', Mr. Thorpe," Pierce drawled. He still looked like a Georgia football lineman despite his thinning hair.

"Bobby Lee," Thorpe grunted cordially.

"Oh, thanks," Pierce said awkwardly. He wasn't ready for that yet. He had been with Southern only a couple of years and Thorpe was still the boss. Bobby Lee could play one of the boys if he wanted to, but Jack Pierce wasn't ready to accept him in that role. He didn't know any of Bobby Lee's sins yet. No man can feel comfortable with another until he knows something bad about him and has forgiven.

"What's on your mind?" Thorpe asked, motioning toward one of the chairs.

"A new case. That is, maybe a new case." Pierce looked at the paper in his hand as if to refresh his memory, but they both knew it was only for show.

"What's a 'maybe new case'?"

"Oh, I don't know. Just a feeling I got." He offered the sheet of paper to his boss. "I took this call yesterday afternoon, after you were gone."

"Hamp Jessup," Thorpe said reading aloud. "I know the place. Pine Hill. Nice little hospital. Quiet little town. Terrible medicine." He scanned the notes on the paper and slid it back across the desk. "What's up?"

"Mr Jessup called to tell you he thinks they might have a claim coming. Pretty light on the details. He said he wanted to talk to you."

"Yeah. They all do. Some of those hospital administrators think I run the malpractice section all by myself."

Pierce could have told Bobby Lee that he *did* run the section by himself but he wasn't ready for that either. "Mr. Jessup seemed to think it could be big trouble."

"In Pine Hill?" Thorpe said, smiling comfortably. "How big can it get? They don't practice three turds worth of medicine up there. What's the name of that asshole GP that runs the place?"

"Cal Brownlea?" Pierce offered.

"Yeah. Brownlea. Remember that rinky-dink barbecue we went to at his place a couple of years back?" Bobby Lee made a face.

"Seemed like nice folks," Pierce said.

"Mountain red-necks. They wouldn't even let 'em empty bedpans at the Emory Clinic. But in Pine Hill!" Thorpe lifted his hand, godlike.

"Small towns are like that, I guess." Pierce had heard Bobby Lee rant about small-town medicine before, and how they weren't worth the risk. But both of them knew it was all just talk. The small hospitals paid their premiums on time and hardly ever generated a claim, despite the poor quality of medicine. Unfortunately, Bobby Lee got most of his information on modern medicine from racquetball partners who practiced at Emory. To them, everything except what was published in last month's *New England Journal of Medicine* was dangerously old-fashioned. The Medical Association of Georgia didn't agree, of course, but few of the young Turks from Emory were MAG members anyway.

"Why don't you hop up there and hold Jessup's hand," Thorpe suggested. He had already begun to lose interest in Pierce's problem and started to pick through other papers on his desk.

"He won't sit still for me, Mr. Thorpe. Not on this one." Pierce hesitated for a moment, hoping he hadn't suggested his own incompetence.

"I suppose he wants *me* to look at his problem personally."

"You just might want to do that when you hear what all it is."

"Brownlea dropped a baby on its head," Thorpe suggested without looking up.

"Not exactly. It seems a surgeon named Thatcher—"

"Thatcher! Oh, my God." Thorpe stopped arranging his papers and began to listen.

"Dr. Thatcher was operating on a black kid and . . ." Pierce was not sure what Bobby Lee's reaction to the news was going to be. Thorpe's closest target often bore the brunt of it, reminiscent of the ancient king beheading the runner bearing bad news.

"And?" Thorpe bellowed.

"And . . . he left some kind of an instrument inside."

Bobby Lee looked at the ceiling and muttered something about fucking veterinarians before waving his hands at Pierce, urging him to continue.

"A lawyer up there has asked for the hospital record."

"A lawyer up *there?* Not somebody from Atlanta?"

"That's what Mr. Jessup said. That's why he started to get nervous."

"What happened to the kid?"

"He died."

"Holy shit," Thorpe said, almost reverently. "What else did Hamp say?"

"Nothing much else. 'Cept he allowed they got a good jump on the case and needs to talk to you about it."

Thorpe looked at his watch. He knew the best way to save the forest was to piss on the campfire. "Have we not both the hospital and Thatcher?"

"Uh-huh. Both of them. A million umbrella on top of one hundred thousand—three hundred thousand for the hospital and a straight hundred grand on the doctor. And their premiums are up to date. I checked them both."

"Just our goddamned luck. Why can't one of these bastards forget to pay his premium before he fucks up? That way we could deny 'em."

"Mr. Jessup said he'd wait for your call," Pierce said, ignoring the question.

"You call him. Tell him I'll be up there in a couple of hours and tell him I don't want to eat his goddamned hospital food."

"You want me to come along, Mr. Thorpe?"

"Naw. I want to get a quiet look at this before anybody notices. I'll make it look like I just dropped by to say howdy. You go to Macon."

"Great ribs in Macon."

"You look out for Dr. Tinsley. He'll have *you* for lunch."

Chapter 13

At six-thirty Eula Pitts dropped the last of the pork chops into the skillet and dodged the spattering lard. Josh was late, but he'd be along. She was sure of that. He wasn't the kind to stop off at McKittrick's and drink up his pay with the rest of the road crew. Oh, sometimes—if there was a big occasion, like the birth of a child to one of the men—he'd take a beer, but drinking hadn't been Josh's problem. She was thankful for that.

The smell of corn bread wafted from the oven and a pot of greens bubbled on the back burner. The cover clattered onto the pot as a teen-aged hand tried to peek and found it too hot.

"You go right ahead and burn yourself, Pearline," Eula invited, poking at the chops with a fork.

"But, Mama, I'm hungry *now*," the girl whined. At fifteen, she was beginning to resemble her mother, with big breasts, bigger hips, and a sad, sagging face.

"Josh'll be along in a minute, so you jes hush. Go read one of yo' movie magazines or somethin'. Watch the TV."

"They ain't nothin' on but the news."

Eula nodded sympathetically. She didn't see any reason to take up good television time telling people about white folk's troubles either. As far as she was concerned they could rerun "The Jeffersons" instead of showing Cronkite.

"What's keepin' ole Josh anyway?" Pearline said. She clumped across the kitchen and threw herself across an old sofa discarded long ago by one of the white families in town. Josh had found it along the road and got the crew boss to let him lug it home on the sand truck after dark.

"Will you hush and give the man some room? He don't

have to show up 'round here to punch no clock. This here's his own home, his and mine, and he got a right to come in and out of it when he's a mind to." The words were Josh's, of course, but they became her own when she needed to point out the facts of life to Pearline or Franklin. She turned the chops over, looking to see if they were beginning to burn.

"But he's always home by six o'clock, Mama."

"Lately, it would be hard for yo' to tell, Miss Run-around. Seems like every day yo' come by with another car-load of boys. I swear, I don't know who half of 'em is."

Pearline rearranged herself on the couch, annoyed by the remark. Despite her obesity and stupidity, she maintained a certain physical popularity with the young blacks. Eula knew that little could be done about it and worried about another pregnancy. Brownlea had never told either of them about the tubal ligation.

The little house had four rooms and a half-closed back porch. There were faded curtains on the front windows and none on the back. Eula and Josh slept in the larger bedroom, and, before he died, Franklin had the other. That put Pearline on a folding cot in the living room and her clothes in a closet Josh built for her near the back door. After her brother died she had waited a day or two before claiming his room, but most of his things remained. Removing them would have to wait for memories to fade. In some ways he wasn't gone yet. Pennants were still tacked to the wall. A basketball remained in the corner next to his bed. Even Eula sometimes found herself setting a place for him at the table.

Eula smiled as a car pulled into the yard, the headlights flashing across the kitchen. "Josh must have found hisself a ride home. You scat now and get washed up for supper. That man'll need some room at the sink before he's ready to eat." The house had an indoor toilet, but the room was so small, Josh had put the cold water sink on the back porch. In the mornings Eula used the sink in the kitchen where it was warmer.

Inspired by hunger rather than obedience, Pearline lumbered from the old couch and headed for the back porch. She hated to wash out there, especially when it was dark and the insects beoynd the yard were making strange noises.

Eula turned the stove down and looked at the corn bread. Almost perfect, she said to herself. It was a comfort to have a man as regular as Josh. Some of the women she knew at church weren't half as lucky, and she told them so, often.

Footsteps came on the front steps, but there was more. There were voices. Now, who could that be, she thought. Maybe it wasn't Josh after all. He never brought anybody home after dark, except one time when his brother in the army stopped by on the bus to North Carolina. But there were voices, sure enough. Men's voices. Friendly voices. And a little laugh. Eula took the corn bread out of the oven and turned down the flame under the chops. "Lordy, if they is stayin' for supper," she mumbled, counting the chops.

"Evenin', Mama," Josh said. His tone announced he wasn't alone. "Got some men here, with me." He held the door open but the man behind him waited on the porch.

Eula wiped her hands on her apron and came to the front door. The kitchen light made it only halfway onto the porch as she squinted to see who could be out there. She nodded to Josh but that was all. Eula didn't abide public kissing, not even between a man and his wife.

"This here's Mr. Thorpe, from 'Lanta," Josh said. The man in the dark held his hand out and Eula touched it warily. She could not remember Josh bringing any white men home before.

"Evening, Mrs. Pitts," Thorpe said. "You remember Mr. Jessup, from the hospital."

"Miz Pitts," Jessup said pleasantly, stepping into the light. He didn't offer his hand. He was afraid she might recall who had had Josh ejected from the hospital, the night Franklin died.

"Evenin'," Eula said cautiously. She stepped out on the porch. Whatever these white men wanted, it had to be trouble. It always was. She studied her husband's face for a hint, but Josh didn't look worried.

"Mr. Thorpe's got somethin' to talk to us about," Josh explained.

Eula turned her attention to the well-dressed man from Atlanta. "Well, yo' could ask the gentlemen in, Josh Pitts."

"No need, Miz Pitts," Jessup said quickly. "I 'spect you're into fixin' your supper, and Mr. Thorpe and me, well, we don't want to trouble you none. We already done talked with Josh and he can tell you 'bout most of it."

"We found Josh at work today," Thorpe added quickly. "They told us at the county road office where we could find him." He said "county" as if it were the seat of the federal government. "That gave us some time to talk."

"And Ah'm obliged for the ride home, too," Josh added, bobbing appropriately.

"Mr. Thorpe is an insurance man, Eula," Jessup explained. "He handles the business for us over at the hospital."

"Uh-huh," Eula said. She was still not comfortable. At the Pitts house, she handled business affairs. Josh knew better than to make any deals without her.

"Well, I done tole Mr. Thorpe about Franklin and how you was lookin' into his insurance and—"

"Insurance?" Eula asked, cautiously.

"The one you got Mr. Marshall lookin' into for you?" Thorpe added, smiling pleasantly.

"Oh yassah," Eula said, feeling her way.

"Well, Eula, since insurance is Mr. Thorpe's business, I thought maybe..." Jessup said.

"Maybe I could be of some help to you and Josh," Thorpe added. "I thought I could save you the expense of hiring a lawyer and going to all that trouble. Besides, like I was tellin' Josh, there's a hospital policy to consider."

"What hospital policy?" Eula asked.

"The hospital covers everybody while they're patients, Eula," Jessup said. "And when they ... when they ... well, when there's a problem, like Franklin had, we try to help out, as best we can."

Thorpe wanted to kick Jessup for suggesting there had been a problem. "We have a basic insurance policy on anybody who passes unexpectedly at the hospital, Mrs. Pitts," Thorpe said quickly.

"Five thousand dollars," Josh blurted.

"Five thou—for what now?" Eula asked squinting again although her eyes had become accustomed to the dim light.

"For Franklin's passing, Eula," Jessup said somberly. "It's like a school insurance policy. Like if he got injured in a game?"

"Mr. Marshall didn't say nothin' 'bout no school policy," Eula said.

"Well, of course, he wouldn't know about it, right off, Eula," Jessup explained. "He does mostly wills and deeds."

"Uh-huh." Eula looked at Josh and noticed the glint in his eye. She took a step closer to him and sniffed his breath.

"We stopped off on the way home so's we could talk," Josh said, exuding guilt.

"Just a social drink at the end of the day, Mrs. Pitts," Thorpe said. In fact, he hadn't touched his. McKittrick's sold half pints, canned beer and paper cups. Josh had accepted a scotch and milk in the back of the car while Jessup mixed his with Coke. Jessup had made one for Thorpe, but Bobby Lee only held it as he talked about the deal. The other blacks at McKittrick's assumed the two white men in the big car were either talking to Josh about a job or were cops. It didn't pay to get too close, and nobody did.

"That's all right," Eula said defensively. "I got no special beliefs against drinkin'. A man's entitled."

Her remark pleased Josh and he smiled proudly for the men. He regretted he didn't have a bottle in the house. Thorpe and Jessup were suddenly afraid he did, and neither of them wanted to use or refuse his glasses.

"All you has to do is sign this form, Eula," Jessup said. He reached into his inside jacket pocket and produced a folded paper.

"Josh has already read it over and signed it, Eula," Thorpe added. "He'll tell you everything's in order." He glanced at Josh and nodded appreciatively. Thorpe produced a small silver Cross pen and held it up to the light as he twisted the end.

Eula took the paper and stepped closer to the kitchen door where the light was better. "What-all do this say, now?"

"Just a formality," Thorpe supplied casually. "You know how those insurance companies are."

"Uh-huh." She squinted at the form and began to read some of the type, understanding nothing.

"It just says we can pay you the money, Eula," Jessup added. "You know we want to do right by you and Josh."

"Uh-huh." She continued to read, losing the train of thought after the first sentence.

"And we're right sorry about how we had to put Josh out of the hospital the night Franklin passed," Jessup continued. "But he understands all that now, don't you, Josh?"

"Yassah. Ah surely does," Josh said, weaving slightly from the scotch.

"All Ah got to do is sign this paper and we gets to keep the money?" Eula asked.

"Got the check right here," Thorpe said, patting his jacket.

"You can sign the check and take it right on to the bank in the mornin'," Jessup said, smiling broadly.

"But we has to pay the hospital and Dr. Thatcher out of it?" she asked, glancing at Jessup.

"We'll take care of that too, Eula," Jessup said.

Thorpe again wanted to kick the administrator's ass. Things were going smoothly. Too many concessions were bound to raise suspicions. "That is, Mrs. Pitts, I think we can make some arrangements for you. I think we can talk to Dr. Thatcher. We'll see how things work out."

"Well, we owes that bill fair and square, Mr. . . ." she mumbled.

"Thorpe," the insurance man supplied. "I know you do, Mrs. Pitts, but we don't want you to feel pressed. The hospital can stand a little reduction, if you know what I mean."

"Well, that's mighty kind, Mr. Thorpe," Josh said, scowling at his wife. "Anything yo' can do is surely appreciated."

"Well, it looks all right to me," Eula said, glancing at Josh for reassurance. "Y'all want me to sign right here? Next to where Josh done already drawed his name?"

"Right below his name, Mrs. Pitts," Thorpe said. "See that line, right there?"

"Jes' let me take it in here and spread it on the table," Eula said. "That way Ah can do a proper job of it."

"Oh, you can just—" Jessup began.

"That'll be fine, Eula," Thorpe interrupted. "You take it on in there and we'll just stay out here admirin' the evenin' with Josh till you get back."

"Jes' take me a minute," she said, disappearing into the house.

"Sorry to bother you at supper time, Eula," Jessup called after her. "Smells mighty good."

"Pork chops, greens, and corn bread," she shouted.

"*Mighty* good," Jessup repeated, shaking his head.

Pearline had already helped herself to a plateful, spilling gravy onto the oilcloth. Eula made a wiping movement with her hand to inspect one corner of the table and carefully put the paper down. She stared at the pen for a moment to make sure it would work and laboriously signed her name.

"What's that, Mama?" Pearline asked through a mouthful of food.

"Hush up, child. Ain't no concern of yo's." Eula blew on her clumsy signature as if to dry the ball-point ink and folded the paper.

"What's them men want, Mama?"

"We jes' got some business, Pearline. Someday, when you is growed, yo'll have business to tend to, too."

"It's about them library books I done lost from school, ain't it, Mama?" The girl was unable to hide her nervousness and stuffed more food into her mouth.

"No, it ain't. Now yo' hush up and eat. That's all yo' has to do." Eula brought the paper to the door and handed it to Jessup along with the pen.

Bobby Lee quickly took both of them out of Jessup's hand and held the paper up to the light. He allowed a small smile and held his empty hand out to Eula. "Thank you, Mrs. Pitts. And here's your check. If you'll just sign it on the back?"

The woman looked at the check for a moment and took the pen again. This time she did not retreat to the kitchen. Thorpe helped her hold it against the house as she signed again below her husband's name.

"You come see me at the hospital if there's anything you or Josh need," Jessup said, shaking hands.

"Yessuh, Ah'll sho' do that," Josh said. "Mind that yard, now, Mr. Jessup. Things get left around out there."

"We'll be careful," Thorpe said, tugging gently on Jessup's arm. "And you folks get right on in there and pay attention to the supper. We're going to get out of your way directly."

"Yessuh, Mr. . . ." Eula began.

"Thorpe," Bobby Lee shouted from somewhere in the yard.

"And good evenin' to you, too, Mr. Jessup," Josh called. He waited on the porch with Eula until the car started and the headlights went on.

Jessup acknowledged Eula's wave with a tiny beep of the horn as he threw the car into gear and drove off. Both men kept poker faces although they could no longer be seen from the house. After a hundred yards down the dark narrow road, neither of them could stand it anymore and gales of laughter filled the car.

"Hot damn, Bobby Lee. I've got to hand it to you. You are the slickest!"

"Thank yo', brother Jessup," Thorpe said in his best black impression. "Thank yo' kindly."

"Can't you see the look on Yancey Marshall's face when you show him that claims release all signed and paid for?" Jessup howled.

"Let's hope he never has to see it," Thorpe said, trying to control his laughter.

"Nothin' like winning a case before it ever gets filed."

"Wallinsky and Bunczkowski would have been right proud of me," Thorpe said.

"Who?"

"Just some old folks I heard about. They're long gone now. Long gone."

"What should I tell Joe Thatcher?" Jessup said.

"Tell him? Tell him nothing. The guy's an asshole and we both know it. The only way he's ever going to pull up his socks is to worry about this lawsuit. If he knows I've just got him off the hook, he'll do it all over again."

Jessup drove in silence for a mile thinking about Thatcher and the hospital. Finally he asked, "Are you going to drop his coverage?"

"Hell no. If we drop him it will be a red flag to every hungry lawyer in the state. They'd go over all his cases with a fine-toothed comb."

"What about his hospital privileges?"

"Right now, Hamp, you've got to carry him. If he doesn't straighten out, you'll have to consider dropping him from the staff. Let him stew for a while. It might do him good."

Chapter 14

Yancey Marshall paced the front porch of his A-frame sipping coffee and listening to the sounds of dawn, alone. Donna had gone off to Charleston to be with an aged aunt who had finally given in to cancer. Donna had hardly known the aunt, but when the good-bye letter had come, she remembered the woman had nobody else. Cancer can't be left totally alone, she had told him.

Yancey didn't mind being alone. Not anymore. He now coveted it, like some precious poem, too private to be shared. He had not shared much of his privacy with Donna, only his body and a part of his loneliness. She was the release, the moment, the occasional laughter at dinner and then, the intruder who reminded him of what he had all to himself on the side of the mountain. He knew this, but he didn't feel guilty because she knew it too and didn't ask for more. She wanted more, but she didn't ask. To ask would be to be refused, and that would bring pain. His love for the place was not confined to the mountain or the A-frame. It extended to all the mountains and to the town and to the people who stubbornly lived there as their own people had. They possessed little and asked for nothing, ignoring but not ignorant of the bustling world around them. All of them had seen Atlanta and some had even gone beyond only to return, symbolically kissing the rocky soil and gulping in the cool air that hummed through the pines around them. Mountain people needed no apology or explanation to simply be there with each other.

He had slept poorly. No, he had not slept at all. After dining alone on a small steak and onions and peppers he

fried all together in an old iron skillet, he had tried to
read. A restatement of the War by a man named Herman
Wouk, but it hadn't kept his interest. Too far away, too
different in its characters, too foreign from his part of the
world, *his* Georgia. The book lay next to his chair in the
big room facing the fireplace. It had been replaced again
by the autopsy report and hospital chart of Franklin Pitts.
He knew the truth was somewhere in those records. He
chased it through the nurses' notes and the mysterious lab
reports with a hunter's instinct, stalking, creeping, retrac-
ing his steps over unfamiliar ground. He made a flow
sheet of the hospitalization on a yellow pad, mapping his
way through a mystery until at last that too had been
thrown to the floor, covering both Wouk and Markham.
It was as if he were deciphering the coded confession of
an accused friend, afraid to learn the truth but driven
toward the discovery.

In bed it had been crumpled pillows and a feigned interest in the late talk show without sound. Even after
sign-off he had left the television on as an eerie night light
protecting him from the darkness of his own thoughts.
The ceiling fan had been studied and restudied, the
shadows counted and measured until calls of early morning birds announced that the world would begin again,
with or without him. It was then that he turned off the
TV and padded to the kitchen to make coffee, still
dressed in his flannel shirt and jeans.

Alone on the porch, he tried to see the Pitts boy and
Thatcher together. He had never known Franklin and the
image came to him blurred and stereotyped with long
black teen-age arms and legs, white teeth behind pouting
lips. The basketball star from a school that Yancey hardly
knew. A red brick building. A driveway with yellow blue-
bird buses. Faceless adolescents and scattered reports of
harmless vandalism. Thatcher came with watery eyes and
tinkling glass. A weaving figure in a styleless dark suit, a
slurred, belligerent voice at a party with the inevitable
Marilyn at his arm.

Yancey banished the image of the drunk, replacing him
with a younger man in a short white coat making rounds

at Grady with other young men, listening and learning from an older physician at a patient's bedside. Thatcher seemed eager then, impatient to be of service, to give it all a try. Yancey saw him in the crowded emergency room, shouting urgent orders to a nurse as he skillfully controlled the bleeding from a black man's neck wound. The blood gushed from between Thatcher's fingers and splattered onto the sleeve of his white coat as he called for the nurse. She was busy at a nearby instrument stand carrying out the orders, her back to the intern. Yancey did not understand what Thatcher called for or what she was doing, but he forced her to turn around in his mind.

Suddenly, the scene froze and began to disintegrate. The nurse was Marilyn. Her uniform changed to a sweater with pearls and a plaid skirt. The emergency room and the intern had vanished, leaving her alone. Then she was gone.

Yancey's coffee was cold and suddenly so was he. The mist in the trees was fleeing from the dawn and the jays began to accuse each other of unspeakable crimes. The lawyer knew it was time to choose sides.

His pickup avoided most of the potholes in the ledge road like a wary packhorse. Inside the cab there were the mixed smells of deodorant soap and aftershave. A shower had given him new energy but a dull ache from his sleepless night persisted, somewhere behind the eyes. The sun was out boldly now and long golden fingers poked at the ground between tall dark pines. In an isolated clearing a deer startled at the sound of the oncoming engine and then chose to ignore it, confidently recognizing a neighbor needlessly on his way to town.

Pine Hill was still asleep. The pigeons near the courthouse stepped back an inch or two as the pickup drove over their breakfast and then waddled back into the middle of the road to reclaim it. Yancey thought about stopping at the office but it was too early. The mail was not in yet and it was too pretty a morning to tolerate a musty office. It was going to be bright and a little too cool. It was a mountain morning!

He drove through the town and turned right on Po

Biddy Road. The section was Pine Hill's answer to suburbia. The newer houses in town had been built out there and white fences contained well-cut lawns, four bedrooms, and two-car garages. Marilyn had chosen one of the first lots although it had taken her a few years to get Joe to build and move. The house was a barn red colonial with white window frames and irregular shingles, and a weather vane on the roof, and a brass knocker in the middle of the front door. Few people used the front door and nobody used the brass knocker, but Marilyn thought it looked nice. Visitors would have agreed but there were hardly any of those either anymore.

The house sat at the rear of a wide cul-de-sac. A neighbor had quipped that Marilyn had made the driveway wide enough for Joe to find without hitting the fence, but actually it had been the designer's idea. It balanced the width of the front elevation, he said. It also made a few hundred dollars more for the builder. Marilyn was an easy mark and everyone knew Joe didn't give a damn what got built, where it went, or what it cost as long as he didn't have to discuss it.

Yancey stopped his truck at the corner. The post light near the driveway was on and the garage doors were open. Her car was there, but Joe's wasn't. Yancey glanced at his watch. Quarter to seven. Surgeons get off to the hospital pretty damned early, he reasoned. The truck motor ran quietly as the lawyer scanned the neighborhood. The Atlanta *Constitution* waited patiently in front of every door except the Thatchers. A sure sign that someone was up. He considered turning around and going back to the office and then decided no dammit, I've come this far, I'm going to talk about it. Surely Marilyn knew how to make coffee, at least.

He parked the truck in the driveway behind her Mercedes and got out quietly. There were expensive lawn tools and an unused boat on a trailer inside the garage. They were Joe's symbols of domestic industry and recreation, neither of which he had time for. Yancey half expected a dog to bark when he knocked on the side door, but Joe hadn't found time for that either. Inside came the sounds of a latch chain being unfastened. Marilyn peeked warily through the crack.

"Yancey!" a surprised voice said. She opened the door widely. "I thought you were the yard man."

"Mornin', Marilyn. Hope it's not too early for you. I need to talk to Joe. I thought I'd catch him before he left for the office."

"He's not here, Yancey." Her voice sounded tired.

"I saw his car was gone." He stepped into the kitchen behind her. The room had originally been done with style, but now showed signs of age and neglect. There was a butcher block serving table in the center of the room and tarnished copper-bottomed pots and pans hung above it on hooks. The walls were covered in a powder blue fabric with a fleur-de-lis pattern and grease spots around the brass eagle light switches. The dining area was a high-backed booth with a heavy dark-stained pine table still cluttered with dinner dishes.

Marilyn reached for the closest dinner dish and then abruptly abandoned the project. "We ate late last night," she said. "Coffee?" She crossed the room to an automatic outfit and reached for a stoneware mug.

"Love some." He sat awkwardly on the end of the bench not yet feeling welcome, although there was nothing inhospitable in her attitude.

"I've been thinking about your case," she said, bringing two coffees.

"So have I."

"I shouldn't have come to your office like that. I could have just sent the report over."

"It was all right."

"No, it really wasn't, Yancey. To be honest with you, I wanted to talk you out of the whole lawsuit."

"Who said anything about a lawsuit?" He put too much sugar into his coffee and stirred it in a rapid circular motion.

"Oh, come on, Yancey. We've known each other for a long time. Something happened to the Pitts boy and you're getting ready to file on it."

"I'm not sure." He sipped his cup and looked at her through the steam.

"You're not—" She stopped abruptly hoping she hadn't interrupted his train of thought. He looked tired; about as tired as she felt.

"I've been thinking about the town and the hospital. And I've been thinking about Joe. I'm not sure what good it would do to stir things up."

"Was it something I said?"

"Partly. But there's more to it than all that. I hate to see a boy get hurt. I hate it just as much as the next guy. But I just ain't the kind to want to hurt somebody else just because of it."

"Like Joe?"

"Like Joe, like you, like maybe a lot of folks before it's over."

Marilyn lit another cigarette and dropped the match into the crowded ashtray. She wore a quilted housecoat and red fluffy slippers that fell off her heels, producing a muffled clack on the tile floor with every step. She had brushed her hair but had not applied makeup. Yancey correctly assumed she had not showered. Marilyn was the type to shower vigorously, hair and all, emerging from the bathroom with a scrubbed, shiny face and a towel twisted into a turban. The housecoat and the soft brown hair falling to her shoulders said she wasn't ready for such athletic ablutions.

"Yancey, before you say anymore, I want you to know something." She slid her hand across the table and put it over his. "Joe didn't send me after you. That was my idea, and I'm not proud of it."

"You did what you thought you had to, Marilyn. Does he know?"

"Only that I took the report to your office. That part of it was his idea." She withdrew her hand when she saw him looking at his own.

"Why do you think he sent you with it?"

"I don't know, Yancey. Not really. At first I thought it was some deadline I had to keep. He came home from the office in a big hurry and told me to hightail it over to you with that copy. Seems like he could have sent his nurse or the boy that comes in nights to clean up, but he wanted me to do it." She glanced at the dinner dishes and winced again. She could remember a time when she would never have left them before going to bed. In those days Joe wasn't as bad.

Yancey thought for a moment as he studied her face. Her eyes were brown and a little too big for the sockets. With sleep and a little attention, they could be beautiful eyes. But now they showed the hurt. Her mouth was firm but sensuous and some army dentist had spent a lot of government money making her teeth nearly perfect.

"But I read that report and read that report and read that report," Yancey said, shaking his head sadly. "I ain't no doctor, but I can't see nothin' in there for anybody to be bent out of shape about. That's why I wanted to talk to Joe. I thought maybe I could straighten the whole thing out, least so's I could explain it all to Eula."

"He went straight to the hospital. It was real early. Hardly light yet. I didn't get up but I heard him go."

"I don't know how he does it," Yancey said. His public admiration for doctors had always been obvious. He also thought doctors' offices and hospitals smelled funny. Leftovers from a childhood mystique.

"Neither do I, Yancey." There were years of concern in her voice. "He was . . . he was kinda bad last night."

"Drinkin'?"

She nodded slowly and puffed on her cigarette. The coffee on her lips made the end of the cigarette brown.

"It's been worse lately," she said.

"Maybe he needs help."

"We tried that a couple of years back, Yancey. We told everybody we were going to South America on a cruise. I took him to Duke to dry out. He was fine for a while after that."

"Maybe he needs another 'cruise.' "

"I asked him to. He won't go. It's like he's driven. He's killing himself, Yancey. And I don't know why." Her eyes had become moist but she was not crying.

"He's unhappy with himself, Marilyn. I saw the same

thing in my daddy. He'd sit and drink and stare and then he'd drink some more. It killed him. Mama, too, by the time it was all over. And you know what was botherin' him? Or at least what he *said* was botherin' him?"

Marilyn shook her head.

"The federal government. Now don't that just take the cake? The federal government! Like they gave a shit about my daddy or what he did. All he was was a farmer. Didn't even make 'shine. But that's what it was for him. The federal government. Said the economy was goin' to hell and that's why he drank."

"They don't need a real reason," she said.

"Who?"

"Drunks. The problems follow the booze and the booze follows the problems. It's an endless supply."

"Not endless."

She sighed deeply. "No, I guess you're right. Everything's got to end sometime."

Yancey reached for her hand and found it. He was no longer self-conscious about it. "Marilyn—does he . . . does he *sleep* with you?"

She shook her head but she didn't look at him. Somehow the question was not personal or intruding. Yancey's tone showed genuine concern.

"I remember how you kissed me at the office," he said.

"I'm ashamed about that, Yancey."

"Don't be."

"I thought I was doing it for Joe, but I've thought about it a lot since then, and now I'm not sure." She raised her head and looked at his face. He radiated the health and confidence every advertising agency searched for. He was Wheaties and the Marlboro man and Dial soap in one tanned face. He was everything Joe Thatcher had never been.

"You can't curl up and die, Marilyn," he said. Unconsciously, his eyes swept from her coffee-stained housecoat to the dirty dishes and the clutter of pots and pans near the sink. She saw his inspection and wondered what he thought. A domestic mess could bother a man who had learned to live alone.

"Sometimes I think there's nothing left," she sighed. She put her cigarette in the ashtray and let her finger toy with the hairs on the back of his hand.

"There's more to life than what you're going through," he said after a while. His thoughts were crowded with woods and streams and mountain trails and frosty mornings and crackling fires and rare roast beef.

"There has to be," she said. She thought of the two of them in bed, holding on to each other, giving everything, begging for more, praying it would never end.

Yancey searched Marilyn's face for the anxieties he remembered around his mother's eyes. His own father's drinking and abuse had made his mother old before her time and Marilyn was traevling the same route. "Could you leave him?" he asked.

She withdrew her hand to smoke and weighed the question. "You mean for good?"

"Yancey nodded.

"He's all I've got, Yancey."

"For better or for worse, eh?"

"Not so noble. It's a lot more practical than that." She glanced around the kitchen. "It's a mess, but it's me," she said.

"You don't see yourself in a high rise in Atlanta or a beachfront on Hilton Head, with a fat check coming in every month?"

"Monthly check? He'd never make it alone, Yancey. He'd fall on his ass the moment I left him, and that would be that." She snuffed her cigarette out and cocked her head toward the ceiling to blow a long, thin stream of smoke at an empty plant hook.

"Maybe you'd find someone else," he said casually. He didn't want to sound like a volunteer.

"Who'd have me? I started out to be a doctor's wife and ended up a nursemaid to a drunk. I don't know which is worse."

"Well, one thing's clear," he said. "You don't need any more trouble than you've already got."

Marilyn stared into her coffee. Unused to kind words,

she was in danger of crying. "What about Eula Pitts," she asked. "She's trouble."

Yancey hesitated for a moment before walking to the cluttered sink. He stood there silently, looking into the yard. The bricked barbecue pit, the tailored lawn, the three-season garden, the painted fence—a microcosm of Pine Hill. It was the doctor's house and the doctor's yard. The townspeople called it that because they wanted to and because they needed to. If someone doesn't make it then none of them does.

Yancey threw his gaze to the ceiling and emitted a moan. "Oh, God! Eula Pitts!" He turned to face Marilyn again. She still had not cried.

"What will she do, Yancey?"

"I don't know."

"But, you're her . . . lawyer." She made it sound like executioner.

"Yeah," he said, through a sigh. "I guess I am. But if I weren't, she'd probably get somebody else."

"Like who?"

"Oh, hell, Marilyn. I don't know. Probably one of the smart blacks from Atlanta. They're not worth a damn, but they can find the courthouse as well as anybody else."

"What's she got, Yancey?" The question sounded genuine and probing.

"Her son, Franklin. He—"

"I know. He died, Yancey. I'm not an idiot. But what's it all about?"

Yancey looked at the woman with sympathy. Maybe he had misjudged her. Joe hadn't told her anything. His suspicions that she had come to him as a conspirator faded. "I don't know it all, Marilyn. At least not yet. The kid died after the operation and she wanted to know why."

"Why didn't she ask Joe or see Jessup?"

"Oh, I guess she tried, but they gave her the usual runaround. That's when she came to see me."

"They wouldn't tell her anything?"

The lawyer shook his head. "That's what starts most of these cases, Marilyn. If the doctor and the hospital would just level with folks when something happens, they'd go away satisfied. But they don't, and people have to go out and hire a lawyer. Then, when the lawyer goes and asks about the case, everybody gets nervous and starts to . . ."

"Cover their asses?"

"Yeah."

"But Joe sent over the autopsy report as soon as he got it. He made the copy himself."

Yancey stared into her eyes from across the room. "I know that," he said softly.

His tone forced her to get up and come to him and take both of his hands in hers. He lowered his head, but she bent slightly to look up into his face.

"What was it, Yancey? It was something in the report." She continued to search his face.

He nodded. He wanted to avoid. He wanted to deny. He fought with the rising urges to disclose everything he knew. "I've examined a lot of evidence in my day, Marilyn."

"The report said something bad? Something that could hurt Joe?"

"That autopsy report was a phoney," he said flatly.

"Yancey!" she scolded. "How can you say that? Who would . . ." Her voice trailed off as she answered her own questions.

"He didn't tell you, did he?"

Marilyn shook her head. She could now let the tears fall. She put her head against his chest waiting for his embrace. It came, but slowly, awkwardly.

"I didn't think you knew," he said. Yancey's arms tightened and he felt her sob.

"Then what really happened to the Pitts boy?"

"I don't know yet. But something they want to hide."

"They? Who they?" She looked up at him, oblivious to her tears.

"They. Him. What's the difference? I just don't think Joe's in it all alone."

She slipped her arms around him and put her head on his chest again. "What happens now, Yancey?"

"I'm not sure. I've got to talk to Eula."

"Does she know?"

"No."

"You've got to tell her. You're her lawyer," Marilyn said softly.

"It's not that easy."

She listened to his heart beating, slowly and quietly. It made her own beat faster. Yancey wasn't sharing her fears and it made her feel terribly alone.

"Take me back to your place, Yancey. Not for Joe. For me."

He held her tighter for a moment and closed his eyes. He hadn't wanted this. He knew he wasn't ready for it.

"Not now, Marilyn," he whispered. "Not yet."

Chapter 15

F O R some, thinking is easier while standing at rain-pelted windows, late at night. For others, it's a quiet corner in a big stone church suddenly off a city street, or a long drive to nowhere. For Yancey Marshall it was an outcrop, a few miles up a trail, foot-dangling into a deep ravine that hid a mountain river. He drove straight to Boar's Head from Marilyn's house and parked his truck at the ranger substation. It was occupied only during extended dry spells as a fire lookout and sometimes when logging permits had been granted. For now, it was empty.

It took Yancey a little over an hour to reach Carson's Rock. The main trail was a feeder to the Appalachian but seldom used due to the steep grade. He took it with long, relaxed strides and deep breaths that announced he had been there before. The granite face had lost its earth and foliage years before, and due to its isolation had remained free of everyone's graduation year. Hemberton's Ravine, hundreds of feet below, lived in perpetual shade and mist, a slippery, moss-covered haven for small animals and bears. The river below roared incessantly like a never-ending train at the far end of an Iowa farm.

Yancey had been coming to this isolated rock for several years to ponder legal problems, generally to think about things and to gaze across the ravine at the Three Sisters. Hardly the Tetons or the Maroon Bells, but in the distance, for peace of mind, they rivaled McKinley or Everest.

He gathered a handful of tiny pine cones and tossed them aimlessly down the front of the outcrop as he thought about Eula and Marilyn and Franklin and Joe.

He was not convinced there was a single happy solution to the whole problem. According to law school ethics, the case belonged to Eula and Josh. But she didn't know there was a case, and possessing something unknown sounded a lot more like mining rights than torts. Eula had asked him to get the report from the hospital for her. She wanted them to tell her why Franklin Delano had died. And they had done that. Not truthfully, perhaps, but then he had no proof they lied to her. His suspicions had come from looking too close. Eula had not hired him as a detective, or at least not for more of a detective than a lawyer needs to be. In fact, he wasn't quite sure if she had hired him at all. She hadn't signed a contract. Nobody signed contracts in Pine Hill. A nod and a handshake was enough to show the "meeting of the minds" where the mountains met the skies. But the absence of a contract might be enough to send the woman away. No charge for the hospital chart, Eula. Jessup hadn't charged for it, so why should I? No charge, no check, no question. Just go. She could take the autopsy report and the hospital chart to someone else, if she wanted. Maybe one of those smart black lawyers in Atlanta would see the smoky photocopy edges on Markham's "reports" and raise an eyebrow. Maybe not. Probably not. Oh, hell, Yancey. Who are you kidding? If you don't want the case and you don't want Eula, tell her, for Christ's sake. Eula, I don't want the case. No, softer: Eula, honey, this don't seem to be exactly my kind of case. Miz Pitts, there ain't nothin' I can do for you to bring back Franklin, so there's no sense in . . .

A jay screamed at a squirrel on a dancing branch that threatened to spill the crafty rodent into the ravine. The squabble brought Yancey back from his conversations with Eula. There *was* something there and a little work would uncover it. Why else would a surgeon like Joe Thatcher bother to phoney his own record? But if the problem were big enough to hide, wouldn't it be big enough to kill when uncovered? Did he care? Could he allow himself to care? A lawyer who didn't care? Was he a lawyer who did?

Yancey threw the rest of the pine cones into the air,

stood up and said "Shit" loudly into the ravine. Some problems, he concluded, are destined to be followed, one step at a time with no solutions preplanned. Giving up his favorite rock and crunching down the trail, Yancey knew he would have to find Eula.

In Ray Dingle's office all the elements of an argument were there, but the voices were kept low, heads close together as Billy Markham and his administrator hunched over the expensive oak and glass cocktail table that separated the two imitation Louis XIV bèrgere chairs. It wasn't that Dingle actually appreciated the subtle good taste of his rust velvet furnishings and the fine craftsmanship of his Chinese rug, but business at the Dahlonega Hospital had been good and he could afford it. Besides, he had a deal with a furniture dealer in Atlanta that netted him a ten percent kickback, making every expensive purchase personally more attractive. Dingle was a far better businessman than he was a hospital administrator. His salary at Dahlonega was a modest thirty thousand a year, but his side deals on purchases brought him closer to a hundred.

"So, as I see it," Dingle continued, carefully placing his Wedgwood teacup onto its saucer, "we have been handed a golden opportunity to help Jessup out and to sweeten our contract with ihm at the same time."

"And all I have to do is to throw out my autopsy report on the Pitts kid," Markham said. He ran his fingers admiringly along the smooth, polished edge of the table. His wife, Carrie, had never ceased commenting on the matched Thomasville wall units since she laid eyes on Dingle's office.

"Not throw out, Billy, just modify."

"Same difference."

"Sooner or later, we might have to produce our copy for some nosy lawyer and we'd look dumb if we didn't have one on file."

"It still stinks," Markham said.

"Everything stinks if you get too close to it," Dingle said.

"Even tea in Wedgewood."

"Look. You get thirty-five percent of the gross lab bill-ing. Everytime the gross increases you win. You're happy with that, aren't you?"

"I was till now," Markham said, studying the sailboat design on his cup.

"What does that mean?'" Dingle asked cautiously.

"It means you need to pull off this deal with Jessup and I want more."

"How much more?"

"Forty-five percent."

Dingle squinted and looked at his pathologist carefully. He didn't like to be outbargained on anything. "An in-crease in your contract percentage would take board ap-proval."

"You could swing it."

"Oh, I suppose I could, Billy, but there would be a lot of questions to answer. The board of trustees is composed of our best community leaders. Mostly assholes."

"They always do what you tell them."

"As long as we make money. The minute we operate in the red, they'll kick my ass all the way to the county line, and you know it."

"Fat chance. You've got a closed market, medicare and all. Where else are people going to go for hospital care? Atlanta?"

Dingle smiled at that one. Mountain people wouldn't even buy a car in Atlanta. "Why don't we do it this way?" he suggested. "The board doesn't review our con-tract with Jessup. They already approved the basic agree-ment to cooperate with Pine Hill and sell them certain services."

"Like pathology."

"Right. The board said I can charge them a fee and even show a profit. But as far as how we split it, well, that's internal."

"Go on."

"So how about if I modify our present arrangement and give you sixty or sixty-five percent of the billing on the Pine Hill specimens to bring you up to, say, forty overall?"

"And no audit from the trustees," Markham said, liking it.

"As long as we don't lose money on the deal, the board classifies Pine Hill work as 'humanitarian.' " He said the word as if it identified the ultimate art of stupidity.

"And what if I don't go along?" Markham knew the answer, but he wanted to hear Dingle say it.

"Oh, you could send out your autopsy report as written and even see that it gets to Yancey Marshall, but nobody on staff's going to like it."

"Call it integrity."

"Try paying off your mortgage with integrity."

"We've got to save something as true," Markham said.

"Uh-huh. And in time you'd find the staff agreeing with me that your work had dropped below our usual standards."

"And I'd walk, right?"

Dingle shrugged innocently. "There's always a younger pathologist knocking at the door."

Markham pretended to think it over. "Forty-five percent overall," he said softly.

"I'll try. But forty anyway." Dingle held out his hand across the cocktail table and waited for the pathologist to shake it.

After putting his teacup down very carefully Markham did.

The Mountain View Motel had twenty-two rooms, and if she didn't stop, Eula could get around to all of them, even on the rare weekends when the No Vacancy sign was lit. She had a cart that supplied her with clean sheets and towels, little bars of soap, and plastic glasses in cellophane. The location of the cart identified the room Eula was working on and her daily progress.

Yancey Marshall knocked softly on the open motel room door. The room smelled of stale cigarette smoke. "Eula? You in there?"

There was a clank from the bathroom as she released

the handle to the mop bucket, and when she stuck her head out into the room, she appeared mildly exasperated. She didn't like interruptions.

"Eula. It's me. Yancey Marshall." He stepped into the room and out of the glare in the doorway.

"Mr. Marshall?" She wiped her hands on her apron and came toward him, exchanging her frustrated expression for a wide smile. "Now, ain't that somethin'? Ah was fixin' to come on down to see you jest as soon as Ah could get free. And here you is! Ah thought yo' was some guest comin' to axe me for somethin' and keep me from gettin' mah work done."

"Well, I don't want to bother you none, Eula, but if you were coming to see me anyway, maybe it'll work out better this way."

"Sit down, Mr. Marshall," Eula said expansively. She had a better right than most to offer the motel as her own.

Yancey sat on the corner of one of the double beds, trying not to undo Eula's work. She sat on the desk chair, a hand on each knee, ready to be attentive.

"You must get tired of straightening up after folks," Yancey offered.

"Ah gets used to it. The women is the worse."

Yancey nodded. It seemed like the appropriate thing to do although he wasn't quite sure what she meant. He waited for an explanation, but none came, leaving him with an awkward void.

"I came to see you about Franklin," he said, filling in.

"Yo' found somethin' out?"

"Dr. Thatcher sent over the autopsy report."

"What do it say?"

"It's what it doesn't say that bothers me, Eula."

"Howzat?"

"I don't know. I just have a funny feeling about that report."

"But it tells why Franklin passed?"

"Uh-huh. It says he had a blood clot in the lung."

Eula nodded solemnly. "That's what Dr. Thatcher done tole me."

"But Franklin never broke a bone or sprained his ankle, did he?"

"Not so's Ah remembers. Why?"

"Just wondering. Those lung clots seem to follow things like that."

"All's he yelled about was his belly hurtin'. He didn't say nothin' about no sprain."

"Did Dr. Thatcher ever tell you that anything went wrong with the operation, Eula?"

She pouted and shook her head slowly.

"Or Mr. Jessup, the hospital administrator?" Yancey continued.

"No, suh. That Mr. Jessup done treated me jes' fine." She patted the pocket in her apron where she carried a small imitation leather purse, held closed by a thick green rubber band.

"He's a fine man, Eula. I went to see him at the hospital. I think he got Dr. Thatcher to send over the report."

"And that other man is nice, too' Eula said.

"Other man?" Yancey asked, not really concerned. He didn't expect women like Eula to get the whole thing straight anyway. This sexist-racist tolerance was almost inborn and would have been blatantly insulting if expressed. But outward expression was unnecessary. His practiced southern attitude was sufficient.

"The man that come out to the house with Mr. Jessup," she explained.

"Jessup came out to your house?"

"Uh-huh."

"When."

"Night 'fo last."

"To do what? Did he say anything?" Yancey was suddenly interested.

"He tole Josh and me about the *in*surance and all like that." She accented insurance on the first syllable, apparently distinguishing it for Yancey from outsurance.

The lawyer began to frown. Hamp Jessup and another man at Eula Pitts's house? That had to be the social event of the year, outshining, by contrast, the biggest party ever thrown by Cal Brownlea.

Eula reacted to his frown by offering further explanation. Without it she was convinced he would think her to
be an idiot. There was no doubt in her mind what this
white Georgia lawyer thought of black middle-aged fe-
males. They could clean and cook and look after the children and amen themselves to death at Wednesday evening
services, but they were too dumb to worry about and too
old and too fat to chase.

"The insurance man was from 'Lanta. Said his name
was Tharp or Thorpe or somethin' like that."

"Why do you think he was an insurance man, Eula?"

" 'Cuz he talked like one and 'cuz he had the check."

"Check?" Yancey shrieked, standing up. She had used
the only word in the entire English language that never
failed to get a lawyer's attention.

"Uh-huh." She reached into her apron pocket and took
out the little crumpled purse. Yancey watched for an eter-
nity as she fumbled with the rubber band. He said nothing
during the process, fearing that question would make her
stop until the answer was found.

Finally, the purse popped open, exposing a small roll of
hundred dollar bills. Sheepishly, she offered the money to
Yancey.

"How much is there?" he asked, counting rapidly.

"Five thousand."

"Five tho—"

" 'Cept fo' twenty dollars. I done bought me some
shoes."

Yancey's eyes flashed to the woman's feet. New shoes.
Bright, shiny, ugly, comfortable, and impractical new goddamned shoes!

"What did you have to sign to get the check?" Yancey
asked in a slow cadence that said he dreaded the answer.

"Jes some paper."

"A release?"

"A wha'?"

"A release. Did it talk about the hospital and
Franklin?"

"Uh-huh. It was all about the hospital and Franklin.

That's what the insurance was fo'." It seemed perfectly obvious to Eula and she showed it.

"Those bastards," he said softly.

"They was real nice. Carried Josh all the way home in their car."

Yancey handed the money back. "I think you ought to put that in the bank."

"Yassuh. I jes wanted to show it to Josh. All at once, like. He ain't never seen no five thousand dollars all at once."

"And maybe you'd better not spend anymore of it just yet."

"Suh?"

"I think those men may have taken advantage of you, Eula. You may have to give the money back."

Eula's eyes became enormous as her mouth dropped open. "Give it back? But—"

"Eula, if they were willing to pay you five thousand dollars for Franklin's death, something must have gone wrong."

"They said it was like a school policy."

"Well they were lying. There ain't nothin' like a school policy involved here, Eula. There wasn't any accident. They're just covering up for some liability."

"Fo' what?"

"For something that went wrong in the hospital."

"With Franklin?"

"With something, Eula. I'll have to find out." He started for the door but paused and turned once more. "Was Dr. Thatcher there when they gave you the check?"

"No, uh-uh," she said, shaking her head, making it a triple negative.

"But I'll bet he's included in the release. They didn't leave you a copy of that paper, I suppose."

Eula shook her head again and stood up, wincing slightly as her weight shifted onto the new shoes.

"I'll call you when I find out something, Eula. Just don't you worry none." Despite the situation, he found himself smiling. He couldn't help it. She really did look ridiculous. Utility apron, her hair tied in back by a kerchief, a fist full of hundred dollar bills, and those awful shoes.

Yancey went back to his office and dialed the hospital. He was outraged and worried at the same time. He wanted to call Hamp Jessup every foul name he could think of and lecture him about honor and decency and fraud. He wanted to yell and scream and shout obscenities. He wanted to punch the son-of-a-bitch in the nose. But he did none of these. When Jessup's office answered he said, brusquely, "This is Mr. Thorpe. Put me through to Hamp Jessup."

Mrs. Maxwell bought it and gave him a subdued "Yes sir" in return.

"Hi there, Bobby Lee. What's up?" Hamp said expansively the instant he was on the line.

Yancey paused for a second. He wished he had asked Eula if Thorpe had had an accent, but decided she wouldn't have known. When you hear hoofbeats, it's probably not zebras, he said to himself. In the South there are southerners.

" 'Ole Eula cashed the check," Yancey drawled carefully. Too southern? Too deep? Almost Faulkner and Oxford, Mississippi. Yancey bit his lip.

"Hot damn!" Hamp exclaimed.

It was working. Yancey wondered how far he could make it go.

"Does that get us off the hook?" Hamp asked.

"Mos' likely."

"Thatcher, too?"

"Uh-huh." Yancey knew he was at risk with every word.

"Well, that *is* good news, Bobby Lee. I'll see that Joe gets the word. He'll be mighty glad to hear about it. I know the whole thing's been worrying him."

Yancey put his hand over the phone and evaluated the risk of another question. He knew it would be embarrassing to be discovered in this ruse. He jiggled the telephone button a few times and reached for his best no-accent accent. "Excuse me," he announced abruptly. "This is the telephone company. We have to interrupt this line for emergency repairs. Sorry for the inconvenience."

"What?" Jessup asked.

Yancey clicked the phone off and hung up. He dialed Atlanta information and asked for the number of one Bobby Lee Thorpe, telling the operator that he wanted the business number, not the residence. When it rang, he listened very carefully.

"Southern Casualty," the receptionist repeated. "Hello? Hello?"

Yancey replaced the receiver on the desk set and treated himself to a satisfied smile.

Chapter 16

I T was a common practice for a hospital to ask for and receive a copy of a patient's medical record from a previous hospitalization. The information provided continuity of treatment, and the exchange required only a printed form signed by the patient. Donna Strickland had no trouble finding a complete chart from Mercy Hospital in Macon on a patient named Johnson. He had had his gallbladder removed in Macon after a stone had lodged in his common duct. His symptoms of chronic cholecystitis recurred shortly after his return to Pine Hill, and after a series of ineffective tests, Charlie Kern had sent for a copy of the man's chart to compare results.

With careful pasting to block out the entries on each page of the chart, Donna had managed to produce a convincing blank set of Mercy Hospital forms. After she and Yancey had transcribed Franklin Pitts's findings, a photocopy of their forgery, bearing a fictitious name, looked good enough to fool the FBI.

Yancey kept this masterpiece in a plain manila envelope as he waited in Dr. Kern's reception area for his turn to be seen. Kern had agreed to see the lawyer only after he was assured the questions would not be about one of his own patients.

It was quarter to five when Dr. Kern's last patient, a young unkempt woman, emerged from the inner office clutching a prescription and thanking the nurse profusely.

"Dr. Kern will see you now, Mr. Marshall," the nurse said. She was fortyish, lean, hard, efficient, and exactly what Charlie Kern needed. She could assist him and manage the office at the same time without intruding. Without her he would have been unable to find a Band-Aid or dial the telephone. Her name was Clara, but it should have been Friday.

Yancey followed her down a narrow hallway past several examining rooms to Kern's private office. She announced him as soon as they reached the doorway.

"Well, hello there, Yancey," Kern said from his desk. "It's good to see you. Have a seat."

Yancey thanked him and took the wide-armed Georgia pine chair.

"Mr. Marshall is the last one," the nurse said. "I'm going to head on home."

"Oh, yes. Please do, Clara. And thank you," Kern said.

"Your list for hospital rounds is next to your bag. First office appointment is ten-thirty."

"Fine."

"Good evening, then. Good evening, Mr. Marshall." She left without waiting for replies.

Kern folded his hands on the heavy pine desk and looked over his half glasses at the lawyer. "How you gettin' on, Yancey?"

"Fine. Just fine, Dr. Kern. 'Preciate your lettin' me come by like this."

"Well, from what you said on the telephone, you got a problem in diagnosis, and if I can help any, it'll be my pleasure." Kern fancied himself as a diagnostician and, in fact, wasn't bad at it. His problem lay in his inability to take definitive action once he made a diagnosis. For Kern medicine was a never-ending series of tests, office visits, and X rays invariably evoking a differential diagnosis of several obscure syndromes for which he prescribed mild tranquilizers and mint-flavored chalky liquids to calm the bowel. If the patient had a real medical problem, such as heart disease or diabetes, he would refer him to Brownlea along with a lengthy consultation note which Cal never read, while potential surgical cases were diverted to Thatcher.

Only Charlie Kern could find incipient lupus erythematosis, borderline adrenal insufficiency, questionable midsystolic murmurs, and idiopathic B_{12} deficiencies in anxious patients with chronic complaints. Only he took the time to look for such conditions because, as he put it, he "studied" his patients (a term he picked up at the Medical College of Virginia) and because those vague conditions posed no threat for either of them. The freshman adage was *primum non nocere,* first do no harm, and for Charlie it was more than a caution. It characterized his whole practice.

"I've been asked to look into this young man's case by his uncle, an only survivor," Yancey said. "I don't think you know the uncle. A chicken farmer over near Brasstown Bald? Like I told you on the phone, the boy was treated in Macon. These medical records are all Greek to me." He opened the manila envelope and removed the chart.

"Mercy Hospital?" Kern asked appreciatively as he took the chart and raised his head to adjust his glasses.

"Yes, sir. About a year ago. Seems like this boy developed abdominal pain and was admitted for tests."

Kern held up his hand. "Please, Yancey. Reading medical records and laboratory results is a special talent of mine. I studied under ole Dr. McDermott and got the prize in physical diagnosis my second year at MCV." That was not true, but over the years, Kern had said it so often, he had come to believe it.

"Sorry," Yancey said, sounding humble. "I'll just sit here quiet as a bird dog on point. But I'd be obliged if you'd call out things when you run across them so's I can understand what it's all about." Yancey was smart enough to be very dumb when he was supposed to be. His rule was to look smart for clients, confident for lawyers, and dumb for doctors from whom he wanted information. A law professor had once told him the key to success was to look Irish, sound British, and think Jewish, but he was unable to do any of those convincingly.

"This boy died," Kern observed gravely.

"Yes, sir. That's right."

"It says on the front sheet an autopsy was done," flipping to the end of the chart expectantly.

"They didn't send the autopsy report with the chart."

"That's a funny thing about medical records departments. Some of the librarians consider the autopsy part of the chart and some don't. I guess some of them hold that the medical treatment ended with the death of the patient. They say the autopsy is separate and administrative. It's a lot of nonsense, if you ask me. Seems like they'd keep it all together. Now, at MCV, years ago . . ."

"Yes, sir," Yancey said, short-circuiting this diversion, "did you notice there's no final diagnosis on the face sheet?"

"Well, there's part of one," Kern corrected. "It says 'pulmonary embolus, pending autopsy.' "

"I guess I missed that."

Kern nodded condescendingly. Of course a lawyer would miss that. "Let's see," he began, turning the pages. " 'This fifteen-year-old Negro male complained of pain in the epigastrium, associated with nausea, vomiting, and anorexia.' That's a good point, anorexia. Kids with appendicitis are seldom hungry."

"Uh-huh."

"The pain and tenderness later localized to the right lower quadrant. Classical. I wonder what his white count showed." He turned to the laboratory pages and studied the numbers listed next to a series of abbreviations, "Fourteen thousand five hundred. With a shift to the left."

"Meaning what?"

"Meaning something was inflamed and his bone marrow reacted by sending out more white blood cells to eat up the germs."

"But you said something about a shift to the left?"

"An old term from the days when blood counts were done by hand. The younger or 'acute' cells were counted on the left-hand side of the little adding machine. Nowadays, it's all automatic and there's no left or right to it. Urine seems normal," he added, continuing to read.

"You can tell that?" Yancey asked, sounding amazed.

"Oh, yes, of course. There's a complete UA." At fifty-two, Dr. Kern was balding, his remaining few strands of gray hair stretched furtively across his scalp, ear to ear.

His half glasses rested on a crook in his nose apparently designed for the purpose, and long white hairs grew out of his ears. His taste in clothes was toward moderate conservatism with only the occasional Izod to break the monotony of white oxford button-downs.

"Probably not a Meckle's diverticulum," Kern said almost to himself, "but we must consider every possibility."

Yancey decided not to pursue that one. He had never heard of a Meckle's and really didn't care to.

"Probably too young for pancreatitis or a kidney stone. But he *is* black."

"Does that matter?"

"Got to consider a sickle crisis." Kern referred to the lab pages again. "Nope. He's sickle prep negative." He read for a while in silence and then announced, "Too bad they didn't do a rectal exam." Kern held his finger in the air instructively. "The appendix hangs down next to the place where the large and small intestine come together. When it gets inflamed, we can sometimes get it to hurt by a rectal exam. But they didn't do one here." He tapped on the chart with the same finger and Yancey half expected it to leave a trail of feces.

"They should have done that, huh?" Yancey asked. In his mind he could hear his old torts professor, Gary Smith, intoning the elements of negligence: They failed to do what they should have done or they did something they shouldn't have done and injuries resulted. Franklin had been injured, all right. He was dead. The damages might have been better if he had survived, half paralyzed, but dead would have to do. Some big negligence lawyer from Miami had once remarked in a seminar that the purpose of that big ax you always see hanging on the wall of the railroad car was to allow the conductor, after a wreck, to go through the train, killing the injured survivors, thereby keeping damages to a minimum.

"Well," Kern purred, "there really aren't many of us who take the time to do a *really* complete physical examination these days."

"Ain't that the truth?" Yancey sighed, shaking his head over the sad state of affairs. "What do *you* think this boy had, Dr. Kern?" He said doctor in the same tone he would have said judge.

"Appendicitis."

"I don't know how you do that," Yancey said, buttering his witness not so much as to be greasy, but just enough to add flavor. He knew as well as Kern that appendicitis appeared as a diagnosis on the front sheet but why not throw the doctor a bone? If he didn't want it, he could throw it back.

Kern, of course, did not throw anything back. "I just put two and two together," he said simply.

"They operated on him later," Yancey supplied, hoping to get Kern off of his self-admiring pause.

"Uh-huh." The doctor continued to read the chart, focusing his attention on the operative report and the pathologist's page. "Nothing special about it," he said. "Routine appendectomy. Garden variety inflamed appendix."

"But the boy died."

"Yes, but not in surgery," he said almost to himself. "He developed something else, postoperatively."

Yancey got up and wandered to the doctor's bookshelf. The collection had been extensive and impressive, thirty years earlier. An outdated Boyd's pathology, an old Christopher's surgery, a Cecil and Loeb actually edited by the late Dr. Cecil. All relics in the world of medical literature. Between the books were plastic anatomic models, supplied by drug companies and bearing the name of some marginally effective drug. There was a half a heart, a quartered brain with red and blue blood vessels, and a multicolored transparent female pelvis with dust in the vagina. Yancey wondered how often dust was the real cause of female complaints.

"It's a real puzzle," Kern said, laying the chart on the desk in front of him. "But I'm sure of one thing."

Yancey brightened and came closer to the desk.

"This young man did *not* die of a pulmonary embolus," Kern said.

"Ahhhh," Yancey breathed, settling into the chair; the student at the professor's feet.

"Follow his postoperative course," Kern said, tapping the medical record with his finger. "The diagnosis of acute appendicitis was right. The pathologist confirms it. After the surgery the boy does okay for a while. Then what happens to him? He gets *new* belly pain, swinging fever, his blood count starts going up again. Hell, he's got infection somewhere."

"Where?" Yancey asked eagerly.

"Can't tell for sure, but if you play the probabilities—and that's all diagnostic medicine is—playing the probabilities. If you play the probabilities, the site of the new inflammation is in the abdomen."

"But the appendix was removed."

"Look," Kern said, explaining on his finger, "the appendix and the whole bowel is full of germs. They're supposed to be there. For digestion. But they're supposed to stay *inside* the bowel. If they get out into the belly, bam!—you've got peritonitis."

"And that's bad," Yanced added.

"Bad? Hell, man, that's worse than the appendicitis was in the first place. You can't just reach in and take out the peritonitis. It's all over the place. A *real* mess."

"Is that what you think this kid had?" Yancey asked.

Dr. Kern wrinkled his nose and put on a pained expression. "Not exactly." He flopped his outstretched hand back and forth, illustrating the choices. "This boy went into sudden vomiting, followed by fever and delirium. Frankly, I'd say he was obstructed and later perforated."

"How could he get obstructed?"

"Any number of ways—most of which don't fit his picture at all. But a couple surer than hell do."

"How?"

"Well, maybe the surgeon put a ligature around a loop of bowel or clamped off a blood vessel and caused an infarction. Or—"

"A what?"

"An infarction—just like in the heart. It's an area of cellular death. It can happen in any organ. Just cut off the blood supply to anything and it's liable to happen."

"It happened here?"

"Hard to say. Probably not. But I sure wish they took an X ray."

"It would show them infarct?"

"No. It would show fluid and gas and maybe—" Kern paused and smirked slightly, obviously pleased with himself. "Instruments are radio-opaque."

"Instruments?" Yancey asked, astounded.

Kern shrugged. "Why not? It would fit the postoperative findings better than anything else."

"But wouldn't the pathologist have found an instrument at the autopsy?"

"We certainly hope he would," Kern said. "He wouldn't be much of a pathologist if he missed a clamp now, would he?"

"But he would have reported it and the surgeon would have added that to the diagnoses on the front sheet."

"Uh-huh," Kern said cynically. "My guess is he either didn't have the results of the autopsy when he signed this case out or he 'ignored' it."

"How can a surgeon 'ignore' an autopsy?"

"Easy. It happens all the time. Who's to know? The pathologist hasn't got time to run down to the record room and read all the charts to see if his autopsy findings were put down correctly in the surgeon's discharge summary. Hell, some hospitals, the pathologist's findings are not binding."

"But he makes the final diagnosis!"

"Says you and Arthur Haley. We've got a lot of prima donna docs out there. Do you think some big heart surgeon is going to let some path resident from Thailand tell *him* how his patient died? Fat chance. So in a lot of places the autopsy report is classified as 'advisory.' "

" 'Advisory,' " Yancey repeated.

"Yeah. Nonbinding. Consultative. Not part of the chart."

"And the pathologists put up with that?"

"Oh, not the big ones. Not the giants who write textbook chapters and work at university hospitals. They're pretty straight. Some of them are tigers, raising more hell than they need to. They seem to thrive on telling a surgeon where he went wrong. But in the smaller hospitals the pathologist would be invited to shut up if he found something bad."

"Who'd tell him to do that?" Yancey asked.

"Whoever's ass was in the crack. The surgeon, the hospital administrator—maybe some politician in the community."

"Pressure from *outside* the hospital?"

"Why not? A lot of times the whole community feels protective of its hospital or its university or maybe its famous surgeon. How long did it take to get the whole truth about Elvis Presley? You don't think there was pressure on those pathologists out there in Memphis?"

Yancey found himself nodding. Maybe Franklin's case was not as simple as he had thought. There were all kinds of possibilities. Markham? Brownlea? Harry Long? As mayor he'd have an interest in hiding a scandal. Yancey ached to ask Charlie Kern whether he put Thatcher and Markham in the category he was talking about, but decided it was too close to home. If Kern hadn't recognized the Pitts case so far, he reasoned, he'd better leave well enough alone. Despite Kern's righteous criticism about the clandestine methods of distant colleagues, there was no doubt in Yancey's mind that he would shut up like a clam with lockjaw and throw his legal ass out into the street if he really knew who was involved.

"Could there be that kind of pressure in Macon?" Yancey asked rhetorically.

"Does a fat baby fart?" Kern chuckled.

Yancey knew he had gone far enough with this doctor. Any more might raise suspicions. He stood up and reached for the chart in a way that announced the conference was over.

"Do you want me to call Mercy Hospital and ask about the autopsy?" Kern asked.

"No!" Yancey said, a little too quickly. "I mean—no, thank you, Dr. Kern. I've already written them a letter."

"Whatever you say, Yancey," Kern said, rising and extending his hand. "Let me know if I can help."

"You've already been a big help, Dr. Kern." Yancey

shook the physician's hand. "Send me a bill for your time."

Kern smiled. He enjoyed sending bills to lawyers for little conferences. He'd charge a patient fifteen dollars for an office visit, but bill a lawyer a hundred and fifty for the same amount of time. If the lawyers didn't get hit with substantial bills, they'd come back too often, Kern reasoned.

"Yancey—" Kern said softly as the lawyer approached the door to leave. "Just remember I can't afford to be quoted down there in Macon. The other doctors wouldn't take too kindly to that."

"I understand," Yancey said. He understood all too well. The medical society was filled with doctors who would listen to a lawyer's problem, read a patient's medical record, and even write an opinion criticizing the care given, as long as they could remain anonymous. But a lawyer needed an expert witness, ready to take the stand and swear to tell the truth, the whole truth, and nothing but the truth, regardless of the consequences.

"It's not that I don't want to help you out, Yancey. It's just that I have an obligation to my patients."

"Sure. But you know? There's one thing I don't understand about doctors."

"What's that, Yancey?"

Yancey continued to move toward the door. "How come that a patient stays a patient as long as he is sick or injured, no matter how much of a pest he is. But the minute he files a lawsuit, he becomes one of the bad guys and even his own physician refuses to see him, or send copies of his records or testify in his behalf? Seems to me that he still needs a doctor. All the lawyer does is change the place where's he been getting treated from the hospital to the courthouse."

For a moment the eyes of the lawyer and the doctor met and searched each other. Neither of them needed to answer the questions.

Chapter 17

L A Rue De Paris La Chaumière, tucked away on an obscure side street in the affluent Buckhead section, was considered by some to be the finest French restaurant in Atlanta. Yves, the owner and attentive maitre d', agreed but thought the title too modest.

The establishment was small, expensive, and ideal for impressing out-of-town guests. Or so Bobby Lee Thorpe thought when he suggested that he meet Yancey Marshall there for cocktails and dinner. The call from Pine Hill's only lawyer was enough to make him sound almost friendly.

"Why, of course I'll be glad to see you, Mr. Marshall," he had said over the phone that afternoon. "I'm not familiar with any actions filed against our hospital up there, but I'd be delighted to discuss any problem you may think you have."

Yancey wasn't delighted with the eighty-five-mile drive to Atlanta and he was generally suspicious of French cuisine, particularly when all the waiters wore tuxedos. He parked his pickup truck two blocks from the restaurant and walked back, fearing they had valet parking. He had arrived before Bobby Lee and was ushered into the tiny bar by the proprietor the instant he mentioned the insurance man's name.

The bar had only six stools and was tended, somewhat unexpectedly, by an Australian with a handlebar mustache. He served Yancey an Ancient Age and ginger without condescension and exchanged light conversation with the lawyer until Bobby Lee swaggered in, his arm around Yves. The bartender automatically began to construct a perfect Courvoisier stinger on the rocks.

"You must be Yancey Marshall," Thorpe said enthusiastically as Yves deposited him next to the only customer at the bar.

"Mr. Thorpe?" Yancey offered his hand.

"Call me Bobby Lee. You've met Yves? He's really something. If you could speak French, he'd tell you a couple of the goddamnedest jokes you'll ever hear."

"I could try in English," Yves said.

"Later," Thorpe said, pleasantly, reaching for the stinger. "Courvoisier, I hope, Tony."

"No, you bleedin' arsehole," The bartender said, "I made it with Christian Brothers." Tony reserved these discourtesies for carefully selected regulars who had grown used to his Brisbane banter without taking offense.

"When you are ready for a table, you will let me know," Yves said, glancing toward the door and a newly arriving party of four. "I'm sure you will be pleased with us," he promised Yancey.

"You can't beat the place," Bobby Lee confirmed. "Best fat back and turnip greens in the South."

"*Mon Dieu*," the restaurateur sighed, flashing his eyes toward the ceiling. In a moment he was gone as Tony occupied himself with cocktail orders from inside.

"I like turnip greens," Yancey said.

Bobby Lee cast an obvious glance to the right and to the left and leaned closer to the lawyer. "Don't let it get around, but so do I," he whispered. "These Frenchies don't know how to cook 'em worth a shit." He took another long sip of his drink and smiled to let Yancey know he was kidding. An instant before Yancey wasn't quite sure.

"I've never been here before," Yancey said needlessly.

"You'll love it," Bobby promised. "Tony! Give Mr. Marshall another drink."

"It's Yancey," the lawyer said.

"Okay, Yancey. That's just fine. Just fine. You one of our outstanding Georgia grads?"

Yancey shook his head. "Woodrow Wilson."

"Fine school, Woodrow Wilson," Thorpe said, immediately classifying Yancey as a legal lightweight. "A lot of lawyers around Atlanta went there." Woodrow Wilson was a local law school unaffiliated with any university and unapproved by the American Bar Association. Its graduates were eligible only for the Georgia bar exam and the entrance requirements were significantly lower than Emory's. It attracted the part-timers and the night owls, but many went on to become outstanding Georgia lawyers and some even judges. Night-school lawyers everywhere tended to be a little defensive, although that feeling of inferiority had faded somewhat when Warren Burger became Chief Justice of the Supreme Court. He was one of them, and his rise to prominence gave the night schoolers a lift. It was also said that his appointment gave several Ivy Leaguers apoplexy.

Tony brought another Ancient Age and one more stinger. He knew Thorpe would be ready.

"Let's see," Bobby Lee continued. "You're from Pine Hill, right? Nice little town. Nice little town." It was incomprehensible to him why anyone would want to live in an isolated mountain town like Pine Hill, but what the hell, they bought policies and their money was as green as anyone else's.

"Yes, sir. That's the only place I've ever wanted to practice. Love them hills." He wanted to add that any place would be better than the war zone they called Atlanta.

"Must be peaceful."

"Most of the time," Yancey conceded.

"But I guess they generate a problem or two from time to time, eh? Otherwise you and me would be out of business." He slapped the lawyer on the back, being careful not to spill his drink. It was Thorpe's style to close as soon as possible. A long delay made it only more awkward to discuss a problem later.

"I represent Eula Pitts and her husband, Josh," Yancey said simply.

Bobby Lee nodded gently. He had never entertained any doubt about that point either, even though it had not been discussed on the phone. As far as he was concerned, nothing else had ever happened in Pine Hill.

"They're not happy with their full and final release?" he asked casually. "It was a standard form."

"And of course you just happen to have a copy with you."

"Uh-huh." Thorpe patted his jacket pocket and sipped his stinger.

"Just what did you-all buy for five grand?"

"Peace of mind, Mr. Marshall, peace of mind." A small smile appeared over the edge of his glass as the ice cascaded onto his nose.

"Another stinger, Mr. Thorpe?" Tony asked. He began to pour without waiting for a reply.

"Send it in to the dining room. I'm about ready to eat. How 'bout you, Yancey?" He took the lawyer by the elbow and wheeled him away from the bar. As expected, Yves's response was immediate, with snapping of fingers high in the air to unleash his impeccable force of continental waiters.

At the table the two men paused in their conversation as menus were presented and water poured. Tony had already sent over fresh drinks, clueing the waiter, so that he did not have to show his lack of professionalism by asking, "Who gets the stinger?"

"Just what was it you paid Eula Pitts for, Bobby Lee?" He had begun to look at the tall menu and was dismayed to find the titles in French.

"Any and all claims . . . on behalf of themselves, heirs, executors, administrators, whoever . . . arising out of the diagnosis, treatment, and death of their *dear* departed son, Franklin Delano . . ." It was obvious that Bobby Lee was comfortable with insurance forms.

"Against?"

" . . . any and all parties . . . the hospital . . . the nurses, the medical staff . . . their executors, heirs, partnerships, professional corporations . . ."

"Including Joe Thatcher?"

"Including Dr. Thatcher. Would you consider splitting the rack of lamb with me? It only comes for two."

"I hate lamb. You don't really think Eula and Josh knew what they were doing, do you?"

"They're both of age. Nobody forced them to do *nothin'*. Try the tournedoes, then. The Béarnaise is magnificent."

"They didn't know what kind of a claim they had. Eula thought it was some kind of a school policy." Yancey put the menu down. "Pick out anything but the lamb, Bobby Lee. I don't understand this French stuff."

"We've never admitted there was any claim, Yancey. Just because we paid out some money and collected a couple of signatures on a piece of paper doesn't mean we admit any wrongdoing. I'm just saving the company a lot of aggravation and trouble."

"Five thousand says there was one hell of a lot of trouble brewin' somewhere," Yancey said.

"Naw. That's standard in a death case for us. I mean, lookit here." He used the edge of his salad fork to make parallel creases in Yves perfectly pressed tablecloth to keep track of his points. "We've got a dead nigger boy. And a high school basketball star, too. Pine Hill's a small town and it's full of mountain folks. Lived there all their lives. Know each other real well. Dr. Thatcher's a fine man and a fine doctor, but . . ."

"But what?" Yancey asked, still staring at the marks on the cloth.

"Well, he ain't DeBakey."

"Who?"

"The big heart man in Dallas or Houston or wherever. Thatcher's good, you understand, but we're talking about Pine Hill, Georgia." Bobby Lee said Georgia in four syllables.

"You're saying Thatcher did something wrong?"

"Hell, no, I ain't," Thorpe said. "I'm just trying to explain to you, best I can, what we-all consider when we make a pay-out like that. There ain't nothin' that says I got to sit around on my ass in Atlanta, waiting for somebody to think up a lawsuit. If I smell trouble I've got the authority to take care of it before it starts. And that's all I done here. Nothin' more than that. Now, let's have the steak Diane flambé. They'll make it right here at the table. You'll like that."

"Sounds good to me. You can never go wrong with steak." Yancey sipped the last of his Ancient Age, now well watered by the melting ice, and watched as Bobby Lee instructed the waiter. He didn't just place an order. Bobby Lee and the waiter had a schooled conversation over the entree, the wine, and exactly how the vegetables were to be cooked. It was definitely not a Morrison's Cafeteria.

"Eula came to me and asked me to look into her son's death," Yancey said when Bobby Lee had finished with the waiter.

"And I'm sure you did that for her. That's your job as a lawyer," Thorpe said.

"I went over to the hospital to read the chart."

"And I trust Hamp Jessup treated you with respect and courtesy? He's a fine man."

"Oh, I have no bone to pick with Hamp. We get along. He gave me a look at about everything he had on the boy."

"And?" The wine had arrived and Bobby Lee sniffed and scrubbed the Châteauneuf-du-Pape, searching without success for imperfections.

"And I found out Franklin had appendicitis and was operated on by Dr. Thatcher." The waiter poured Yancey's wine after Thorpe had blessed it with the slightest nod of approval.

"No surprises so far," Bobby Lee said.

"The blood clot to the lungs came as a bit of a surprise."

Thorpe's face remained carefully unchanged. "I'm an insurance man, not a doctor," he said, supervising the filling of his own glass.

"Well, they don't teach much about that in law school either."

"There's no way Joe Thatcher could have caused that blood clot in the lung, you know."

"That's what I found out when the case was explained to me," Yancey said, playing his first card.

"Somebody went over the case for you?"

"Uh-huh. A doctor friend of mine. He gave me some damned good idea."

"Like what?" Bobby Lee moved in on a chilled crab claw with a little urgency that showed anxiety over Yancey's remark.

"Oh, he explained to me what a pulmonary embolus is and how they get made and what happens to the lungs when they get there. Things like that." Yancey poked at his salad as if it were terribly unimportant.

"Your consultant from around here?"

"Atlanta?"

"No, I mean 'around here.' Atlanta, Pine Hill, wherever." Bobby Lee made himself a large forkful of salad by several stabbing motions, occasionally striking the plate.

"I'm not going to tell you who he was, if that's what you're after, Bobby Lee. I had him go over the boy's medical record, including the autopsy report and then tell me what-all he thought." He nibbled absently at the edge of a crab claw. Actually, he was starved, but knew that Thorpe was gauging his level of confidence.

"Did he agree with the pathologist's diagnosis?"

Yancey turned away slightly to watch the waiter set up his alcohol stove, and begin to melt his dollop of clarified butter. He raised and rotated the pan as he painted the meat with a mixture of dry mustard, garlic, and brown sauce. It smelled delicious, but to the mountain lawyer, it looked like raccoon shit.

"With all due respect, Mr. Thorpe," Yancey said, still watching the waiter, "I don't think I'm in a position to disclose *any* of my expert witnesses' findings."

Bobby Lee did not like the sound of 'expert witnesses.' That implied a lawsuit.

"Oh, I understand, Yancey. I'd never ask you to do a thing like that. It's just that I'm a little surprised. I didn't think there was anything to this case."

"Maybe you're right." Yancey felt the presence of another waiter to his left and turned from the flaming of the steak to find a tiny serving of lime sherbet in a long-stemmed glass. He was visibly confused by the sight.

"Yves thinks it clears your palate from the seafood and improves your appreciation of the meat course.

"Oh."

"I think it's half a dessert in the middle of supper," Bobby Lee said. "You don't have to eat it. Just mess it up with your spoon and they'll take the sucker away."

Yancey did better than that. Assuming that Yves probably knew best, he ate the sherbet, and found it light and distracting.

"Yves used to serve the salad last for the same reasons, but nobody would go along with that one. He says that's the way they do it in France, but I find that hard to believe," Thorpe said. The flames on the brandied steak having died, the meat was quickly sliced and served with the remaining sauce.

"Everything is hokay?" Yves said, inserting his version of the Luchow rule. Yancey had never heard of the Luchow case and didn't know that the question, when asked after the first bite, removed liability for defective utensils.

Bobby Lee made a circle with his thumb and index finger, a sign that Yves vaguely associated with an American cigarette advertisement. Nonetheless, he got the message from Bobby Lee's smile and half-filled mouth and went away pleased with his restaurant and himself.

"I'm inclined to sue you for fraud," Yancey said softly. He wiped his mouth on the stiff yellow napkin and wondered why people went to so much trouble to spoil a steak.

"Fraud?" Bobby Lee asked, lightly.

"Uh-huh. Ole Eula didn't know what she was doin'."

"So how has she been harmed? Where's her case?" Bobby Lee asked, pouring more wine.

"It's there."

"Who's at fault? The hospital? Dr. Thatcher? For a blood clot in the lung?" Thorpe dissected his steak Diane with a precision that demonstrated the return of his confidence.

"All of the above?"

"Come on now, Yancey. That's not reasonable and you know it. There ain't no way we caused that boy's death."

"I'm not so sure."

"Your expert says that? I mean, we're straight shooters. You show me how we killed that kid and I'll talk settlement with you. How's them beans?"

"They forgot to cook mine."

"Hell, man. That's the way they're supposed to be. A little crisp. The Eye-talians call that *al dentey,* or something like that.

"I like mine boiled with a hunk of ham."

"My mama used to boil 'em up like that. Mmmmmmmmmm." Bobby Lee managed to make three syllables out of his lip-smackin', finger-lickin', Aunt Jemima growl of general appreciation for all things fried, boiled, or smoked, southern style.

"Why did you take Hamp out there with you?" Yancey asked.

Bobby Lee shrugged. "Goodwill, I guess. I don't go trampin' around them nigger shacks all by myself."

"I'll take seven hundred and fifty thousand," Yancey announced, catching Bobby Lee with a mouthful of Châteauneuf-du-Pape.

Bobby Lee smirked, recovered his poise, and wiped his mouth. "Why not make it a million?"

"Only if I have to go to trial," Yancey said. He was careful not to smile.

Bobby Lee stared at the lawyer from Pine Hill. There was something dangerous about the man and that bothered Thorpe. The eyes were steady and clear. The hands were thick and strong. The hair was a little too short around the ears. This was not one of those downtown Atlanta lawyers willing to settle short to pay off their office rent. This was a true mountain man and Thorpe knew that could be trouble.

"You talked this case over with Dr. Brownlea, yet?" Bobby Lee asked.

"Brownlea? Thatcher's the one that operated on the boy."

"But Brownlea runs the medical show up there and we both know it. You talk to Cal and see what he says."

"Brownlea ain't about to help me sue Thatcher, or the hospital or anyone else."

"You just go talk to him, that's all. I got a lot of faith in ole Cal. He'll straighten you out on this stuff."

Yancey tried to find motive and truth in Thorpe's face but it was too flushed and too watery in the eyes from the stingers and the wine.

"Brownlea doesn't run the courthouse," Yancey said. The remnant of his steak had grown suddenly cold and the flavor of the conversation had made it unpalatable.

"I'm not so sure," Bobby Lee smirked. "Pine Hill's not all that big."

Yancey leaned toward the insurance man. "It's big enough to insure that when somebody is injured by another person's negligence, justice will be found and damages paid." There was something about this Bobby Lee Thorpe that Yancey could intensely dislike and that quality was becoming more and more apparent.

"*If* you can find a case . . . and a jury . . . and a judge who'll be willing to hear it," Bobby Lee said through his teeth. He stared at Yancey Marshall but gestured toward the waiter.

"*Monsieur?*"

"*Cafe.*"

"Your usual style?" the waiter asked, his enthusiasm rising.

"Yeah. Two."

The waiter sensed that the two men were engaged in serious conversation and moved to a nearby empty table to begin the concoction Bobby Lee thought of as coffee. College girls waiting tables in local restaurants invariably saw dinner for two as a date and constantly intruded with inane questions about the ice water, the ashtray, the coffee and, God forbid, their service. Yves hired only men proud enough to be servile without feeling inferior and mature enough to know that even the most pleasant dinner could serve as a battleground for two civilized men.

"I'll find the case," Yancey said slowly. "It's in there

somewhere. Otherwise nobody would have given a damn about Eula or Josh or Franklin. No more than they ever did. But when I see you and Hamp Jessup runnin' out to Eula's place wavin' a check and soundin' like Sunday-after-service callers, I smell a rat."

"A rat's not worth much in court," Bobby Lee said softly. "The smell is worth even less." He paused to supervise the construction of his special coffee. The glass was sugared and flamed into a crystalline frost coated the rim. The coffee was added and to that the several rums, brandies, and liqueurs, allowing easy ignition and a display of graceful pyrotechnics as the mixture was poured from glass to glass. Extinguished, it was served with a gob of whipped cream, a twisted dinner napkin insulating the customer's hand from the hot glass. With a professional lack of passion, Thorpe quietly wondered how much the Rue de Paris would have to pay when one of the coffee-making acrobats missed and flamed the tits off of some doctor's wife.

"*Magnifique,*" Thorpe said as the coffee was placed before him. "You'll like this, Yancey. Too bad they burn off all the good stuff."

"They might not be the only ones. I mean this, Bobby Lee," Yancey said, trying to sip the coffee and negotiate the tied napkin around it. "This Pitts case ain't goin' away. You'd better understand that. I think what you did to Eula stinks, and I'm out to prove it."

"Be my guest."

"Somehow, Thatcher killed that kid and I think you and I both know it. He's dangerous."

"What are you, some kind of a medical crusader?" It was obvious Thorpe didn't believe the title.

"Just a small-town lawyer, Mr. Thorpe. That's all. And I've got a job to do for a client."

Thorpe nodded and ran his fingers rhythmically along the rim of his coffee. "What's a 'small-town lawyer' make these days? Thirty? Fifty thousand a year?"

Yancey felt his molars grind together. This was no casual economic survey. Not from Thorpe. He didn't give a damn how much money lawyers made, small town or not.

"Maybe less. Maybe a hell of a lot less, Bobby Lee," Yancey said, rising, "But I'll tell you one thing. They sleep well."

"Maybe it's the mountain air," Thorpe said, rising and holding out his hand.

The handshake was brief and insincere on both parts. "Maybe," Yancey said. "And maybe it's because they know there's something left to fight for. Something more important than influence and political contacts and big expense accounts. Maybe there are still little people to represent and maybe that can be done honestly, without regard to reward."

"Maybe," Thorpe said, withdrawing his hand. "But anyway, Yancey, I enjoyed meeting you." He looked around the Rue de Paris, obviously pleased. "You couldn't ask for anything better, could you?"

"Maybe," Yancey said. "Next time, the lunch is on me. And it will be at Howard Johnson's."

Chapter 18

THE next day Yancey filed the civil action of *Josh and Eula Pitts* v. *Joseph Thatcher, M.D., and Pine Hill Hospital, Inc.* He knew there might be more defendants, but under Georgia law he could amend his complaint later. The basic case would be sufficient to evoke an answer, undoubtedly a general denial. With a case filed, he could send written interrogatories and take depositions, marrying people to their stories under oath. He had seen the change that could occur after a witness was sworn in and forced to answer questions in front of a court reporter. Only calculated, guarded responses would be tendered, carefully boxed, and protected by the objections of opposing counsel.

Outside the Office of the Clerk of Court, Yancey smiled and tried to imagine Thatcher's face and the sound of Jessup's voice when they were served by the sheriff. With a little luck, Yancey thought, all hell would break loose and the tight little team of conspirators would begin to break apart, each seeking a better defensive posture. According to the Rules of Civil Procedure, they would have twenty days to answer. Twenty days to notify their insurance carrier and begin a defense. Yancey assumed that Bobby Lee, not being an attorney, would assign the case to one of the big Atlanta law firms that handled everything for Southern Casualty. In a way Yancey regretted that. He would have preferred dealing with Thorpe directly, jabbing him wherever he could and watching him bleed. Instead, he assumed he would have to contend with some old fart from one of the hip pocket law firms that depended on the steady hourly rate an insurance client provided. Southern Casualty would have to collar its house tiger and unleash the snail.

Yancey instructed Eula and Josh to speak to no one about the case and to refer all questions or comments to him. At first she had been reluctant to turn over what was left of the five thousand so he could put it in a trust account. They were totally incapable of providing any expense money, but with a forty percent contingency contract, the case was a reasonable bet. Legal ethics, designed almost entirely by the defense bar, prohibited a plaintiff's lawyer from paying the expenses on behalf of his client. But the rules did not forbid a quiet "loan" as long as the client remained liable for repayment. Without cost advancement and contingency contracts, poor clients would never be able to afford a lawyer, even with the best of cases. Doctors universally complained that contingency fees encouraged hungry lawyers to invent a suit where none existed. Their reasoning was correct, but they were unwilling to admit the justice of a system that let a lawyer work his ass off in a case and receive nothing when he lost. All the doctors could see was the forty percent fee when the case brought in a six-figure judgment.

The deputy caught Joe Thatcher in the hospital parking lot a few days later. He had come to serve Hamp Jessup, but was happy to kill two birds with one stone. Typically, the doctor registered embarrassment when the paper was handed to him.

"Probably just a mistake," the deputy said sympathetically.

"I don't know what the world is comin' to," Thatcher said, squinting as he opened the folded document.

"Ain't that the truth," the deputy said. He glanced sheepishly at the doctor and knew there was nothing he could say to make the moment lighter. "Excuse me, Dr. Thatcher," he added. "I've got one for Hamp, too."

"He's inside," Thatcher said, throwing his head toward the hospital. "Who else you got one for?"

"That's all. Just the hospital and you."

Thatcher shook his head slowly. "I did everything I could for that Pitts boy."

"Yes, sir. I know."

"Everything." When he looked up, he was alone. Experience had taught the deputy to serve the paper and get the hell out of the line of fire. Not everybody took kindly to bad news.

Thatcher's response would be embarrassment, then anger, leading to heavy drinking and deeper resentment followed by a smoldering hate. He stalked to the car, viciously stabbed the lock with the key, and threw open the door with such force, the window cracked. The car started obediently as if sensing that any hesitation would evoke a beating from the master. The car screamed out of the parking space and raced through gear levels that threatened to tear out the automatic transmission. Local police had seen him drive like that before, but had never said anything. They needed a surgeon in town and they knew he wasn't drunk. When he had been drinking, he drove fifteen miles an hour and hunched forward over the steering wheel like a myopic turtle groping for a familiar lily pad.

Thatcher made it home without passing through the center of town. That was fortunate since Josh Pitts had been assigned to a crew repairing potholes near the town square. The sight of Josh Pitts in his windshield might have been irresistible.

Leaving the car still rocking in the driveway and the kitchen door wide open he marched to the bar in the den and filled a glass with Jack Daniels. He had no time for ice for this one, or for the next one either. The warm liquor grabbed at his throat and convulsed his stomach into several spasms which he grimaced to control. The Black Jack was down and would stay there if he relaxed and gave it a little time. Time enough to ice the glass and light a cigarette.

Suddenly, he sensed he was not alone and turned abruptly to find Marilyn in the doorway, her expression approaching contempt.

"Getting an early start?"

"That son-of-a-bitch!"

"Who?"

"That bastard of a lawyer. He *sued* me!"

"Yancey Marshall?"

"Yancey Fuckin' Marshall. You said it. I just got the papers." Thatcher reached into his jacket pocket and produced a wrinkled printed form, crumpled it into a baseball and threw it at his wife. It hit the wall above her head and rolled halfway across the room on the shiny planked floor. She knew she should leave it there and walk out, but she had to see the paper.

Thatcher made himself another straight Black Jack as Marilyn smoothed the complaint on the bar with the edge of her hand. The words brought no surprises. The terms were nonspecific and the charges somewhat vague, alleging conduct below the standard of care, negligence, and wrongful death.

"He's not going to get away with it," Joe muttered. He was beginning to move on to drunken hostility.

"This is the boy in the autopsy report," Marilyn blurted.

"I been in this town too goddamned long."

"Won't Hamp report it to some insurance company, Joe? Isn't that what he's supposed to do?"

"Piss-ant lawyer." The ice survived two more quick shots.

"Maybe we can talk to Eula. She ain't got a mean bone in her body," Marilyn whined.

" 'Course she ain't, Marilyn. This ain't Eula. It's all that lawyer. He done talked them niggers into all of this."

"She's probably upset about her boy."

"Oh, I know that. Any mother's going to be upset 'bout her boy dyin'. But nobody like ole Eula Pitts goes and files a lawsuit."

"Times change, Joe."

"Not in Pine Hill they don't." He gulped the last few drops in his glass, tossing the tiny remnant of ice to the back of his throat.

"Maybe we can . . . maybe we can offer her something," Marilyn said.

Without warning, Thatcher threw his glass at the wall behind the bar, shattering a half a dozen wineglasses on a shelf. He turned on Marilyn, his face a Halloween mask. "Offer *her* something?" he snarled. "I ain't payin' that nigger bitch a dime. It's that goddamned lawyer that's going to get something from me, that's who."

"Yancey Marshall won't take anything, Joe," she said, glancing at the broken glasses. "It'll only make him mad if you offer him something." She thought of the lawyer, troubled and hesitant in her kitchen. He was not the bloodthirsty tiger Joe imagined.

"*I'm* not going to offer him nothin'," Thatcher slurred. "I got a couple of 'good ole boys' on the other side of the mountain that owe me since their last car wreck."

"Joe—" she said warily.

"They got ways of settlin' accounts." He picked up a fresh glass and poured another.

"They'll only get you into trouble, Joe," she said cautiously. She was careful not to mention the broken glass. When he was drinking, he would not tolerate correction, especially from Marilyn. She tried that once and had to hide a black eye for two weeks.

"Not these boys. Maybe they got no brains, but they've sure got loyalty. It grows pretty thick in the mountains. When they like you, they'll do anything for you." He took half his drink in one gulp and winced as it burned its way to his stomach.

"I don't know," she said. "It scares me. If Yancey finds out, he'll sic the sheriff on you for sure."

Thatcher turned on her in a flash and grabbed her by the arm. She knew she'd have black-and-blue marks from the grip, but didn't cry out. It was safer to be quiet.

"If he finds out, it won't be from any of my boys and it better not be from you. You hear?" His grip increased as he stared into her face.

"Joe, don't hurt me," she pleaded. "I won't say a word."

He looked at her for a moment longer and then pushed her away. "See that you don't," he warned.

"Let me fix us something to eat," she cooed pleasantly, edging toward the door.

"I'm not hungry," he said, gulping the rest of the drink.

"You might be later," she called from the kitchen. She knew he wouldn't be. He'd be drunker and angrier, but not hungry.

At ten-thirty Joe passed out in a chair. Marilyn tested the depth of his stupor by forcefully removing his shoes. His only movements were deep, rumbling breaths that half trapped a bubble somewhere in his chest. When he got like that she knew it was safe.

Chapter 19

DONNA Strickland called Yancey at his office and asked him to take her out of town for a day or two. Her aunt had died of the cancer and it upset her more than she wanted to admit. The whole visit to the dying woman had been unpleasant. The tumor had spread to the liver and some surgeon had implanted a thin plastic catheter into a vessel near the bile duct and had brought it out to a little rubber plug on the skin. He had taught her how to shoot drugs into the little tube to slow down the growth of the cancer and had convinced her she was saving herself a fortune in hospital bills by doing it herself at home. The drug had caused her hair to fall out and her intestine to painfully shed its lining as her jaundice grew deeper and deeper. In between she gave herself Demerol in the thigh and felt absurdly guilty about it. Donna knew immediately she couldn't help. She couldn't bring herself to administer either of the injections, and the sight of her yellowing, shriveled aunt made her want to run away and cry. She had come back to Pine Hill to avoid it all and to find Yancey.

She had felt strangely relieved when the undertaker called to say the woman had passed, and even more relieved that she had left instructions for a cremation without a service. At that moment she didn't want to be alone and had turned to Yancey for help. He was ready for a day or two away from his desk anyway. The timing was perfect, even for Donna's aunt.

It was Friday. Weekenders were already buzzing around Pine Hill looking for antiques, homemade jams, and quilts. Partly to avoid them, Yancey had suggested driving to Stouffer's Resort on Lake Lanier. Nobody from Pine Hill ever went there. The hotel depended on people from Atlanta. The hotel offered golf and tennis, which neither of them played, boating and swimming, although it was too cold, a respectable bar, and an outstanding restaurant. It was just what the two of them needed.

They arrived at dusk and Yancey checked them in as Mr. and Mrs. Morgan Young from Hickory, North Carolina, serving their secrecy and adding to the enjoyment of getting away.

On the way down to the lake, Donna had cried a little before telling him how her aunt was probably better off. Later, she had started to play with his pants and by the time they got to the room, he was overdue. They made love for an hour before showering, unpacking, and heading for the bar. A combo was playing on a little elevated stage in front of a postage-sized dance floor. The place was surprisingly crowded and most of the tables were taken. Yancey thought the music was too loud and asked to be seated in the corner, out of the way. Donna said it was too dark in the corner, but agreed to give it a try. As he sat down Yancey realized he couldn't have picked a better table. Across the room, seated with a beautiful girl in a long black expensive dress, was Billy Markham. Yancey's first urge was to get up and leave, but then he realized Markham had not seen them yet. He ordered a pair of stingers and tapped Donna on the back of her hand.

"Don't look," he said, smiling at her, "but Billy Markham is sitting across the room."

She immediately looked across the room. "Who's that with him?" she asked.

"I don't know and stop staring."

"That's not his wife," Donna said.

"Look at me, dammit," Yancey said, still smiling. The force of his hushed tone made her turn and look at him.

"You want to leave?" she asked, returning his smile, less convincingly.

"Not yet." He picked up his drink and offered a low toast.

"I hate stingers," she said, returning the salute and sipping the drink.

"An insurance man said they were great."

"I didn't know Dr. Markham had a girl friend," Donna said. "What's his wife's name?"

"Carrie. And why do you assume that's his girl friend? Can't he have a sister or something?"

"In a long black slinky? Come on."

"Women have evil minds," the lawyer said softly.

"That's because we're usually on the bottom. When you're the fuckee you learn to think dirty. How else can us poor women break even?"

Yancey stole another glance at the couple, using his glass as a shield. The girl with the pathologist was in her early twenties and wore her honey brown hair on her bare shoulders. It was obvious she was very interested in the doctor, hanging on his every word and smiling with enthusiasm. She had to be a date, Yancey reasoned. People who knew each other well were never that attentive.

Yancey watched Markham slide his hand across the table, touching the girl as he reached the end of his story. She laughed a little and dabbed her mouth with her napkin while he maintained a practiced deadpan.

"He's telling her a dirty joke," Yancey said.

"So? What are you? The Lake Lanier chaplain? She looks old enough."

"I wonder who she is," Yancey said.

"I'll run right over there and get her phone number for you."

Yancey wasn't listening. He was thinking. Suddenly, he turned to Donna and reached for his wallet. He put a twenty on the table to cover the stingers and began to write a note on the cocktail napkin.

"What are you doing?" Donna asked, craning her neck to see.

"I'm playing according to their rules." He finished the note and turned it around to her. After she had read it, he said, "Give me two minutes and then pay the waiter. Tell him to keep the change and to give this note to Markham's girl."

"But . . ."

"Tell the waiter you know the girl and that it's all a little joke."

"Then what do I do? Sit here and wait for her?"

"No. Leave the bar as soon as you give the waiter the note. Tell him he got the note from a bellboy from the lobby."

"I don't really get it."

"I'm playing a hunch. Billy didn't bring her down here from Dahlonega. He couldn't have kept her hidden up there for long."

"So?"

"So when she gets this note saying that someone has backed into her car, she's going to run right out to the parking lot to look at it." Yancey smiled, pleased with himself. "I'll pick up the license number."

"What if she didn't drive up here?"

"Then I'll go back to our room and show you my other talents."

"You already did."

"Only twice so far tonight," he said, heading for the door without looking back. With that fox at his table Yancey knew Markham would not see him leave.

In the lobby he looked for a place to hide and smiled as he thought that if it were an old John Garfield movie, he'd be reading a newspaper behind a potted palm. Stouffer's didn't provide such classic props but there was a display of scenic photographs for sale in a corner that would do nicely. The photos were placid, pastel, and phoney and no one was inspecting the display.

In three minutes Donna came down the hallway, turned left in the lobby, and took the elevator to their room, but there was no one behind her. After a few moments Yancey began to feel foolish. It hadn't worked. The girl didn't fall for it. Or maybe she didn't drive there after all. . . . Damn. It would have worked for John Garfield.

Then, just as he was about to give up, the girl in the long black dress appeared in the hallway clutching her napkin and looking concerned. The doctor with her glanced around the lobby for a moment and followed her into the parking lot.

Yancey watched them from behind the photographs, but the parking lot was not well lighted. He cupped his face to the window and strained to follow any movement. The lights on the tall poles made round amber pools between the darker rows of cars. Yancey felt a growing sense of failure growing inside him. Then, suddenly, a light went on inside a car as the door was opened. Somebody went in through the driver's side and fumbled with the latch on the glove compartment. The dome light was replaced by the piercing beam of flashlight as the couple carefully inspected the car. He didn't wait for them to return. He took the elevator to his room.

"Row six, three cars to the left of the pole," he told Donna excitedly.

"And I suppose you want me to run out there and get the number," she sighed.

"No, honey. I'll get it as we leave." He began to open his suitcase.

"Leave? We just got here."

"Yup. And in less than an hour we'll be at the Atlanta Hilton. I'm not through with you yet."

Chapter 20

B O B B Y Lee told Hamp to call a meeting of everybody who had anything to do with Franklin Pitts. "I don't care if all they did was dump the shit out of his bedpan," he had said. "Get 'em all together so we'll know where we're goin'."

The meeting was held on the evening shift in the small dining room. Jessup checked them in personally and then locked the door. Most of them had no idea why they had been summoned, but when the administrator said come, they knew it was wise to come.

They became quiet when he stood in front of the group with Bobby Lee. "This here is Mr. Bobby Lee Thorpe," Hamp said, injecting awe into the announcement. "He's *our* insurance man." He pronounced insurance on the first syllable so that even the nurses' aides would properly understand.

"Thank you, Mr. Jessup," Thorpe said, taking over. He paused to let Hamp take a seat in the front row. Only one speaker was needed and there was no doubt in Thorpe's mind who that was going to be. "Is everybody here?" he asked, scanning the dozen or so present. Self-consciously, the nurses and the aides began to steal glances at each other. Only Brownlea and Kern stared straight ahead. They had been previously briefed by the administrator.

"All, I think, except for Dr. Thatcher," Jessup supplied, half rising in his seat to join in the inspection. "But he'll be right along."

As if cued by some off-stage buzzer, Thatcher arrived at the door and began to rattle it against its lock. Jessup made finger and eye movements at the nurse nearest the door. For a moment Bobby Lee was upstaged as Thatcher entered dressed in a long white coat over a green scrub shirt, mumbled greetings to the nurse, and took his seat in the front row next to Brownlea.

"Thank you for coming, Dr. Thatcher," Thorpe said without sounding condescending.

"I had to check a patient," Thatcher explained.

Bobby Lee nodded. His eyes wandered over the group a little more carefully, gaining their attention by his silence and his deadly serious expression. Gone was the affable salesman. Replacing him was the captain of the defense team, a role he enjoyed as much as the hand-shaking, drink-spilling doctor recruiter.

"I asked Mr. Jessup to call this meeting to tell you about some trouble that we are facing. Facing together." Togetherness was to be his theme. Thorpe didn't need ideas or strategy from any of them, Thatcher included. He needed loyalty and was confident he would get it, at least temporarily. There was always the danger that as more and more facts emerged, some would defect to the other side, but as long as he could hold them together he would stay ahead. There was no substitute for them all starting off arm in arm.

"Several weeks ago we treated a young man for appendicitis," he continued. The presence of several black nurses' aides kept him from other racial references. "The patient was Franklin Pitts. I'm sure you all remember him. But because you each took care of this boy in a different way, depending on your assignments, you may not know the complete story. That's why we're here. Dr. Brownlea admitted the boy, and together with Dr. Thatcher the correct diagnosis was made. After the appropriate tests, Dr. Thatcher performed the surgery and the appendix was removed. That operation, ladies and gentlemen, was necessary to save the boy's life. There is no question in my mind that Dr. Thatcher did his usual skillful operation and that all of you who assisted in the operating room performed properly. Mr. Jessup joins me in congratulating all of you for a job well done." He paused to nod appreciatively toward Thatcher as the surgeon modestly studied the palms of his hands.

Thorpe lowered his voice to a raspy whisper as he continued. "The boy died during his postoperative stay in the hospital." One of the black aides thrilled Bobby Lee by emitting a small gasp followed by "Lord, Jesus." Thorpe was sure he was scoring points.

"Let me make it perfectly clear that nothing went wrong," Thorpe continued. "No one did anything he or she wasn't supposed to. Nobody could have asked for better care from any of you nurses and nurses' aides." Thorpe radiated appreciation for the untiring efforts of the ladies seated in front of him. If this asshole in the front row was half as bright as you nurses, he thought, we wouldn't have our collective tit in the proverbial ringer. That reminded him to survey the individual tits. Some of them weren't bad at all.

"Now, I'm no doctor, so you'll have to forgive me if I make a technical error in my explanation of this case. I'm sure the good doctors here will correct me where I'm wrong." (One word from any of those idiots and I'll kill him, Bobby Lee thought without breaking stride.) "It seems that a couple of days after his successful appendectomy, the boy developed a blood clot, probably in the vein from his leg. This clot broke free and without warning"—he paused, finger in the air—"it was carried to his lungs and caused his heart to stop." Thorpe looked at Brownlea and the doctor responded by nodding vigorously. (Reinforcement, Bobby Lee told Brownlea before the meeting. We have got to have it. Otherwise the nurses and those other lard asses will think I'm selling them a bunch of shit. When I look at you, you clap and yell hallelujah.) Brownlea had agreed to do it. They knew they could not depend on Thatcher, and Kern was only hearing the case for the first time. He had never directly participated in the case and had artfully avoided all discussions of it afterward. Trouble is like sand spurs, Kern had said. If you don't want any sticking to you, then you shouldn't get too close.

"Many of you know Eula Pitts and her husband, Josh.

He works with the town maintenance crew. Some of you
might even know their charming daughter, Pearline. She
was a patient here, sometime back, I understand." Thorpe
kept a straight face, but Jessup was forced to cover his
break-up with a coughing fit and fumbling for his handkerchief.

"Those good people will miss Franklin and so will
many of us," Bobby Lee said. The nurse who had said
Jesus before, now added an amen. "And you can understand why these folks might get upset, not knowing the
true facts about the case like we do."

Dr. Thatcher shifted heavily in his seat. Despite his
resolutions to remain poker-faced, his mouth twitched and
his palms were wet. There was a bead of perspiration
somewhere on his neck, itching just below the ear, but he
refused to touch it, fearing that despite Bobby Lee's lecture, all eyes were on him. Only Mary Atkins stole a
glance at him now and then, but her interest had nothing
to do with Franklin Pitts.

"But I *believe*," Bobby Lee intoned, sounding a little
like Martin Luther King, "that it wasn't Eula Pitts or Josh
Pitts that brought this lawsuit." There was a small collective murmur. The cat was coming out of the bag, and just
in time, Jessup thought. Any more delay and some of the
women would have been looking at their watches and
worrying about getting supper ready at home. Put it in,
Bobby Lee, Thatcher thought. Put it in before she cools
off.

"Oh, yes!" Thorpe said, raising his eyebrows. "*We* are
being sued! But I don't want any of you to be afraid or
nervous about anything. I'm here to tell you that no matter what happens, not a single one of you will ever have
to pay out a penny." He held his arms wide like Christ on
the mountain. "The Southern Casualty Insurance Company will cover everything. We owe it to you. *You* are
our family." The arms dropped to his side with an exhausted slapping sound that evoked applause from several
of the women. It was as if they had been miraculously
snatched from the jaws of bankruptcy. As employees of
the hospital, Southern Casualty covered them all anyway.

Bobby Lee's reassurance was both priceless and cost-free. With Thatcher it was a different story. He had his own policy with Southern and they were stuck with him.

"There is a lawyer in this town named Yancey Marshall," Thorpe said without condemnation. He had to be careful. Yancey had probably done legal work for some of the nurses. "And he represents Eula and Josh Pitts in this lawsuit against the hospital and against Dr. Thatcher." *Now* all the eyes flashed to Thatcher for a moment. Now he was free to wipe that damned drop of sweat off his neck.

"You see they *have* to name Dr. Thatcher in the suit because if they didn't, we could say he did something wrong, and if they didn't name the hospital, he could say it was all our fault." Thorpe smiled and tried to look a little perplexed. "That's a little confusing, but that's the way the lawyers for the insurance company explained it to me. And let me tell you we got some of the finest lawyers in the world working for us." He thought for a moment about the adolescent he had just hired to sign the pleadings and felt his stomach tighten.

"Now Mr. Marshall may come around to talk to some of you, and that, of course, is his right. His job is to represent his clients. He's supposed to nose around and ask a lot of damn-fool questions. But don't any of you let him get you mad. He may insinuate that one or more of you did something wrong and somehow caused poor Franklin Pitts to die. But I don't want *any* of you to get mad." He gave them a moment to glance at each other and mumble something stupid.

"Of course," he continued, a little slower, and a little more slyly, "there's no rule that says any of you have got to waste any time with him. You don't have to talk to him at all. Not unless he files some papers and calls a hearing. And if he does we'll have our laywers right in there beside you. There's no way that Southern Casualty is going to let any lawyer trick any of our good and faithful employees. No siree."

The team ate it up. They sat closer together, arms touching without self-consciousness. Ten more minutes of

Thorpe talk and they'd be willing to share toothbrushes and sell their children to benefit their mutual defense fund.

Bobby Lee gave Brownlea the eye. It was his turn.

"Dr. Brownlea? Do you wish to add a few words? I'm sure the ladies . . ."

Brownlea stood up slowly and majestically. He turned to face the women and without looking placed his hand on Dr. Thatcher's shoulder. It was a physician's skillful hand on a surgeon's broad shoulder, white coat and all.

"Mr. Thorpe, we here in Pine Hill have faced trouble before," Brownlea said firmly. "But we've always come through before and by God we'll come through it again." Cal paused and swallowed hard, causing Bobby Lee to wonder if the old fart was buying some of this crap himself. "The mountains and the snow kind of draws us together. We're sort of a family, I guess."

Bobby Lee looked at Thatcher. He was hanging on Brownlea's every word. Thatcher's eyes were slightly red, but Bobby Lee correctly blamed it on booze rather than contrition. Brownlea seemed stuck. He just stood there looking at Thatcher with Thatcher looking at him.

Shit, Bobby Lee thought, they're both going to cry, for Christ's sake. "Well, thank you, Dr. Brownlea," he said abruptly. "I'm sure we can count on you for professional support." He nudged him toward his seat. "Maybe we could hear from Mr. Jessup."

Hamp rose as Brownlea sat down, his hand still resting on Thatcher's shoulder. "We've kept these ladies here long enough, Mr. Thorpe," Hamp said. "They know my office door is always open to them. I'm willing to discuss any problems they may have anytime, day or night." Nurse Atkins smirked at that one and Bobby Lee caught it.

"They'll probably want to talk to you if that Yancey Marshall comes by to ask them any questions, Mr. Jessup," Thorpe suggested. They'd better, he thought. If they didn't, he'd make Hamp fire their asses—after the lawsuit was over, of course. Nobody could be fired *during* a lawsuit. It always looked like hell.

"They'll do that, I'm sure, Mr. Thorpe," Hamp said as

Brownlea nodded in agreement. "And all of us thank you for coming up here from Atlanta to explain all of this to us."

Move 'em out, Hamp, Bobby Lee telegraphed silently. We don't need a lot of bullshit questions. Jessup's announcement and his offer to shake Bobby Lee's hand caused everyone to rise. The early unity had been achieved. The well was carefully poisoned. Yancey Marshall could now swim upstream against the tide of assembled opinion as best he could with Bobby Lee cheering for him to drown.

Thorpe, the three doctors, and Jessup formed a receiving line to shake the hand of each of the ladies as they left and to exchange a few more personal words of encouragement and support. Mary Atkins's parting remarks to Thatcher were careful and formal, but their eyes met and said much more as she squeezed his hand.

Alone again, the men stood in a small circle, fumbling for cigarettes and asking each other with eyebrows and grunts how everyone thought it had gone.

"They'll hang in there, most of them," Bobby Lee said, his expression challenging Hamp Jessup to agree.

"I think you scared the bejesus out of them," Thatcher said, his little laugh identifying his anxiety. No one rushed to join Thatcher in his remark. He was becoming the leper, and in private, no one wanted to stand too close, although the public displays of support for him would continue.

"We may have more of a problem than we think," Dr. Kern said slowly. His hands were stuffed in his pants pockets and he studied his shoes as he spoke.

"How do you see it, Charlie?" Brownlea asked.

Ordinarily, Brownlea sent Kern cases to be studied a little more slowly and a little more carefully than he himself had time for. He was not always impressed by Kern's eccentric diagnoses, but he often enjoyed the man's reasoning. Thatcher thought Kern was an asshole, but had been forbidden by Brownlea to tell him so. At home he did it anyway. He told Marilyn that the man didn't know any medicine at all. Asshole was the name Thatcher gave anyone he didn't understand.

"Tell us what you think, Doctor Kern," Bobby Lee said.

"I think I've been had," Kern replied.

Chapter 21

FOR privacy Jessup brought Bobby Lee and the doctors to his office. Thorpe was pleased with the nurses' pep talk, but obviously upset with his doctors.

"How the hell could you let a hick lawyer like Yancey Marshall just walk right into your office and hand you a chart to review?" Bobby Lee asked. He had assumed Jessup's seat behind the desk.

"Like I told you, Mr. Thorpe," Kern began. "He said the chart was from Macon. I never thought it had anything to do with the Pitts boy." Kern was appropriately standing on the carpet in front of the desk, his weight shifting nervously from one foot to the other.

"But where the hell would he find a chart like that in Macon?" Thatcher asked. At times his stupidity amused Brownlea, but this was not one of them.

"It's not a Macon chart, for Christ's sake, Joe," Brownlea said derisively, "it's your chart, lock, stock, and barrel."

"But—" Thatcher began, confused.

"Yours?" Bobby Lee asked Hamp, pointing his trigger finger.

"No way," Hamp said confidently. "Mine's locked tighter than a drum in my file cabinet."

"One key?" Brownlea asked.

Jessup nodded and patted his pocket. "For that drawer, yes. Not even Mrs. Maxwell."

"Then, how the hell . . . ?" Thorpe asked generally. He turned to look at Thatcher. "You didn't."

"Didn't what?" Thatcher asked. The other men began

165

to glance at the ceiling or their shoes, once again embarrassed by and for their surgical colleague.

"The chart, Dr. Thatcher. The fuckin' hospital record," Thorpe said through his teeth, "Did *you* give it to Yancey Marshall?"

"No!" Thatcher said, resenting the accusation.

"Or to Eula Pitts?" Bobby Lee persisted. All heads were turned to Thatcher now, his replies too important to be missed.

"No! What is this anyway?" Thatcher said.

Bobby Lee sighed. It was time to calm down and explain. Whatever Thatcher might have done, he had to be kept on the team. "Evidently, Yancey has copies of the chart *and* the autopsy report. Somehow he's changed the name on the pages and suckered a review out of Dr. Kern." He caught himself immediately and said, "Sorry, Dr. Kern. Just an expression." A wave of the hand from Kern put him back on the track. "But we don't know how much Yancey really knows about the case or how he got the copies," Thorpe said.

"He got the autopsy report from me," Thatcher said slowly. "I told Hamp I was going to do that. But it's okay. It's one of *my* copies."

"What difference does it make whose copy it was?" Kern asked. "Can't a lawyer come over and get the record if he wants? I mean with a proper release and all?"

"Sure he can, Charlie," Brownlea said, "but there's a little something extra here. We probably ought to bring you up to date." He glanced at Jessup and then at Bobby Lee. Their gentle nods were enough. "The autopsy report that Joe gave Yancey Marshall isn't the same as the one in Hamp's file."

"Wait a minute," Kern said, holding up his hand. "Run that by me again. The autopsy report Joe gave to Yancey is different than Hamp's?"

"Uh-huh," Brownlea said.

"Well, what the hell?" Kern asked. "Who's fault is that? Markham's?"

"I don't think Billy knows a hell of a lot about any of this," Thorpe said.

"Then, how . . . ?"

"Tricky photocopy," Thatcher said. "The same way he must have made the Macon chart you received."

"Son of a bitch," Kern said softly.

"What did the Macon chart say about the appendix?" Thatcher asked cautiously.

"The appendix?" Kern repeated. "Gangrenous, I think. Or, at least, severe acute inflammation. But the autopsy report wasn't included."

Thatcher nodded knowingly. He was confident no copies of the chart had been made before he replaced the pathologist's report on the appendix. Markham's report on the normal appendix had arrived the day after surgery. He had made the switch soon after Donna had added it to Franklin's record. Thatcher had correctly reasoned that the records librarian had more to do than read every incoming pathology report, particularly those that were normal. Until the boy died, Thatcher was confident no one but himself would give a damn about the report. It had only taken him twenty minutes in his office to type out a new report on the appendix, upgrading the diagnosis from normal to gangrenous. An old report on another patient had served as a perfect model.

Brownlea stared at Thatcher for a moment and frowned. He closed his eyes as if to remember and then sighed deeply. What the hell, he thought, they were all into it now, anyway.

"We may have to take another look at this mess," Hamp said, obviously worried.

"Why?" Thorpe asked.

"Well, I was under the impression we had the jump on Yancey," Hamp said.

"We do, don't we?" Thatcher asked.

"Maybe," Hamp said. "I'm just not sure anymore."

"He's got *my* autopsy," Thatcher said. "And it says the boy died of a pulmonary embolus, just like we told his mama."

"Just like the kid in Macon," Kern added.

"Oh, who gives a shit about that phoney Macon chart?" Thatcher said bravely. "All it shows is that

Yancey's a little smarter than we gave him credit for. You're probably just pissed off about him out-foxin' you, Charlie."

"It wasn't me he out-foxed, Joe," Kern said. "He knew whose chart it was all the time."

"Uh-huh," Thorpe said, "but you done told him a pulmonary embolus is one of them things you can't foresee. Happens all the time, right?"

"I wish that was what I did tell him," Kern said.

There was a moment's silence as everyone studied Dr. Kern, the diagnostic curiosity collector.

"What *did* you tell him, Charlie?" Brownlea demanded.

"I think I said something to the effect that the boy's swinging fever and rising blood count suggested an inflammatory site. Something in the belly. Something other than a pulmonary embolus."

"He'll need more than that," Thatcher said confidently.

"I don't want him to have nothin'!" Bobby Lee snapped. "Give him a fact or two and he'll have some medical whore come up here and testify the whole treatment was negligent." In Bobby Lee's mind, a medical whore was any doctor willing to testify for the plaintiff against another doctor. To him it didn't matter whether the expert witness was telling the truth or not.

Bobby Lee got up and faced the window behind the desk. He was exasperated. His defensive line was developing holes before the first play. Or at least before the first play he cared to acknowledge publicly.

"I'll take care of Yancey Marshall," Thatcher said grimly.

"From here on in," Thrope said, turning on the surgeon, "you let me handle this, you hear? When I want any help from you, I'll ask for it."

Chapter 22

YANCEY arrived at the hospital in Dahlonega a few minutes early for his appointment with Billy Markham. The pathologist had postponed the meeting for a couple of days to give himself a chance to talk it over with Ray Dingle, his administrator. They had agreed that a flat refusal to see the lawyer would look too suspicious. Dingle had immediately phoned Hamp Jessup and had promised to report back to him the moment the meeting was over. There was an air of nervous confidence among them. Even Bobby Lee had concurred when Jessup told him what Yancey was up to. Thorpe was convinced that Marshall was only fishing despite his conference with Kern. His confidence was infectious and Markham had felt reassured by it.

"I'll try to be as quick as I can, Dr. Markham," Yancey said as he took a seat in the pathologist's office.

"No problem, Yancey," Markham replied comfortably. "I'll help you however I can.

"Just some routine questions. About the Pitts boy." The lawyer opened his briefcase and began to rummage through some papers, although the autopsy report was on top of the stack.

"Pitts . . . Pitts . . ." Markham squinted as if to recall the name.

Yancey was tempted to say the kid Joe Thatcher killed. "A young black boy who died over at Pine Hill after an appendectomy." He slowly produced the autopsy report and paused to review the front page.

"Oh, yes. Now I recall."

"Dr. Thatcher gave me a copy of the autopsy you performed, but you know the kind of words you pathologists put in them."

"I suppose we do get a little technical." Markham wanted to grab the report out of the lawyer's hand and see what the Thatcher version said, but busied himself with the clicker on his ball-point pen.

"I promised Miz Pitts I'd hightail it on over here and let you explain all this stuff to me so's I could make some sense of it for her. She's really a nice woman."

"I'm sure she is, Yancey. Too bad about her boy."

"And her husband, Josh, too. Awfully nice colored folks. Honest as the day is long. He works for the county."

"Oh?" Christ, Markham thought, when the hell will he get on with it.

"County road department. Fixes potholes and things like that." Yancey continued to scan the report, flipping the pages slowly, hoping to increase the pathologist's interest. Yancey was not satisfied that Markham knew what the report said despite his signature on the front page.

"Sorry I don't have any coffee, Yancey. They shut everything down at seven. Maybe I could call one of the nurses' stations?"

"No, that's all right. I had some on the way over." Marshall paused for a moment and then asked, "Do you have your copy of the autopsy?"

Markham made an almost imperceptible move toward the center drawer of his desk before he caught himself. "I'm sorry, Yancey. Paula Dixon locks up my files when she leaves. If I had only known . . ."

"No problem, Dr. Markham. We can work with mine." He scanned the pathologist's face for signs of nervousness but was unconvinced. If he had had X-ray eyes, he could have seen Thatcher's clamp in the desk drawer lying on top of Markham's report.

"They're all the same," Markham said lightly. He held out his hand. At last, he thought, he'd get a chance to see what that idiot surgeon said.

Yancey wasn't quite ready to surrender the report, but the pathologist's timing had upstaged him. The only thing left to harvest was the expression on Markham's face when he got his first look at the front sheet. To Yancey's disappointment, the pathologist remained a poker face as he read in silence. He flipped to the second page and nodded slowly.

"Uh-huh," he said. "I remember it now. Pulmonary embolus."

"It hits you all of a sudden, doesn't it?" Yancey asked coyly.

Markham's eyes flashed at the lawyer. He was forced to a double meaning but still wasn't sure it was there.

"They seldom give the patient any warning," Markham said steadily.

"A postoperative complication?"

"Sometimes. Sometimes not."

"Pregnancy? After a fractured leg?" Yancey had to show he had done his homework.

"Yeah. That kind of thing." The pathologist continued to read. Incredible, he thought. Thatcher had totally rewritten the front page and then had altered enough of the text to omit all references to the peritonitis and the clamp. Markham had to give the surgeon credit. The forgery looked authentic. He wondered how Thatcher has mastered the pathological jargon, not realizing he had simply lifted appropriate paragraphs from other autopsies in his office files.

"Too bad your copy is locked up," Yancey said. "Who did you say had the keys?"

"My secretary, Paula Dixon."

"Does she type them, too?"

"Uh-huh. The transcribing pool won't touch an autopsy report. Too technical. Too—"

"Gruesome?"

The pathologist thought for a moment. Why would Yancey care who typed the report? Then he saw the typist's initials, "tm," at the bottom of the front sheet. "I suppose you could say that," he said, almost stumbling. "Some people are funny about autopsies. I don't know why. They're no worse than surgical reports.

"How long has Paula been with you?"

"I don't know. A couple of years." Markham's hand felt for the point of his chin.

"Funny," Yancey said. "I thought you used somebody else. Somebody named Judy Ward?"

Markham looked up from the report, half stunned. "Where did you hear that name?" He was suddenly not the same calm Billy Markham. The eyes had widened and a frown had appeared.

"A little luck and a lot of hard work," Yancey said casually. "Does Carrie know?"

Markham's face became stony hard. "You're a son-of-a-bitch, Yancey Marshall," he growled.

"Sometimes it comes with the job."

"I ought to break your nose and kick your ass out of my office."

"Under the circumstances, I don't think that would be appropriate," Yancey said, smiling a little to rub it all in.

"That kind of shit's not fair," Markham said.

"Neither is a phoney autopsy report, Billy."

The pathologist paused for a moment. "It wasn't my idea," he said, already half defeated.

"And Eula Pitts wasn't mine. Look, I don't give a crap who you take to Stouffer's for the weekend. It's none of my business. But I'm gettin' fucked around by the whole bunch of you bastards. All I want is the truth about this Pitts kid."

"It might not be that easy," Markham said. "At least not now."

Marshall nodded knowingly. "Everybody's in too deep?"

"Well it's Thatcher. He's unstable as hell."

"You're right enough there, Billy. Personally, I think he's a dangerous goddamn drunk. He scares the shit out of me."

"Scares *you?*" Markham asked, unbelieving.

"Oh, not personally, you understand. I can take care of myself. But he's a surgeon and he operates on people. He's dangerous, Billy. Even his wife says so. She can't control him."

"I've seen a lot of drunk doctors," the pathologist said

softly. "I remember one that tried to deliver a baby that was too big for the mama. He had to cut off its head to get it out."

"But you're willing to protect them?"

Markham threw his hands wide. "What can I do? Take them all on?"

"Pathologists are supposed to tell the truth. Like lawyers. Or at least like lawyers promise to do." Yancey gave a shrug to soften the example.

"Like lawyers who sneak around to find out some girl's name?"

"It's her real name, isn't it?"

"You're still a prick," Markham said.

"You don't have to believe it, Billy, but I really don't like to play the game this way at all."

"Shit."

"Hamp Jessup and that bastard from the insurance company went over to Eula Pitts's house in the middle of the night, got her dumb husband half drunk, and sweet-talked the both of them into signing a release," Yancey said indignantly. "They gave her five thousand dollars."

"I don't know what's fair and what's not in the insurance business. I figure they're all crooks," Markham said.

"You may be right, Billy. But that ain't the way to treat Pine Hill coloreds. They may not know too much, but you can't fuck 'em over like that and forget about it."

"Yancey Marshall, the civil rights crusader," Billy sneered.

"Screw civil rights," Yancey said. "I don't give a shit about civil rights or integration or school busing or any of that liberal crap out of Washington. I liked it the way it was. Everybody knew where everybody else stood. But this ain't no way to treat 'em. I can't put up with cheatin' 'em out of what's rightfully theirs. No matter who they are."

"This case is liable to ruin Joe Thatcher," Markham warned.

"Sure. *Now* it might," Yancey said, getting up to pace the narrow office. "When it started he could have just authorized Southern Casualty to pay it off, quietlike. Nobody would have known the difference. But now it's gone beyond that. Now there's all kinds of people involved. People who should have known better. He's got Jessup and Thorpe and, for all I know, Cal Brownlea mixed up in it. And maybe you, too. It's not worth it, Billy, No matter what they pay."

"Sometimes things kind of snowball," Markham offered limply.

"Oh, hell, I can see that, Billy," Yancey said, still pacing. "But somehow we've got to find a way out of this mess."

"*We?* I suppose if I don't help, you'll blow the whistle on me."

"I don't want to."

"You're willing to trade me and Carrie and all the rest for Franklin Delano Pitts and his mama." Markham said the boy's name like he had been a criminal.

"I'm between a rock and a hard place, Billy. I ain't sorted it all out yet." He stopped pacing and faced the pathologist. "Not yet," he added.

"A lawyer doesn't have to take every case that comes along, Yancey. Isn't that right?"

"Oh, hell, yes, that's right. No more'n a doctor's got to treat everybody that stumbles into his office."

"Maybe you could drop this one."

Yancey shook his head. "It wouldn't work, Billy. Eula knows something happened. She'd only get somebody else."

Markham looked at the autopsy report again and then exhaled loudly. "Have we got room to trade?" He stared at the lawyer to see if there was any room at all for a deal.

"What have you got in mind, Billy?"

"That depends. What about Judy?"

"She doesn't have to be involved. It's up to you."

"It would really hurt Carrie," Markham said.

"Somebody you just met?"

"A friend of a friend, I guess you could call it." Markham ran his hand across his forehead, grabbing his temples. "I don't know why I went along with it."

"Men have been doing it for centuries," Yancey offered philosophically. "But why Stouffer's at Lake Lanier?"

"That was her idea. I wanted to meet her in Atlanta."

"Okay, so she wanted to get out of town, too. I can understand that. She was afraid her friends might see her."

"Yesterday I would have said the same," Markham said. "But not now. I think I've been set up."

Yancey smiled at the pathologist. "Who'd give a shit who you met for the weekend, besides Carrie?"

"Thorpe."

Yancey closed his eyes and winced. He was beginning to believe he had badly underestimated the insurance man. "Jesus," he said softly.

"They've got me coming and going," Markham said. "I met this guy Thorpe at one of the staff meetings. He was explaining the insurance coverage to the hospital-based physicians. You know, like me and the radiologist and the anesthesiologist?"

"Uh-huh."

"And we got talking and had a few drinks afterward. He said something like, 'You must be tired and bored being a one-man path department.' And I allowed how I was kind of fed up with routine surgicals and repeat lab work on the same old diagnoses. This place isn't Johns Hopkins, you know."

"Or Pine Hill," Yancey needled.

"Yeah. Well Thorpe said he knew this honey in Atlanta that liked to try something new every now and then, and that he'd have her call me."

"This was before the Pitts kid died or after?"

"Oh, before. Maybe a year or so before."

"So you dated this Judy Ward before I saw you at the lake?"

"Yeah. A few times. But what were you doing at Lake Lanier last weekend anyway?"

Yancey held up an index finger and waved it back and forth. "No, no, no, Billy," the lawyer chanted. "That's not the way these things are played out. In order to get me to tell *you* who I was with at Stouffer's, you've got to get the table in the dark corner."

Markham nodded his head. "I guess that wasn't very smart. But we got away with it before and I guess I got careless."

"What makes you think you got away with it before? Doesn't Thorpe have a camera?"

"He wouldn't—" the pathologist froze. "Hell, Yancey. Do you think that's been his game all along?"

The lawyer knew he was in danger of losing his advantage. If a witness began to feel hopeless, he would cave in completely. Yancey needed him to see some glimmer of hope, a way out, in exchange for cooperation. It was an old police technique Yancey remembered from criminal law.

"He was just a blow-hard salesman, Billy. He just wanted to keep you happy and maybe bank something he could use later. He probably set up a lot of guys with a girl."

Markham thought that one over for a moment before nodding. "She always was a little too comfortable. She never asked for anything. Never crowded me the slightest. Everything I wanted to do was all right with her."

"A pro?"

Markham shrugged. "I never actually paid her. Maybe a little help with car fare, but nothing right up front."

"Subsidized by the home office," Yancey suggested.

Markham got up from his desk and stood at the window for a moment. Scenes of a new hospital, somewhere far away, raced through his mind in unconnected patches. Thoughts of Carrie's anger and later her disappointment made him wince. News of the affair and the divorce raced through the medical staff in his mind. Some of them wouldn't care and some of them would say they were proud of him for getting "a little strange," but most of them would question his integrity and be reluctant to trust his diagnoses on difficult tumors. Their wives would force them to avoid him, and he wouldn't ever quite know when. He would be unsure who was still being genuine regardless of what they said. That is unless he admitted it and flaunted it and showed them he didn't give a damn— a damn about gossip, about Carrie, about the rest of the medical staff, and most of all, about their clucking, hand-wringing wives.

"It's probably not all that bad," Yancey said, pretending to read Markham's thoughts.

The pathologist turned around suddenly as if he had just been interrupted. "Maybe not," he said. "But either way I'm screwed. If I don't play ball with you, Thorpe gets me. Isn't that the way it is?"

"That's the way Thorpe would like you to see it. But you've got more to worry about than what Carrie might do to you. You could be involved in an insurance fraud."

"An insurance fraud?" Markham repeated. He said the words like tax evasion or criminal conspiracy. All those things sounded like enormous legal problems to him, although as a pathologist, he didn't know what they really meant. Yancey would have felt the same ill-defined discomfort had he been forced to use words like sarcoma, or myeloma, or amyotrophic lateral sclerosis to explain a vague ache in his back. Comfort came from early familiarity where one could develop contempt and disappeared much later when the real gravity of the same words properly understood became inescapable.

"I'm not sure how the Insurance Commissioner would classify the deal Thorpe and Jessup pulled on Eula and Josh," Yancey said, "but, I'll tell you one thing, he won't like it."

"I didn't have anything to do with that," Markham said.

"Okay, but you let this phony autopsy report out, and surer than hell, that's going to look like conspiracy." Yancey tapped his finger on the report, still lying on the pathologist's desk.

"But Thatcher—"

"Yeah, I know," Yancey said snidely, "you didn't have anything to do with that either, Thatcher did it all. And I suppose he faked the report on the appendix, too."

"The appendix?" Markham tried to sound genuine.

"The boy's chart says it was gangrenous."

"Jesus. How could Joe think—"

"Let's face it, Billy. Thatcher's sick. He thought he'd

get away with it. The booze has pickled his brain, what's left of it."

"Do you think Cal knows all about this?" Markham asked, sounding more anxious.

"How could he not know? Shit, they all must know. Or at least that's what a jury will think." He gave the pathologist a moment to think about it.

"Is it too late to fix it?"

The lawyer shrugged. "That's hard to say. Some of it. You can hang in there with them and go down with the ship or you can help me straighten it out. It's up to you."

"I need time to think about it," Markham said.

"Sure," Yancey said, standing up again. "Keep that copy of the autopsy. It'll give you something to show Thatcher or Brownlea. I'm not going to be hard-nosed about it. I don't need all of you. I can be satisfied with Joe's license and Thorpe's money. So far there isn't any need to tell the State Medical Society about your involvement."

The two men stared at each other for a long time. Markham could feel the hairs on the back of his neck. Yancey wanted the pathologist to feel nervous but not panicked. Once Markham decided there was no way out, he'd join the others and help build a defense. There would be nothing to lose.

"Can you give me some time?" Markham pleaded.

"A little, Billy, but don't sit on it too long." Yancey picked up his briefcase and reached for the door. He knew he had to give Markham a day or two to talk to the others, but only a day or two. More time would give Thorpe an opportunity to talk the pathologist out of everything.

Before the lawyer could open the door, the phone rang. Billy answered it, and held up a finger at the lawyer.

"For me? Who knows I'm here?" He returned to the desk and took the phone from Markham.

"Everybody knows you were coming to see me. I told Ray Dingle about it."

Marshall was still frowning at the pathologist as the hospital operator made the connection.

"Mr. Marshall?" a female voice said.

"Yes, this is Yancey Marshall."

"Mr. Marshall, this is the clerk in the ER at Pine Hill."

"Yes?" That had to be trouble, Yancey thought to himself.

"We have just received Donna Strickland and she . . ."

"She what?" the lawyer demanded. He glared at Markham. If they have done something to Donna for getting him the records, he'd kill them all, he vowed silently.

"She asked me to call," the clerk said. "There was an accident. Her car—"

"Was she hurt?"

"Yes, sir. But she's stable. They are going to take her to surgery."

"Surgery? Who is?" Yancey was almost yelling now.

"Dr. Thatcher and Dr. Brownlea. They're going to operate on her right away. Dr. Thatcher said she is bleeding inside."

"I'll be right there," Yancey said. He put the phone down and turned toward the door again.

"Trouble?" Markham asked.

"Accident. A friend. I'll call you in a couple of days." In a few minutes Yancey's pickup was roaring down the valley road toward Pine Hill.

Chapter 23

TELEVISION programs had led Yancey to expect pandemonium in the ER. Instead there was an ominous silence. The clerk and a uniformed deputy stood in the doorway, their backs to the entrance. The clerk's white dress and stockings outlined her skinny frame and contrasted with the forest green the paunchy sheriff wore. Generous rolls of fat hung over his wide black gun belt and threatened to burst his collar.

"Excuse me," Yancey said almost apologetically.

The clerk waved her hand at him without turning around. She obviously did not want to be bothered. The deputy, equally reluctant, turned halfway and recognized the lawyer.

"Oh, howdy, Mr. Marshall."

"Is that Donna Strickland in there?"

"Yes, it is," the clerk said. "Are you Yancey Marshall?"

"Yeah. How is she?"

"She didn't look so bad when she arrived," the clerk said. "But Dr. Brownlea's been with her a long time."

"Went off the road just beyond Cedar fork," the deputy said. "Rolled it. But she wasn't throwed out."

Yancey nodded his head. "That's a bad curve," he said, straining to look beyond the officer. There were several people in white standing around a wheeled cart. Brownlea was in his shirtsleeves with his back to the door. There were two IV stands at one end of the cart. A unit of blood dripped from one of them and saline from the other.

"Dr. Brownlea's a good doctor," the clerk said encouragingly.

"Yeah," Yancey said. He scanned the crowd around the cart. "Where's Thatcher?" he asked.

"Dr. Thatcher's been called," she said.

"I thought you said on the phone that Thatcher and Brownlea were taking her to the operating room."

"They're fixin' to," the clerk said.

"Dr. Thatcher just got here," the deputy said. He nodded toward the staff dressing room.

"But you can't . . ." the clerk called after him.

"He's expecting me," Yancey replied as he opened the door and went into the dressing room. Thatcher was propped against the steel lockers, trying to force a wobbly leg into a pair of green scrub pants. A cigarette dangled from the corner of his mouth and the smoke curled up to his left eye. His face was flushed and his hair was mussed. The white shirt he wore had obviously served all day and his tie had been pulled loose.

"Jesus Christ," Yancey mumbled. He closed the door and leaned against it for a moment, studying the surgeon.

Thatcher made one more attempt at the scrub pants and almost fell on his face. He glanced at the door, having either seen Yancey come in or out of general self-consciousness. He squinted at the lawyer and stepped out of the scrub pants, his white half-hairless legs appearing like spindles.

"The goddamn lawyer," he growled.

"Thatcher, you're absolutely fried."

"Not quite." Thatcher lurched toward the low bench in front of him and sat heavily on it, renewing his struggle with the pants.

"You're not thinking of operating on Donna," Yancey said slowly.

"No choice. She'll be dead in an hour if we don't." The first leg slid on halfway, increasing the surgeon's difficulty with the second.

"But you could transfer her. Send her to Dahlonega or Atlanta." Yancey moved away from the door and came closer to the surgeon. The smell of bourbon was unmistakable.

Thatcher shook his head slowly and leaned to his left to let the cigarette fall to the floor. "We'd never make it to the ambulance," he said.

"I'll arrange for a chopper."

"Hah!" Thatcher laughed. "Just like that! It'd take a couple of hours to get one up here from Atlanta. By then you'd be flying a dead girl." He pulled the other leg on and stood up, weaving back and forth as he fumbled with the drawstring.

"Joe, I can't let you do this," Yancey said, grabbing Thatcher's shirt.

The surgeon glared at the lawyer and began to peel his hands from his shirt. "This ain't some law court, *Mr.* Marshall. This here's still a hospital and you've got nothin' to say." His rising anger made his voice remarkably steady.

Suddenly, the door burst open and the deputy stuck his head in. "Dr. Brownlea says you'd better come back in there right away, Dr. Thatcher." He looked at the two men facing each other, their four hands on the surgeon's shirt. "You all right?"

"I'm fine, Buford," Thatcher said. "Mr. Marshall here was just helping me with my shirt." The remark made Yancey relax his grip. His hands fell helplessly to his side.

"I want to talk to Brownlea," Yancey said, heading for the door.

"Cal's busy," Thatcher yelled after him. He tore his shirt open, spilling the buttons onto the tile floor. Then, with another lurching motion, he pulled the shirt off, still buttoned at the wrists and inside out.

"What's that lawyer up to?" the deputy asked him.

"He'll be all right, Buford. He's just worried about the girl. Throw me one of them green shirts." He pointed at a stack of neatly folded surgical laundry.

Yancey's attempt to enter the emergency ward was partially blocked by the clerk. The deputy could hear him shouting something at Dr. Brownlea and abandoned Thatcher with a shrug.

"I've go to talk to Brownlea," Yancey yelled. "Tell him! Tell him or I'll go in there myself." The clerk held desperately to one arm, delaying him until Buford arrived. The deputy pushed Yancey against the wall and grabbed him by the wrist.

"You just hold on there, Mr. Marshall," Buford said. His jaw was clenched and his heart pounded in anticipation of a fight.

"You saw Thatcher's condition, Buford," Yancey said. "You know what's going on. Let me talk to Brownlea."

"What's your problem, Yancey?" a familiar voice said behind him. The lawyer looked up to see Cal Brownlea's face. He wore rubber gloves and there was blood spattered on his shirt. Evidently, he hadn't had time to change into greens.

"Cal, goddammit," Yancey said, struggling against the deputy's grip. "Joe's drunk. And he's changing into operating clothes. You've got to stop him."

Brownlea put his hand on the lawyer's shoulder and nodded at the deputy. "Let him go, Buford," Brownlea said. "He'll be all right." The deputy complied, but stood ready to grab the lawyer again.

"I saw him in the dressing room, Cal," Yancey said. "He's shitfaced."

"Yancey!" Brownlea said sharply. "Donna is bleeding inside her belly and maybe into the chest, too. We can't do much about the chest. Not here. But we can open the abdomen and see what's going on. "I've already put some stitches in her face and we got her leg in an inflatable splint. But she's got to be opened, and right now."

"But, Joe is—"

"Joe's all I've got," Brownlea said firmly. "He'll be okay, Yancey. I've seen him work like this before. I don't know how he does it. I'll be right there with him every minute."

"Can't you get Dr. Kern?" Yancey pleaded.

Brownlea shook his head. "Kern's great with the bullshit diagnoses, but he's hopeless in the OR." He looked beyond the lawyer and watched Thatcher emerge from the dressing room. The stagger was unmistakable. Everyone watched in awe. Buford fumbled with the coins in his pocket, convinced that Thatcher could not pass a field sobriety test.

"What's her pressure?" Thatcher asked thickly as he approached the door.

"Sixty over forty," Brownlea said.

"Pressure cuff the blood," Thatcher ordered.

"I did, Joe. This is the second pint."

"Call the lab and tell them to release all the type specific they've got, followed by all the O neg they can find. Then the O pos."

"Full type and cross match?" the clerk asked.

Thatcher wobbled his head. "Uh-uh. Just major group. Start with whatever she is."

"She's A pos," Brownlea said.

"Okay. A pos or neg," Thatcher said to the clerk. "Go to the lab and get it all. And I don't mean stop and fill out the forms. I mean put the units under your arms and *run* back here. You understand?"

The clerk nodded, wide-eyed. She had never been asked to do such a thing before. Her job was to fill out admitting forms and take insurance information from the families. She didn't know anything about the blood bank.

"But how will I know which is which?" she asked.

"Ask the goddamned lab tech, stupid," Thatcher yelled. He pushed Yancey aside and tried to enter the ward, bumping against Brownlea.

"Thatcher," Yancey growled, "if she dies, I'll kill you with my bare hands."

Thatcher turned to look at the lawyer. "You want to kill her? Just continue to stay in my way. If I don't get her into the OR and open the belly, she'll be gone. Now what'll it be?"

Yancey looked at Brownlea, but the physician was staring at the surgeon. Cal could not understand where Thatcher got his strength in times of stress. With the same blood alcohol at a lawn party, he'd be falling on his ass. And here he was barking coherent orders and challenging the town's only lawyer.

"Does Hamp know what you two are up to?" Yancey asked.

"What the fuck can Jessup do for us now? Tell us to fill out some goddamned consent form?" Thatcher turned away from the lawyer and took a large awkward step toward the cart. "You'd better change, Cal. We haven't got all night."

"Two minutes," Brownlea promised.

"Where's Mrs. Gunsby?" Thatcher asked the small crowd of nurses around Donna's cart. Gunsby was Thatcher's favorite nurse-anesthetist. She had seen him through many storms. She had also watched him sink when everything was over.

"She's gone to the OR," one of the nurses said.

"This lady tubed?" Thatcher demanded. He approached the head of the cart and raised Donna's right eyelid as he simultaneously felt for a pulse in the neck. The eye looked at him and searched his face. The lips moved slightly, causing the untrimmed sutures to flop up and down like whiskers.

"Not yet, Dr. Thatcher," a familiar voice said from his right. "Gunsby was afraid she'd aspirate."

Thatcher glanced at the nurse and saw Mary Atkins. She allowed a little smile that ended in a firm jaw and a reassuring wink.

"What are you doing here?" Thatcher asked.

"I heard the ambulance call over my CB at home," Mary said. "I thought you might need me."

Thatcher put his hand on hers, oblivious to the other nurses. She couldn't tell whether he was trying to let everybody know or whether he was too drunk to worry about it. Either way she didn't let it go on for long. She slid her hand out from under his and placed her fingers on Donna's wrist. Thatcher looked at her for a moment, weaved, blinked, and then swallowed hard. He was genuinely glad to see her. She made him feel more confident.

"Nothing goes wrong when you're around, Mary," he slurred.

She glanced away from him and stared at the unit of blood. An inflated blood pressure cuff had been wrapped around it to force the blood out of the plastic bag more quickly. In the old days they had to pump air into the blood bottles, risking a massive air embolism when the setup was forgotten. The newer plastic bags simply collapsed under the added pressure, forcing the blood into the IV line without the danger of pushing air into the system.

"That unit's getting pretty low," she said, trying to sound professional.

Her remark forced Thatcher to look at the blood. "I've ordered more," he said. "Hang it and squeeze the minute it arrives."

"Yes, Doctor," Atkins said stiffly. She needed to perform in front of the other nurses.

"And don't give me any crap about the type and cross-match forms," he said, running his hands expertly across Donna's abdomen. He felt gingerly for the spleen, intuitively convinced that it was ruptured and bleeding. "Lay out a full lap set," he mumbled. "Let's hope to hell she ain't bleeding in the chest."

Brownlea came out of the dressing room looking like the jolly green giant in a scrub suit that was too small for him. His belly showed above the drawstring and his ankles stuck out of the pants like an adolescent.

"Any change?" Brownlea asked, approaching the table.

"She's slipping, Cal," Thatcher said. "Bet you my ass she's busted her spleen. Maybe the liver, too."

Brownlea nodded. Trauma surgery was not his chosen field, but he could follow Thatcher when he was needed. He knew that Joe was no wizard either. In the few big accident cases they had tackled together, they had won some and lost some. There hadn't been any other choice.

"Think we ought to get some more X rays?" Brownlea asked.

"What for? The skull's negative, as far as I can tell. Let's see what's what in the belly. We can't do a hell of a lot about the chest."

"I'm always worried about the neck in these crashes, Joe," Brownlea said softly.

"Sure," Thatcher said mockingly. "Get a dozen views

of the neck. And then take your time reading them, because she'll be long dead by then. You can show them all to Billy Markham at the post."

Brownlea looked at Thatcher and knew the surgeon was right. There was a brief time available to go for the "fixable," as Thatcher's old surgery professor used to call it.

"When your chances aren't worth a rat's ass anyway, Cal, you go for the most important thing you can fix," Thatcher said. "If it works, it works. And if it don't . . ." He took his hands off Donna's abdomen long enough to hold them in the air helplessly.

"You're the man with the knife, Joe," Brownlea said.

"And if you're lucky, Cal, I won't cut *you*." Thatcher allowed a thin smile. His eyes were watery and his mouth was beginning to dry. Inside, his whole body ached for another drink.

Thatcher tossed his head toward the rear exit. The door led through a short corridor to the operating room. Mary Atkins did not need explicit orders from Thatcher. She knew what they would need, and more than that, she knew what they had to offer.

The group began to move like some many-legged creature, with IV stands for antennae and a wheeled cart for a body. It was hard for Yancey, restrained in the other doorway by the deputy, to make out specific parts that had to be Donna. There were arms and legs and sheets and uniforms everywhere. The foot that stuck out from the inflatable splint was certainly hers, and as they reached the rear door, Yancey said good-bye to it.

Thatcher turned around and looked at Yancey as the cart disappeared down the corridor to the operating room. The empty room between them was a scarred battlefield with bandages, wrappings, and plastic debris abandoned on the floor. Thatcher took a few lurching steps back into the arena and stopped. He stood silently with his hands hanging limply at his sides. This was not the champion pausing to receive the accolade but a weary and worn field commander whose outfit had been hammered too often.

Yancey struggled past the deputy, stumbling into the room with an unsteadiness that matched Thatcher's. He came close to the surgeon and they stood face to face. Yancey's heart pounded from the struggle and his mouth was dry with anxiety.

"I want you to save her, Joe," Yancey said softly.

"I'll do the best I know how."

"I'll be mighty obliged to you, Joe."

"My obligation is to Donna. None of this is for you, Yancey."

Yancey felt the muscles of his jaw tighten. "I know I pissed you off with the Pitts case, but I had a client to represent."

"Then you go play lawyer and represent her, Mr. Marshall," Thatcher said, tapping his finger on Yancey's chest. "And I'll play surgeon and see to Donna Strickland." He glared at the lawyer with bleary eyes and then turned toward the operating room.

"I could talk to Miz Pitts, Joe," Yancey said, hopefully. The suggestion made Thatcher stop in his tracks. He put his hands on his hips and looked at the ceiling, his back still turned to the lawyer. "You can talk to anybody you fuckin'-A please, mister," Thatcher shouted without turning around. "Just remember, whenever you get through with whatever you think you have to do for that colored woman, I'll still be here, doing what *I* have to do." Thatcher's hands fell to his side, the hands knotted in tight fists. He walked toward the door and then paused to look once more at Yancey Marshall.

"And by the way," he added, "it's *doctor* to you."

In a moment Yancey was left standing alone in the middle of an empty emergency room. Everyone else had gone. Suddenly, he felt unsure about everything: the case, the law, and the value of life.

It was time for him to cry. And he did.

Chapter 24

J ESSUP'S call caught Bobby Lee in his high-rise condominium. He had told his secretary that he would be spending a quiet evening at home reading an early Le Carré spy story and that he was not to be bothered. In fact, he hated spy novels, especially British ones. The characters were always a little too clever and cultured for Thorpe. He felt intimidated by characters that seemed better educated than he was.

His true purpose was to pry the pants off an Eastern stewardess he had met on a flight from Memphis a few weeks before. The hour in the air had given him time to find out her name, her phone number, her roommate's name, her address, the fact she had been married once, and that she thought artichokes were a dietary joke. She had learned from him only the few facts he wished to disclose. He sure as hell didn't want her calling him at the office. He had enough trouble keeping Mrs. Dillard's nose out of his personal affairs.

The stew hadn't arrived yet, although he had made her promise to be on time. He claimed his busy schedule would not allow him to pick her up at her apartment, but actually he didn't want to be bothered driving all the way down beyond the airport where the airline people invariably lived—new, cheap, lots of jet noise, and predominately black.

"But why the fuck couldn't you have called over somebody from Dahlonega? They've got a couple of decent surgeons, haven't they?" Bobby Lee twisted the extra long telephone cord around his fingers as he paced around the living room and looked out at the downtown lights. The apartment was on Peachtree Street, almost in Buckhead, just below the cathedrals, a fairly new conversion from expensive rental units. His was a three-bedroom unit on the southwest corner of the eighteenth floor, three floors from the top. At the end of most days he could enjoy the reds and oranges of the sunset as it painted the downtown buildings one by one and transformed the Peachtree Plaza Hotel into a temporary holiday candle. Visitors found it breathtaking, but Bobby Lee had become bored with its repetitive beauty and preferred sunsets at Harrison's, a bar for three-piece suits and auburn-haired honeys with charge accounts at Lord & Taylor's.

"The only one in town was Bert Livingston and Cal thought he was just too old to be of much help. He says Joe's not too bad off," Hamp explained.

"Not bad off, my foot. He's probably hanging on with both hands."

"We have the shittiest luck," Hamp said. "Of all the women in town we have to get Yancey's."

"Of all the gin joints in all the world she had to walk into our place," Bobby Lee paraphrased, almost to himself.

"Howzat?" Hamp was not a fan of old movies on TV.

"Nothing. But at least now we know where he got his copy of Pitts record."

"The bitch."

"Be nice. She's dying in your fuckin' operating room."

"Cal says she's holding her own."

"She'll be holding mine and yours too if she doesn't make it," Thorpe said. The doorbell chimed like the end of round two. "Hold on a second, Hamp. I've got to answer the door." He threw the phone onto the blue velvet couch and padded to the door. He hated to wear shoes at home, even when there were guests.

"Come in, baby, I'm on the phone." He brushed her with a ceremonial peck on the cheek and recognized her Halston. Somehow he knew she resented being called baby, but he really didn't give a shit. She was goddamned good looking, but not good enough to grow new manners for. At least not at his age.

As far as Thorpe could recall, Gigi Cavanaugh was twenty-four, a graduate of some obscure college in the Midwest and had a pair of thirty-eights. In fact, they were forties, and the college was just outside Chicago. The age and the name were correct. She had always felt that Gigi was a little tacky, especially after the Caron movie, but it was still better than Gertrude. She was born on November sixteenth, and her mother, in a belch of recurrent piosity, had named her after the saint whose day it was. Lucky for Gigi she hadn't been born on the feast of Eusebius.

Bobby Lee had returned to the phone before Gigi cleared the foyer. The wall hangings were beautiful, matched, expertly framed, and totally irrelevant, since they had been selected by an interior decorator. When she came into the soft-lighted living room she emitted a long, low "Ooooo-wow," despite her promises to herself to stop using the term.

"Pretty, isn't it?" Bobby Lee said, holding his hand over the mouthpiece.

"Incredible." She stepped closer to the window to block the reflections.

"They are," Bobby Lee said, looking at her chest.

"There just wasn't any other way to handle it," Jessup said. "Cal said she had to be opened up right away."

"We've got to take it the way it comes, Hamp. What's Yancey said about it so far?"

"I guess he's taking it pretty hard. A deputy I've known for years said he broke down in the ER and then left for a while. I understand he's back now."

"Well make him happy, Hamp. Let him know we're doing everything we can. Get him a drink. Shit, get him a whole bottle. I'd rather have him walleyed if she dies."

Thorpe squinted to admire the curve of Gigi's ass. He tapped her on the shoulder and offered her a drink by pantomime. She held up an index finger, delaying the drink for a few more minutes at the window.

There was a pause on the other end of the phone. "I don't think I can hold it together, Bobby Lee," Jessup said. "Not if the whole thing starts to unravel off the pool. Not if she—"

"Listen, Hamp. There's a lot at stake here," Thorpe said. "It's not your job or mine to run into some operating room and steady the hand of a drunk surgeon. The doctors have got to look to themselves for that kind of kindness. You and me, well, we're better fixed for keeping the books and sizing up how things come out once somebody steps in the shit. Then it's up to us to show 'em how they can get their tit back out of the ringer. You see what I mean?"

Gigi felt for her left breast and was subsconsciously happy to find it intact. The downtown Coca-Cola sign blurred by her astigmatism, blinked on and off like a distant Christmas tree bulb.

"That's easy for you to say. You're down there in Atlanta. You haven't got to put up with the kind of folks we have up here. Yancey Marshall's not just gonna file another lawsuit if she dies. He's going to take this place apart, brick by brick. And I can't handle that kind of stuff." There was an obvious tremor in Hamp's voice.

"You just hightail it over to Yancey Marshall and tell him we're doing every goddamned thing we can to save that girl's life." Thorpe shouted. The hairs on the back of Gigi's neck began to prickle. Bobby Lee sensed her uneasiness and put his hand over the mouthpiece. "Redneck, chicken-shit hospital administrator," he explained. "I'll be with you in a minute. Think about what you'd like to eat." He knew what he'd like to offer her to eat, but the Rue de Paris would have to come first. The law of the modern jungle.

"You know how Joe is," Hamp pleaded.

"Eye like an eagle, heart of a lion, hands like a lady and head like a cabbage," Thorpe said. "A surgeon."

"Why don't you just fart *your* way into the OR and give him your little words of wisdom personally?" Hamp asked.

"And what else," Thorpe taunted, "read him a couple of chapters from Christopher?" Bobby Lee was proud of his reference to a classical but outdated surgical text, but Hamp missed it altogether.

There was a pause at the northern end of the phone until Jessup said. "I'm scared, Bobby Lee. Plain scared."

Thorpe could tell that the hospital administrator really was. This problem didn't call for glad-handing a member of the board of trustees or bullshiting with Harry Long about his rose garden in the park. This one was liable to have Hamp Jessup coming apart at the seams.

"I'll tell you what, Hamp," the insurance man said, admiring Gigi's ankle. "Let me take care of something down here and I'll be right up. How long do you think Thatcher will stay in the OR?"

"Hell, I don't know. Maybe a couple of hours. Maybe more. Who knows?"

"You tell him for me to keep his ass in that OR no matter what happens. I don't want him talking to Yancey. You understand?" Thorpe shrugged helplessly at the Eastern stew as she began to get the drift of what was happening to her big night out on the town.

"But what if she . . . ?" Hamp stammered.

"No matter what," Thorpe said, measuring each word like a submarine commander. He visualized Hamp nodding obediently.

"I'll tell him." Hamp paused and added, "You could be here in an hour if you stepped on it."

"I need a little longer than that," Bobby Lee said. "Give me an hour and a half to two hours."

"Why, for Christ's sake?" Hamp demanded. "We got troubles. Big troubles."

"Uh-huh. But I want to see if Eastern has earned her wings today."

"You what?"

"I'll be there as soon as I can come," Bobby Lee said, grinning to himself.

The floating nurse dutifully wiped the perspiration from Joe Thatcher's brow. Mary Atkins had established an eye contact signal system with the OR personnel who were not scrubbed in. An Atkins frown or raised eyebrow could produce instant adjustments of gowns, sponges to

foreheads, and sometimes a back scratch for a weary surgeon, imprisoned by his sterile costume.

"Let me see that edge of the liver again, Cal,"
Thatcher said, squinting into the gaping abdomen incision.

Brownlea obliged by raising the liver slightly with his
retractor.

"Light, please," Thatcher said mechanically. The beam
moved a half inch to the right, directed by Atkins, using a
sterile attachment.

"I thought there was an ooze there when we looked before," Cal said.

"It must have come from the tear in the spleen,"
Thatcher said, dabbing a slightly dark area on the under-
side of the left lobe. "There's nothing here. One thing
about livers. When they want to bleed, they bleed. You
can always find the hole . . . not that you can always stop
it."

"How's she doin', Gunsby?" Brownlea asked without
looking at the nurse-anesthetist.

A voice behind the sterile drapes at the head of the
table said, "Hundred over sixty. Second unit of blood in-
fusing well."

"Her pressure stopped dropping when you clamped the
spleen," Cal said to Thatcher.

"Yeah. We'll go back and get it out just as soon as I've
checked everything else. A tear like that in the spleen
could mean something else is busted, too. I remember a
hot-shot resident at Grady that operated on a little girl
with a bike accident, found a torn spleen, took it out, and
closed over a ruptured small bowel. He'll remember that
lesson for the rest of his life."

"Did she do okay?" Atkins asked.

Thatcher shook his head. "Peritonitis and died. Went
to the medical examiner's morgue across the street. The
forensic resident came over to the surgical mortality conference and ate our asses out over it. Had slides and every
thing." The retelling of the Grady peritonitis case gave
him an uneasy feeling. When Franklin Pitts had died of
peritonitis there was no forensic pathology resident to at-

tend the conference and present the autopsy findings.
There had been no constructive criticism from surgical
colleagues. No mea culpas in front of the associate professor of surgery. Instead there had been a private report.
The catharsis of the teaching conference was missing.
There was no board-certified white-haired chief to say,
"You know what went wrong, now don't do it again." At
Grady the march of patients was endless, faceless, and often without names. Cases, that's what they were, Thatcher
recalled, cases. But in Pine Hill they were people with
memories and relatives and continuing problems even if
they had surgery; even if they got better, or died.

Brownlea noticed that Thatcher had not moved for an
unusually long time. He was still staring at the little darkened area on the liver, but there was no bleeding. There
was nothing wrong with the spot. Thatcher was fogging
out.

"Joe," Brownlea said, touching the surgeon's gloved
hand with his own. "Move on, Joe." He watched the surgeon's strained eyes twitch in the bright lights of the operative field. "Are you all right?"

"Yeah," Thatcher said slowly. "I'm all right." He
leaned away from the table and rested his hands on
Donna's draped abdomen. "Just give me a minute." He
stood there for more than a minute, his eyes closed and
head thrown back, weaving in the spotlight like some ancient Hindu blinded after years of religiously staring at
the sun.

"Joe, you want me to look around in here some more,
or . . . ?" Brownlea looked at Nurse Atkins but received
only a helpless shrug.

"Just give me a min—" Thatcher said, as he collapsed
to the floor, emitting a long hissing grunt that sounded
like an alligator begging for marshmallows.

"My God," Brownlea said reverently. He started to
leave his side of the table when he remembered his job. If
he broke scrub to look at Thatcher he could jeopardize
Donna's life. Atkins and Brownlea stared at each other
over their surgical masks without speaking.

Gunsby got up and took charge of Thatcher's body in a

flash. She flipped the eyelid and touched the cornea, noting the reflex. Simultaneously, her experienced fingers pressed on a pulse in the surgeon's neck. There was respectful silence in the operating room as Gunsby made her diagnosis.

"I don't think it's cardiac," she said, looking up at Brownlea. "He's regular and full and running at about eighty."

"Get him some cold towels," Atkins barked at the floater. Atkins held her scrubbed position beside Brownlea, fighting the urge to attend Thatcher.

Gunsby pulled Thatcher's mask off his nose and mouth and returned to her anesthesia machine. Donna Strickland was intubated and had to be manually bagged if she was to breathe at all. Gunsby could spare Thatcher a few moments at a time from her life-supporting duties. "Hook him up to a cardiac monitor anyway," she said, reevaluating Donna's condition.

"It's the booze," Brownlea said somberly. "Drag him out where we can all see him."

The floating nurse strained with Thatcher's arms and scrub shirt. The crumpled mass beneath the operating table became corpselike in the corner near Gunsby.

"Get Travis in here," Mary Atkins said. She knew the ER nurse would be better able to handle Thatcher than the floater. At Pine Hill and other places floaters got to that position by proving they could do almost nothing right.

"What the hell am I going to do now?" Brownlea asked. "I'm no surgeon." He looked into Donna Strickland's gaping abdomen helplessly.

"You've scrubbed in with Joe dozens of times," Mary said encouragingly.

"Yeah. I held what he told me to hold and I cut the ends off his sutures after he tied a knot. But dammit, Mary, you know I'd never take on something like this all by myself."

"You want me to call Dr. Kern?" Mary asked. She watched Brownlea's eyes flash from Thatcher to the abdomen and back again in search of help.

"Charlie couldn't lance a boil," he said softly. It was traditional not to malign a colleague in front of the nurses. He looked at Thatcher on the floor again, "How is he, Gunsby?"

"He's got good color, Cal," Gunsby said. "He'll be all right, I think. But I'm not sure about our own lady at this point." Gunsby pumped on the blood pressure cuff and squinted at the dial.

"What do you mean, 'you think'?" Brownlea said, moving toward Thatcher despite Atkins's restraining. "Give him something, Gunsby."

"It'll make him wild," Atkins warned.

"He's got to hold this thing together," Brownlea insisted.

"She's dropped to ninety over sixty," Gunsby announced.

"Joe!" Brownlea shouted. "For Christ's sake, Joe!"

Chapter 25

M O R E composed, Yancey knew it was time to come in from the cold. Mountainmen were supposed to look strong and show no emotion. After an hour alone in the parking lot Yancey felt he could play that role once more. The emergency room had been cleaned up and the deputy was gone. The clerk maintained her vigil behind the desk. The medical equipment, again ready for anything, looked as if nothing had ever happened.

Yancey took a seat in the visitors' corner and picked up an old issue of *Popular Mechanics*, staring blankly at the plans for a pedal-powered lawn fertilizing machine.

Suddenly, a nurse in green burst into the room and yelled, "Where's Kitty Travis? Dr. Brownlea wants her in the OR stat."

The clerk stammered something about the coffee machine and pointed down the hall. As the floater passed by Yancey's corner, he grabbed her by the arm.

"What's going on in there?" he demanded.

"It's okay," she blurted. "Donna's . . ." the words were frozen in her throat by the lawyer's flinty expression.

"I want it straight."

"Thatcher's collapsed," she said, pulling her arm free. "I've got to find Travis. She can help." She darted down the hallway half searching and half escaping.

Yancey stood in the corner of the emergency room, stunned. Thatcher has collapsed, he repeated to himself. Did that leave Brownlea with two emergency cases on his hands? Would he abandon Donna to help Joe? The mental scene made him panic.

"Call Mr. Jessup," he shouted at the clerk.

"But . . ." she said, hesitating. The lawyer looked at her with wild eyes. She considered calling the deputy back.

"Call Jessup!"

"But Mr. Marshall, he's no doctor. He can't do anything."

"I want him *here*, goddammit," Yancey shouted. He ran his hand wildly through his hair. "I want him to see what goes on in this place. I want him to see for himself."

"I'll have to call him at home," she said, making it sound like she would have to disturb the pope in the toilet.

"That won't be necessary," a voice behind Yancey said. The lawyer turned quickly to see the administrator coming through the door.

"Hamp!" Yancey said in a mixture of desperation and relief.

"I heard about Donna Strickland, Yancey," Jessup said, shaking the lawyer's hand with both of his own. "They ought to do something about that curve."

"Thatcher took her to the operating room," Yancey said softly and heavily.

Jessup nodded and placed his other hand on Yancey's shoulder. "I know," he said, his tone promising that everything would be all right.

"But he's drunk, Hamp," Yancey said, raising his voice slightly. "I saw him. I talked to him."

"Nobody can deny that Joe drinks," Jessup said, "but he's used to it and Cal's in there to help him."

Yancey shrugged the administrator's hand off his shoulder, wrenching himself free. "*Cal*," he said derisively, "just sent out for the ER nurse to help him after 'good old Joe' collapsed on the floor."

"God," Jessup breathed, instinctively glancing at the ER clerk.

"I'll kill him, Hamp," Yancey said, slowly and deliberately. "If Donna—" He turned away and stared at the ceiling, his eyes blinded by tears and an ache tearing at his throat.

"Stay here," Hamp said. "I'm going to the OR. I'll come right back and tell you what's going on in there."

Yancey let him get several steps toward the door before he shouted, "You were the administrator when the Pitts boy died, too."

Hamp heard him but kept going.

In the OR Thatcher had awakened in the corner and had torn the EKG leads off his chest like poisonous snakes. He was unsteady, but at least he was on his feet. The nurses struggled to get him regowned and regloved There was no hope of sending him out to rescrub. Atkins knew the best she could do would be to fence out the germs with a new outfit on top of his contaminated set.

"Light up the left gutter," Thatcher said, craning his neck to look deeply into Donna's abdomen.

"Are you sure you're all right, Joe?" Brownlea asked.

"Move the fuckin' light," Thatcher snarled. He glared at Brownlea over his mask. "Think I'm a goddamned cardiac?"

"I couldn't have finished it without you, Joe," Brownlea repeated, gratefully.

"It ain't over yet," Thatcher said. "Hemostat." He held his palm out and waited only an instant for Atkins to slap it with the handles of a clamp. His hand was remarkably steady as he identified a tiny bleeder in the mesentery and snapped the points of the instrument on the vessel and rapidly executed a double knot as Brownlea removed the clamp.

"You did a good job on that spleen," Thatcher grunted.

"Mary and Travis were a big help," Brownlea said.

"You got it done," Thatcher said. He reinspected the splenic stump and poked at the vessels Brownlea had tied off.

"I'm no surgeon, Joe," Brownlea said.

"Neither am I," Thatcher said. He glanced at Atkins and Travis but neither of the nurses would meet his eyes. Nurses can glare at doctors only when they are angry. In Thatcher's case they were too embarrassed.

"Systolic's holding at one hundred, now," Gunsby said,

peering over the head drapes. "You want to run in another unit?" She tried to keep her tone light, almost flippant, the way the combat nurses did. She knew how Thatcher felt. She wanted to tell him that he was still a good man, despite it all, but the words stuck in her throat.

"Hold up after this one," Thatcher said. "If she's not bleeding in the chest, we'll get an overload on four."

"Jesus, Joe," Brownlea said. "You're not going to crack her chest, are you?"

Instinctively, Atkins began to survey her instruments. She wasn't fully prepared for a chest, but she wasn't far from it. "Get me a rib spreader," she whispered to Nurse Travis.

"We'll try a needle first and see what we get back," Thatcher said cautiously. The slur was less distinct when he spoke slowly and carefully. Over the years he had learned that.

Brownlea put a bloody gloved hand on Thatcher's. "Joe, you're not in any shape to—"

Thatcher snatched his hand back angrily. "You want to transfer this woman to the Mayo Clinic, Cal? 'Cuz if you do I think you ought to close the belly first." He held out his hand in Atkins's direction and received the correct needle holder loaded with suture for closing the peritoneum. Mary had had that ready for an hour, hoping there would be a chance to use it.

Brownlea could feel the muscles of his jaw flexing under his surgical mask as he held, tied, and cut, silently assisting Thatcher's retreat from the abdominal cavity. Suddenly, the OR door swung open and a pudgy man in loose-fitting greens came in, his head and face hidden by a mask and cap.

"Who the hell is that?" Thatcher asked Travis, a little too loud.

"Hamp Jessup," the man said, moving awkwardly into the corner, carefully avoiding everything. He kept his ungloved hands behind his back, convinced that whatever he did, it would be terribly wrong.

"Hamp?" Brownlea asked, smiling. "You've never been in here before. Not during an operation."

"Never been invited," Jessup said, hoping everything would stay that light.

"You ain't now," Thatcher snapped. "Cut that damned suture, Cal." He tapped his needle holder on the back of Brownlea's hand like an assistant professor of surgery working with an intern who was more interested in the scrub nurse than the procedure.

"They said there was trouble in here," Jessup said coldly.

"And you brought your first-aid kit," Thatcher taunted.

"How is she, Cal?" Jessup said, ignoring the surgeon.

"Her blood pressure stabilized after we removed the spleen and tied off a couple of bleeders," Brownlea explained.

"She might live to pay her bill," Thatcher quipped. His humor seemed particularly inappropriate and insensitive.

Jessup stood on tiptoe to improve his view but by then there was really nothing to see. The abdominal wall was half closed, but it still looked incomprehensible to the administrator. He watched Thatcher put in two interrupted sutures before he realized Brownlea was staring at him over his mask. The administrator returned the stare for a moment and then followed Brownlea's eyes to the surgeon. There was urgency in Brownlea's rapid eye movements.

Jessup telegraphed back, Is *Joe* going to make it? without speaking a word and Brownlea silently replied that he wasn't sure.

"You can sign Cal up for full surgical privileges," Thatcher said. "He did a first-class job on the spleen."

"Yancey's still outside," Jessup said, getting on with it. In less stressful times Thatcher's wry comments were more acceptable than his stone-sober cynicism, but this was not one of those times.

"Why don't you bring him in too, Hamp?" Thatcher snapped. "The more the merrier."

"Shut up, Joe," Brownlea said softly.

"Yancey knows," Hamp said.

"Has he said anything?" Brownlea asked.

Jessup shook his head. "He's worried, Cal, And so am I."

"Cut." Thatcher said, holding up the two ends of his newest suture.

"Joe's concerned about her chest," Brownlea said, snipping the excess suture evenly and raising his eyebrows.

Jessup felt panic race through him again. "Are we prepared for chest surgery, Miss Atkins?"

"As an emergency," Mary replied evenly. A good scrub nurse was not to become excited no matter what happened. Even if the patient was hemorrhaging to death right in front of her eyes, her job was to follow orders, pass instruments, and remain calm. Some hospital lawyer, concerned with the patient's welfare, had once suggested that all operating-room conversation be recorded, like the little black box on a commercial jet. Had they done that the tape would be filled with lousy jokes and off-color remarks by the surgeons on good days or selected obscenities when everything went wrong, punctuated with the calm, measured cadence of the scrub's professional replies.

"Can't we avoid that, Dr. Thatcher?" Jessup asked. His use of the more formal style meant he wanted a serious answer.

"If Gunsby can hold the pressure up, we can sit on her for a while," Thatcher said.

"Long enough to transfer?" Jessup asked. For a moment there was no reply. Thatcher tied his last abdominal suture and Brownlea cut the ends. "Gunsby?" Jessup demanded.

"She seems to be fairly stable, Mr. Jessup," nurse-anesthetist Gunsby replied formally. As a CRNA she was an employee of the hospital and answerable to the administrator except for professional demands made on her by the surgeon-in-charge.

"Dr. Brownlea?" Jessup said firmly.

"Yes, Mr. Jessup," Cal replied. Hamp had successfully telegraphed his mood.

"Is this patient stable?" Jessup asked.

"I believe so," Cal said.

"Has the present surgery been completed?" Hamp asked in the same even tone.

"Yes, sir," Cal said, "we have closed."

"Miss Atkins?" Hamp asked.

"Yes, sir?"

"Is the instrument and sponge count correct?" Hamp asked.

"Yes, sir. Instruments and sponges are correct."

"Dr. Brownlea," Jessup said slowly, "may I remind you that you are the current chief of staff?"

"I am," Cal affirmed.

"Then as administrator of this hopsital I am informing you of my formal request that you take charge of this patient's care, terminate the surgery when you deem appropriate, and relieve Dr. Thatcher of all further responsibility."

Atkins was stunned by the announcement while Gunsby busied herself behind her anesthesia machine and Travis looked at her hands. Brownlea stood almost at attention, staring at the administrator, as Thatcher mutely studied the surprisingly neat row of sutures he had made. Despite her iron-willed training, Mary Atkins began to cry, the tears making ridiculous dark green half moons in the upper edges of her mask.

Brownlea turned slowly toward his colleague and waited for the man to lift his head. After several moments in which the surgeon neither spoke nor moved his hands Brownlea said, "Joe, I—"

Without warning, Thatcher turned from the operating table, glared momentarily at Jessup, and snapped his surgical gloves onto the floor like a duble-barreled sling shot. As he left the OR, Mary Atkins mentally screamed for him to come back, to take charge . . . to be himself again, but her mouth formed no words.

Chapter 26

B O B B Y Lee Thorpe was roaring mad, or at least that was how Hamp Jessup would later characterize the man pacing around the administrator's office, waving his hands, shouting questions, and seldom waiting for answers.

"But I *told* you to be extra nice to that drunken son-of-a-bitch," Thorpe said.

"I know," Hamp said calmly. He sat behind his desk, occasionally tapping a pencil, like the host of a late-night TV program.

"You don't even know where the hell he went," Thorpe said. "Neither of you."

"He probably went home to tell it all to Marilyn," Cal Brownlea said from the chair in the corner. Both he and Jessup had changed back to street clothes.

"Went home to drink up everything he has in the house," Thorpe snorted.

"As administrator I *had* to relieve him of duty," Jessup said. "It seemed appropriate under the circumstances."

"Sure," Thorpe snapped. "I'm up to my ass fightin' off this malpractice case for you and you fire the fuckin' defendant. I might as well hand my checkbook over to Yancey Marshall and let him write his own, for Christ's sake."

"If you knew where *he* was," Cal added coyly.

"I suspect you'll find him when you find Thatcher. Yancey took off out of here the minute he found Joe gone," Hamp said.

"That's just fine," Thorpe sneered. "That goddamned lawyer will catch up with him just about the time he gets his skin full and then Joe will tell him anything he wants to know."

"Or Yancey will kill him with his own hands and settle both cases for us," Cal suggested.

"Just can that kind of talk, if you don't mind, Dr. Brownlea," Thorpe said. "So far we don't have two cases. You said that Strickland bitch was going to be all right."

"Miss Strickland has been a loyal and dedicated hospital employee," Jessup said flatly.

"Loyal and dedicated goddamned spy, you mean," Thorpe said.

"We don't *know* she ever took any records out of the hospital," Jessup said.

"And we don't *know* the astronauts went to the fuckin' moon, either," Thorpe said, pacing to the window and looking out at nothing again.

"She's innocent until proven guilty," Brownlea said softly.

Bobby Lee turned from the window to face them, his face contoured in rage. His voice began in a low, rasping hiss that somehow filled the room. "God, I'm sick of you, Cal." He shook his head sadly and took a step toward the center of the room. "And you, too, Hamp, and all of you asshole mountain people, doctors, and niggers alike."

"Bobby . . ." Jessup said, hesitantly.

"Y'all are something else up here. Your medicine is twenty years out of date and your goddamned hospital should have been closed when they discovered penicillin." Thorpe closed his eyes in a painful acknowledgment that he was deeply involved and didn't want to be.

"It's a good town, Thorpe," Brownlea said firmly.

"Good for what?" Thorpe returned. "For hiding from the world? For operating on nigger boys and telling their mamas they just got treated as good as Emory?" He paused to look at Jessup and Brownlea individually. "Red-and-black checkered shirts and some goddamn fish in a mountain stream?"

"It's not Atlanta," Hamp admitted.

"It's nowhere, Hamp," Thorpe said.

It was time for Brownlea to get up. "Yes, it is, Bobby

Lee," he said. "It's a place for people. Real people. People who are interested in each other. We don't need Atlanta. And we don't need their crime and their violence. Not here. Not in Pine Hill."

"You don't need Atlanta," Thorpe sneered. "You need me. You need to be insured. You need to have your ass bailed out when you fuck up, that's what you need."

"We paid our premiums," Jessup said defiantly.

Thorpe wheeled around, looking at the ceiling. "Thirty-seven hundred lousy bucks. You want it back, Hamp? You want it all back in old one-dollar bills?"

Jessup hesitated, glancing at Brownlea.

"You bet your ass you don't want any of it back," Thorpe continued. "What you want is me. Somebody to take the heat off while you guys go on in your dream world, with your mountains and your antique shops and your phoney way of life up here."

"We do the best we can," Brownlea said.

"The hell you do, Cal," Thorpe snapped. "There ain't none of you that's been to a postgraduate seminar in ten fuckin' years and if your ass was on the line you couldn't collect a nickel bet by producing the latest surgical journal anywhere in this hospital. And I don't call that staying up to date."

"I read when I get a chance," Brownlea said.

"Sure," Thorpe said. "*Brown's Guide to Georgia*, that's what you read. You think the *New England Journal of Medicine* is some kind of a radical publication for liberals in Boston. Shit, your idea of medical literature is the *Reader's Digest*."

"And I s'pose you read all that stuff," Brownlea said.

"Not all of it, Cal. Not all of it. But I read more of that crap than you do and all I got to do is run an insurance company." Thorpe stuffed his hands into his pockets and scuffed the carpet with the edge of his shoe. "When I was young, Cal, I wanted to be a doctor, but I couldn't get in. I didn't have a father who was a doctor. I had to make my own way. And all and all I haven't done too bad, either." He paused to point a finger at the physician. "But I'll tell you one thing. If I had made it, I wouldn't be here

with you. I'd be out there looking into every goddamned
thing that would be important to me as a doctor." He said
"doctor" as if it were a title descended from British roy-
alty.

"You'd do that like we all did," Cal said. "When we
were young and still had time and idealism."

"Before you started making money," Thorpe said.

"Before we lost our first couple of patients," Brownlea
countered. "Before we found out they don't care, no matter how good we treat 'em."

"These doctors work hard up here," Jessup offered.

"With their CPAs," Thorpe said.

"With their patients," Jessup added.

"And their patients' mothers?" Thorpe taunted.

"*I* didn't mislead Mrs. Pitts," Brownlea said, defensively.

"Oh, I'll go along with that, Cal," Thorpe said. "But
you didn't go out of your way to tell her the whole truth
either."

"Did you want me to?" Brownlea asked.

"Hell, no, I didn't want you to. I just want to set you
straight. You're no goddamned hero either. You'd just as
soon screw Mrs. Pitts in the ear to win the case. So don't
give me any crap about that Strickland bitch being 'innocent till proven guilty.' "

"Joe did all the talking with Mrs. Pitts," Brownlea said.

"Not all of it," Jessup added. "Ole Bobby Lee here had
some papers for her to sign, too." He raised his eyebrows
to complete his indictment.

"It could have worked," Thorpe said flatly.

"Except for Yancey Marshall," Brownlea added.

"I'm *sure* I could have talked some sense into him before it was too late," Thorpe said. "He had his day. He
gave me all that crap about stickin' up for the Pitts kid
and how it was a cryin' shame to let Thatcher go on like
he does. But in the end, he would have settled the case."

"Why?" Jessup asked.

Thorpe's expression suggested Hamp was some kind of
an idiot. "White lawyer, black client, small town, white
doctor defendant."

Brownlea nodded in agreement. The analysis sounded foolproof to him. With minor variations that's how everything was worked out in Pine Hill.

"But that's all down the tube now," Jessup said. "He's not going to let up on Donna Strickland's case."

"Will you stop saying Donna Strickland's case," Thorpe said impatiently. "If she makes it, there won't be a case."

"But, Joe—"

"Yeah, Hamp," Bobby Lee said, "I know. Joe fell on his ass in the operating room. And you're thinking that would sound like hell to a jury, even in Pine Hill. Well let me tell you. Falling on your ass in the OR isn't enough." He paused to let the two men think that one over. He could tell from their blank stares they were puzzled.

"A malpractice case stands on two legs or it doesn't stand at all," Thorpe continued. "Liability isn't enough. There has got to be damages."

"So if Donna makes it . . ." Cal mused, ". . . and nothing goes wrong . . ."

"We tell Yancey to kiss our respective asses," Thorpe said. "You sewed her up, didn't you? You and Mary Atkins?"

"And Travis," Cal added.

"The law doesn't require you to be an expert in everything if nothing goes wrong," Thorpe said.

"I never took out a spleen by myself before," Cal said.

"So what?" Thorpe asked. "If your stitches hold and she doesn't get infected we might be out of the woods."

"And if there's nothing wrong in the chest or head," Cal said, looking at Jessup for support.

"You took X Rays and all that crap, didn't you?" Thorpe asked simply.

"You can't always tell on X Rays," Cal warned.

"Gunsby says she's doing okay," Jessup added encouragingly.

"I told Gunsby to stay by her bedside," Cal said. "She's more than just a nurse."

"Maybe we should transfer Donna to Grady," Jessup said.

Thorpe threw his hands in the air at the suggestion. "That would be all we'd need," he said. "Send her down there with her chart and eighteen surgical residents will point out what went wrong with everything we did up here. A transfer would be suicide."

"It might save her life," Brownlea said.

"And cook our goose," Thorpe said. "You've got to keep her, Cal. You've got to maintain control."

"But with Joe gone, I'm over my head," Brownlea admitted. "He does all the postoperative care."

"He doesn't do shit around here," Thorpe said. "He writes down some routine orders that have worked for him for years and lets the nurses solve all the problems."

Brownlea caught himself nodding along with Jessup. "But she really might die on us," Cal said.

"She might die at Grady," Thorpe said. "Frankly, I'd rather keep the case in this county. We don't need any hotshots from the Atlanta Medical Examiner's Office poking around."

"But it would be a coroner's case up here, too," Hamp said.

"Uh-huh," Bobby Lee agreed. "And just who is the coroner?"

"I am," Jessup said unconvincingly.

Bobby Lee pouted and showed the palms of his hands, his shoulders raised around his ears. "You see? That's what I mean by control."

"But there would have to be an autopsy," Brownlea said.

"Not until Hamp ordered it. He's the coroner. Elected fair and square."

"Nobody else wanted the job," Hamp said.

"Shit, nobody wants it now, but I'm damned glad you got it," Bobby Lee said.

"Markham said he was too busy to look at traffics and cases like that in the middle of the night," Hamp said. "That's why he wouldn't take the coroner's job."

"Thank God for small favors," Bobby Lee said. "But look on the positive side of things. She's not going to die because Cal isn't going to let her."

"I'll need a consult," Cal said.

"Get one from Kern," Thorpe said. "Let's keep it in the family."

"What about Joe?" Cal asked, glancing at Jessup.

"If he sobers up, use him, for Christ's sake," Thorpe said.

"But I yanked his privileges," Jessup said.

"Yeah, yeah," Thorpe said, glopping his hand impatiently. "I know all that. You and Hamp flexed your muscle and moved Joe over a little. Who knows? Maybe he deserved it. But that's all over now."

"What do you mean, over?" Jessup asked. "As hospital administrator I have a duty to protect—"

"You've got a duty to protect your ass," Thorpe said.

"I ordered the chief of staff to relieve the chief of surgery of his privileges," Hamp said stiffly.

"What the hell do you think you're running here, the Mass General?" Thorpe asked. "I mean, less than a hundred beds? A medical staff of three? Smarten up, Hamp. This isn't some medical-legal seminar."

Brownlea bristled at the characterization and adjusted the knot in his unattractive tie. "The staff may be small, but we do have rules and regulations," he said.

"All of which you can cram up your ass," Thorpe said. "Right now, I want to put us in the best possible position to win a lawsuit."

"At the risk of Donna Strickland's life?" Cal asked softly.

"You like your house and your fancy car, Doctor? You want to spend the rest of your life paying off a judgment?"

"But the insurance—" Hamp offered weakly.

"The insurance is just the first line of defense," Bobby Lee said. "A big judgment could gobble it all up and leave you guys holding the bag for all you're worth." Thorpe knew that was less than a remote possibility, but fear was a great ally.

Thorpe put his hands on his hips and squinted at the ceiling; his "figgering" pose. "Let's see," he said. "The Pitts kid could come to a million and a half—if he was white."

Jessup and Brownlea nodded understandingly. There were two price lists for everything, including liability.

"As it is, I figure a mixed jury might award half a mil, maybe a little more. The kid played high school basketball, right, Hamp?"

Hamp nodded again.

"Six . . . six and a half tops," Thorpe said. "But the Strickland woman is another problem altogether."

"I don't think she's got any kin," Brownlea offered.

"Good point, Cal," Thorpe said. "If she dies an orphan, maybe we can walk away from it."

"She *can't* die," Hamp said, breaking his pencil single-handedly. The sudden crack was much less annoying than the tapping had been.

"If this was a Catholic hospital, you could get all the nuns down to the chapel to pray," Thorpe said, smiling.

"Do they do that?" Cal asked.

"Yep. But only for their own lawsuits. You mountain red-necks will have to toot your own horns."

"What do you figure Donna's case is worth?" Jessup asked.

"The problem we've got there, Hamp," Thorpe said, "is punitive damages. Surer than hell Yancey would go for punitive, and when the judge hears about Joe showing up drunk again and falling on his ass in the OR, he'll probably award her the whole hospital and throw in Thatcher as a houseboy."

"But the hospital wasn't at fault," Jessup pleaded.

"Ever hear of *Darling* v. *Charleston Board of Hospitals?*" Jessup smirked. "That case started it. The court is going to say that you knew and everybody on the staff knew Joe was a hopeless boozer. And that everybody conspired to keep him on the job in spite of himself. That's where they'll hang the hospital. And if that doesn't work, Yancey will scream 'outrage!' That's a new brand of claim that says the whole thing was so goddamned bad the plaintiff ought to be awarded several bushels of hundred-dollar bills."

Jessup was looking paler and Cal a little sicker as

Thorpe droned on, painting the worst picture he could imagine.

"So, if either of you have got any heroic ideas, you just keep them to yourselves," Thorpe said. "What we need here is teamwork and control over Thatcher."

Upstairs, the bedside team of Atkins, Travis, and Gunsby monitored the blood pressure gauge, the EKG blips, the chest sounds, and Donna's level of unconsciousness.

Chapter 27

WHEN Thorpe and the others arrived at Thatcher's house, none of them was surprised to see Yancey's pickup. It was half on the driveway and half on the lawn. Thatcher's car was closer to the garage door.

It was past midnight now, and there were no lights on in the front rooms of the house. Thorpe stopped the car in the street and turned off the lights. For a moment no one spoke as Brownlea, Jessup, and Thorpe stared at the apparently lifeless house.

They exchanged glances as they got out of the car and shut their doors silently. The night was clear and almost cool enough to see one's breath. Each of the men silently wished he had dressed a little warmer.

"Has Joe got a dog?" Thorpe whispered as they walked up the driveway.

"No, uh-uh," Cal grunted.

"Has he got a gun?" Thorpe asked.

"Somewhere," Cal said. "I saw it a couple of years ago. He said he wanted to go rabbit hunting. I think Marilyn hid it someplace."

"Maybe we ought to call the sheriff and have him send a car over," Jessup suggested.

"If we're ever going to work out a deal with Yancey, it's got to be right now and right here," Thorpe said. "A deputy would spoil the whole thing."

"Not if we get our asses shot off," Brownlea said softly.

"By who?" Thorpe said with fake bravado. "By Joe? What for? All he'll want is another drink. And Yancey's not mad at any of us. Least, not either of you two. And

214

all I did was try to screw him out of a few bucks in the Pitts case. I'll offer to settle it and he'll calm down."

"I hope the hell you're right," Brownlea said as they approached the side door nearest the garage. He quietly stepped onto the porch and tried to look through the curtained windows into the kitchen. There were cracks of light and glimpses of the room, but no movement and no voices.

"You think they're here?" Jessup whispered.

"Got to be," Thorpe said. "Probably somewhere else in the house."

"Joe's got a bar in a den off the kitchen," Brownlea said. "We wouldn't hear them if they were in there."

"Shall I knock on the door?" Jessup asked.

"Try the knob first," Thorpe said. "With all that's happened, they surer than hell ain't playing love games in there. I think we should just walk in. What do you think, Cal?"

"Marilyn won't give a damn," Brownlea said. "We used to drop in at all hours."

Jessup slowly turned the door knob, half expecting it to be locked. He looked quite surprised when it quietly opened. The door swung inward without a sound and the three men gathered in the entrance, unconsciously waiting for someone to go first. Small lights were on in the breakfast nook and over the stove, but the kitchen was empty. Thorpe entered first and stood in the middle of the room, his head cocked, listening, his hand waving behind him to signal the others to remain quiet. There were muffled voices in the den. The door to it was partially closed.

Thorpe nodded toward the den with his head and pushed Brownlea to the front of the line, leaving Jessup to bring up the rear as they crossed the tiled kitchen floor with small careful steps. Cal paused at the door to the den and looked at the others as if to solicit suggestions. Thorpe urged him on with his eyes, but Brownlea was unable to proceed without announcing his arrival.

"Joe? Marilyn?" he called as he rapped gently on the door. "It's Cal. Are you decent?"

The voices inside stopped momentarily and were replaced by Thatcher's unmistakably slurred tone. "Come in, Cal," he shouted. "You come alone?"

"Bobby Lee and Hamp are with me," Brownlea said, pushing open the door.

"Good," Joe shouted jubilantly. "The more the merrier."

Brownlea stepped into the semidarkened den and waited for his eyes to adjust. He had expected to see Joe sitting in his favorite reclining chair opposite the door, but it was occupied by Marilyn. She did not speak. Her eyes flashed a hurried message that Joe was somewhere in the corner, nearer the bar, totally hidden from Brownlea's view by the door. Her eyes and her face said even more. It was apparent that Marilyn was afraid of something.

"Evening, Marilyn," Cal said. He wanted to hesitate longer in the doorway, but Bobby Lee, unable to see Marilyn or the expression on her face, crowded the physician into the den and immediately followed. Inside, Cal looked around the room and began to raise his hands above his head. Thorpe and Jessup imitated Brownlea's movements after the administrator half-stumbled over the doorsill.

"Put your goddamned hands down," Joe said from behind the bar. "You look like the three stooges." In his hands was a 12-gauge automatic shotgun.

"Joe, for Christ's sake," Cal said softly.

"You come to see the lawyer get it?" Thatcher asked. He motioned toward the end of the bar. Yancey Marshall sat on the last stool, nearest the wall, his hands palms down on the bar.

"God," Thorpe said in one, long, exhaled breath. "Are you all right, Yancey?"

"So far," Yancey said through clenched teeth.

Jessup lowered his hands slowly and looked rapidly from Marilyn to Joe to Yancey and back again, saying nothing.

"The son of a bitch followed me home," Thatcher said. "Want a drink?" He took a pull on a half empty quart bottle of Jack Daniels without taking his eyes off the lawyer or his hand from the shotgun.

The three newcomers shook their heads in unison.

"Is that thing loaded, Joe?" Brownlea joked as pleasantly as he could.

Thatcher continued to stare at Yancey as he pointed the weapon toward the ceiling with one hand and pulled the trigger. A roar filled the room to drown out Marilyn's scream as shotgun pellets ripped another pattern in the ceiling, sending bits of acoustic tile into the air along with the smoke and the acrid odor of gunpowder. The three men in the middle of the room ducked instinctively as Marilyn covered her ears. Her scream faded into a plaintive cry and died in a desperate moan. With apparent nerves of steel, Yancey refused to flinch.

"The lawyer asked me the same question," Thatcher said, a twisted smile contorting his face. The ejected shell fell into the far end of the bar and rolled around in a short erratic spiral, its open end smoking slightly.

"Donna's going to be all right," Brownlea said, slowly standing again. "Atkins and Gunsby are watching her."

Yancey didn't move or believe him.

"It doesn't make any difference now," Thatcher said grimly.

"We've got to talk about all this," Bobby Lee said, smiling unconvincingly.

"I've had just about all the talk I can stand from you, Mr. Thorpe," Thatcher said. "Now you just sit down."

Thorpe and Jessup looked in different directions for a suitable place to sit before either of them moved.

"Right where you are," Thatcher added. "So's I can see you. You too, Cal."

The three men obeyed without comment and sat on the floor in front of the bar as Thatcher slipped another shell into the automatic and took another drink from the bottle.

"Maybe you've had enough of that stuff," Jessup said his voice shaking.

"Good old Hamp," Thatcher whined. "The asshole administrator. In medicine, the only thing you could administer is an emena."

"Joe—" Jessup said softly. "Don't be ugly."

"Ugly?" Thatcher snapped. "I'll show what's ugly.

How 'bout a fuckin' lawyer's head splattered all over the wall?"

"For what, Joe?" Brownlea said. "What will it prove?"

"Prove?" Thatcher repeated. "Are we proving things now? We got enough lawyers and enough half-assed insurance men running around proving things. You don't have to start with that kind of shit, too. You're a *doctor*, for Christ's sake, Cal."

"And so are you, Joe," Brownlea said.

Thatcher stole a glance at his wife. She had taken her hands from her ears and had stopped crying. She seemed exhausted and drained. "What about that, honey. Am I still a doctor?"

Marilyn bit her lip and tried not to cry, but she couldn't help it.

"Your old man said I should quit surgery in the middle of my residency. You remember that?"

She nodded enthusiastically, tears and all.

"And he said I'd make a fortune if I opened an office in some rich neighborhood and sold eyeglasses to schoolgirls." Thatcher smiled at the memory. "Maybe he was right, babe. Maybe all those nights on call were for nothing. Holding idiot sticks for some goddamned senior resident when my legs felt like rubber and my underwear was wet Kleenex. What the hell was it all for?"

"It was for all those gall bladders you took out without getting paid, Joe," Brownlea said. "Over the years—" He nudged Bobby Lee in the ribs gently.

"And the kids with scraped knees and fishhooks in their fingers," Thorpe added.

The thought seemed to mellow Thatcher a little. For an instant, he looked far beyond Marilyn's tear-stained face at something that had happened a long time before.

"Dickie Mitzel stepped on a piece of glass at the school picnic," he mused. "His mama said it was just a little cut and all he needed was a tetanus shot and a couple of stitches."

"I remember," Marilyn said softly.

"And I looked at his foot—I was only a second-year resident—and told the senior man the kid probably cut the plantar arch. And the senior said, 'What the hell is the plantar arch?' but the chief heard him and put me in charge of the ward for the rest of the month. If I hadn't thought of that plantar arch in his foot, the kid would have gone home and bled to death in his sleep, surer than hell."

"Sorta like the Pitts boy," Yancey said from his corner.

The comment snatched Thatcher from his reminiscences. He wheeled the shotgun around and put the muzzle just below the lawyer's chin. Thatcher's eyes were wild again and his mouth twitched without forming words.

"There's been trouble enough, Joe," Brownlea said gently.

"And we all know who caused it," Thatcher hissed. He raised Yancey's still defiant head slightly on the muzzle of the gun.

"We still got ways of fixing things," Thorpe said. "Ain't that right, Yancey? We can still settle things, can't we."

Yancey continued to stare angrily at Thatcher but did not speak or move. The gun under his chin had stopped feeling cold and was now only uncomfortable. He had never seen a hard contact shotgun wound of the head and luckily had no concept of the total destruction the 12-gauge could inflict. The holes in the ceiling above him were deceptively benign because, unlike his head, there was space behind the fiberboard to absorb and dissipate the energy from the blast. His skull—sealed shut by bony unions since infancy and filled with a semisolid mass of brain, blood, and spinal fluid—would react to the blast by literally exploding, splattering the walls, the ceiling, and most of the people in the room.

"I saw your brand of 'fixin' with Mrs. Pitts," Thatcher said to Thorpe. "She took your five-thousand-dollar check and filed suit anyway."

"We made her a reasonable offer," Thorpe said defensively. "It could have worked."

" 'Cept for him," Thatcher said, tossing his head toward Yancey. He put the shotgun on the bar again in favor of the Jack Daniels.

"Well, he wasn't the only problem, Joe," Cal said, sounding as friendly as he could.

"I performed one of best appendectomies on Franklin Delano Pitts." Thatcher said, pronouncing the name derisively.

"Joe . . ." Brownlea began.

"He would have made it, too, if it weren't for his sickle cell anemia. Lots of them coloreds have that." Thatcher seemed to be talking to someone else, someone beyond the people in the room.

"Check 'em all for sickling, boys," he said a little louder. In front of him he could dimly make out the outlines of the heads of medical students hunched over notebooks. A crowded amphitheater of steep rows, with each student's feet at the level of the head of the man in front of him. They looked downward at a brightly lit ceramic autopsy table that was primarily used to demonstrate specimens. His palms on the bar, Thatcher could feel the cold, smooth surface of the autopsy table at which Dr. Ewing, his surgery professor, stood to deliver his repetitive and boring lectures from faded and dog-eared notes that he stuffed into his inside jacket pocket at the end of class. Thatcher had always resented Ewing for making surgery sound so dull. Later, when he became a senior resident himself, he vowed to make it interesting and exciting to junior house officers, but he was never quite able to.

"Them darkies will fool you, if you don't watch 'em close," Ewing said through Thatcher to his all male, all white audience of captive medical students. "Check 'em out, each and every one of them for sickle cell anemia. It's a simple test. They do it down in the lab. You'll hear more about that from Dr. Stivers in Pathology. But, right now, right here, all you got to remember is to check 'em. Check 'em all. Else they'll thrombose on you postop and die no matter how good a job you done on 'em." Thatcher paused to look up at the last two rows of medical students and pointed his finger at one of them. "You'd better get more sleep, Mr. McKay. This here is surgery. We got no time for you if you're too sleepy to pay attention." He held his finger extended as he slowly relaxed his too-stern expression into a half smile calculated to reassure the young man.

"Joe," Marilyn said soothingly. "Don't go on like that. Not now. Not again. Doctor Ewing has been dead and gone for years."

Joe turned slightly to look at her, his eyes blinking and squinting as if she were difficult to remember.

"You should have told me, Marilyn," Brownlea said without turning around.

"Lately, he's been worse," she said simply.

Suddenly, Bobby Lee let out a laugh, as if he had just thought of something. "By God, Joe, I think I will have that drink with you." He struggled to his feet with exaggerated awkwardness and stepped closer to the bar, smiling his salesman's smile. As he rose, he gave Brownlea a little kick.

"I just might do the same," Cal said, struggling to his feet. "It's been a long day." He managed to exchange a knowing glance at Jessup. Hamp was reluctant to get up until he saw how Bobby Lee's diversion worked.

Thorpe's affable manner diverted Joe from his alcoholic delusion. The medical students and the amphitheatre and Ewing vanished as suddenly as they had appeared.

"About time," Thatcher said pleasantly. "What'll it be?" He made a sweeping gesture toward his well stocked bar. "Nothing too complicated now. I'm just a poor country boy."

Brownlea was astonished by Thatcher's abrupt mood change. His dim recollection of psychiatry, based on outmoded concepts and totally ignored during decades of general practice, gave him little clue to the severity of Thatcher's condition.

"A little of that Daniels would suit me fine," Thorpe said, trying to sound casual.

"Same," Brownlea said.

"Me too," Jessup added, sensing it was time to join in.

Thatcher put three glasses next to the shotgun, oblivious to its menacing presence. "What about you, Marilyn?" he asked affably.

His wife had either brought her silent crying under control or had run out of tears. Her expression was blanker now, and she felt totally drained. She stared straight ahead, accepting but not comprehending the fact that her husband had just switched from being an assassin to an expansive host. She had given up trying to understand his abrupt mood changes.

"Yessir, Cal," Thatcher said, pouring himself another Daniels, but this time using a glass. "There's been good times and bad times up here, but I wouldn't have traded a minute of it. Would you, Cal?"

"Not a minute, Joe," Brownlea lied.

"You've done the town a great service, Dr. Thatcher," Jessup added.

"That's what medicine's all about," Thorpe said expansively. "Isn't that right, Yancey?" He smiled and frowned simultaneously at the lawyer in an attempt to keep Thatcher's good mood rolling.

Yancey was having none of it. He had been sullen and silent for several minutes as the medical team mixed drinks and traded compliments. Yancey was aware of what they were trying to do. He could see that Thatcher was sick, sicker than any of them had ever imagined, but the smiles and the drinks struck Yancey as totally inappropriate for Donna's condition.

"How long is this bullshit going to go on?" Yancey asked loudly.

There was a stunned silence as all eyes looked at the lawyer and then flashed to the surgeon. The remark caught Joe with a raised glass, his lips already pouting in anticipation of the whiskey. He seemed suddenly frozen in midair.

"We all need time to relax," Brownlea said with a quivering laugh.

"While Donna dies?" Yancey growled.

Thatcher put his glass on the bar and ran his fingers along the rim. The muscles in his jaw flexed rapidly as he made nervous pill-rolling movements with his right hand. Donna's name had evidently triggered some fragmented memories for Thatcher, but no one was sure what they were.

"It's the spleen, Cal," Thatcher said loudly. He continued to stare at his drink, "There's a tear in the spleen."

"I know, Joe," Brownlea said quickly. "I took care of it."

"She'll need another half a dozen units of blood if we don't get in there."

"It's okay, Joe," Brownlea continued. "I found the bleeder and tied it off. The spleen is out." He glanced at Thorpe, but the insurance man's attention was riveted on the surgeon.

"Get a monitor in here, Cal!" Thatcher shouted. "We're going to have to crack her chest."

"Joe—" Thorpe said gently. He extended his hand toward the surgeon's arm.

Suddenly, Thatcher wheeled around and glared at Thorpe. "The lingual nerve took a downward curve around the hyoglossus," he recited slowly and bitterly. " 'Well, I'll be fucked,' said Whatton's duct, 'the bastard's double-crossed us.' You didn't think I remembered that much anatomy, did you, Thirsty?" Thatcher stood there for a moment, staring at Thorpe and weaving from side to side. "Thirsty Thurston. You couldn't hack it in clinical practice so you came back to teach anatomy. Thurston the hatchet. How many guys have you flunked this semester, Thirsty? Huh?"

"Joe, please," Marilyn sobbed from her chair.

Thatcher began to count awkwardly on his fingers. "The olfactory, the optic, the oculomotor . . ."

"It's all your fault, Brownlea," Yancey shouted. "You knew how bad he was. The Pitts kid died because you didn't do anything about it."

"Yancey, I swear . . ."

"And God knows how many others," Yancey yelled. Suddenly there were tears in his eyes and his voice failed him. "Donna."

"Hospitals can't watch everybody," Jessup offered weakly. "There just isn't time."

" . . . trochlear, trigeminal, abducent, and the facial,"

Thatcher continued. Thorpe had not moved a muscle since the recitation of the cranial nerves had begun. He was transfixed.

"There's time enough to do the billing," Yancey shouted. "You've got time enough to send your delinquent accounts to collection agencies and to sue old ladies when they can't pay."

"We worked hard to keep the hospital doors open, Yancey," Brownlea said.

"You worked hard lyin' and coverin' up for each other," Yancey said. "You and Kern and this asshole here."

"Acoustic, glossopharyngeal, vagus, accessory, and the hypoglossal!" Thatcher finished. "How 'bout that, Thirsty? Gonna flunk me too? Like Hinchey and Tyler and Corcoran? They were good students, Thirsty. They studied hard. But you didn't care."

Thorpe had heard enough. He made a lunge for the shotgun, but Thatcher was quicker.

Chapter 28

BILLY Markham showed up at the Pine Hill hospital waving a clamp and shouting that he had to see Joe Thatcher. The night clerk at the ER entrance didn't recognize him and thought he was either crazy or drunk.

"I'm Dr. Markham from Dahlonega, goddamn it!" Billy said loudly. "Where is he? And don't tell me he's home. I just called there and nobody answers."

"I'm sorry, Dr. Markham," the clerk stammered. "I haven't seen Dr. Thatcher for hours."

"And Brownlea? Nobody answers at his place either. What the hell is going on over here?" He didn't wait for an answer. He brushed by the clerk's desk and rushed down the hall toward the stairs to the second floor and Donna Strickland's room. He didn't stop at the second floor nurses' station either. The door to Donna's room was partially closed and the lights were on inside. He adopted a more hushed tone as he came up to the bedside behind Atkins and Gunsby.

"How is she doing?" he asked softly.

Nurse Atkins paused in the middle of her blood pressure routine to look at the pathologist. She shook her head slowly.

"She's down to sixty over forty," Gunsby said.

"Did you tell Thatcher?" Markham asked.

"We haven't been able to reach him," Atkins said. She stared at the surgical clamp in his hand.

"Who *have* you notified?" Markham said. He slipped his fingers onto Donna's wrist and frowned as he felt for the feeble pulse.

"No one, Doctor," Gunsby said nervously. "We . . . we couldn't find anybody."

"Jesus," Markham said softly. He glanced up at the IV set up above the bed. Donna was receiving lactated Ringer's. "Has she had any blood?"

"Four units in the OR and recovery," Gunsby said. "That's all we had."

"Who started the Ringer's?"

"I did," Gunsby said. "I didn't know what else to do."

Markham moved to the head of the bed and lifted Donna's eyelid. The pupils were still reactive but she was deeply unconscious. "Let me have that thing for a moment," he said to Atkins.

The nurse handed over her stethoscope without hesitation.

Markham slipped the clamp into his pants pocket and began to listen carefully to Donna's heart and lungs. The sounds were weak and distant.

"How long has she been like this?" he asked without taking the stethoscope from his ears.

"She was all right when we left recovery," Gunsby said. "But after that, she started having trouble holding her blood pressure."

"She's got to be bleeding somewhere," Markham said, almost to himself. He slid his hand onto her tense, bandaged abdomen. "Let's move her back to the OR."

"But . . ." Atkins began.

"Yes, Doctor," Gunsby said obediently. "Shall I set up a lap tray?"

"Set up anything you think is right," Markham said. "You know more about that stuff than I do." He handed the stethoscope back to Atkins and walked quickly to the nurses' station. He picked up the telephone and dialed "O".

"This is Dr. Markham," he barked. "I'm going to call Atlanta. You stay the hell off my line but start calling Dr. Thatcher and Brownlea and call Dr. Kern, too."

"At home?" the hospital operator asked. She was a kindly old lady who had taken the job because she didn't have anything else to do.

"At home, at a bar, at their girlfriend's house, I don't care where you call them. Just call them. And don't stop until you've called every goddamned number in North Georgia. You understand that?"

"Yes, Doctor."

"And get a hold of Hamp Jessup while you're at it. He might as well know what's going on here." He depressed the button on the phone without waiting for her to reply. Then he dialed for an outside line and called Atlanta.

It took Walter Church, the Chief of Trauma Surgery at Grady Memorial, an hour and a half to get there. A helicopter team from Dobbins Air Force Base made it all possible and if anybody short of the President could scramble a helicopter out of Dobbins, Walter Church could. He had brought along his chief resident, Jim Metcalfe. Together, they had opened more emergency chests and abdomens than any other team in the state.

Donna was in the OR, prepped and ready when Church and Metcalfe joined Dr. Markham. They gowned right over their street clothes and reviewed Donna's vital signs as Atkins guided their hands into sterile gloves.

"You've got blood running," Church observed. "That's good, Billy." At fifty-two, Church was tall, athletic, and wore his hair in a gray crewcut.

"I sent the sheriff over to raid my blood bank in Dahlonega. It's only type specific but it's the best we could do."

"What did they do the first time around?" Church asked Gunsby.

"Splenectomy," She said flatly. She had already re-intubated her patient and was quietly bagging her.

"Cut these sutures, Jim" Church said to Metcalfe. "Let's get in there as fast as we can."

Metcalfe's hand trembled a bit as he cut and removed the sutures on Donna's abdomen. "Excuse me," he said, breathing deeply to steady himself. "That chopper ride scared the shit out of me."

"At least no one was shooting at us," Church said. "Clamp." He held his hand out to Nurse Atkins and felt the instrument slap his palm.

Unconsciously, Markham felt the resistance of another clamp in his pocket as he leaned against the operating table.

Blood flowed freely from Donna's abdomen as Church reopened her incision. "It's in here, all right," he said softly. "Sucker, please."

The operating room was filled with the disgusting sound of the suction apparatus slurping the free blood in the abdomen into a small nozzle and then spitting it into a plastic bottle under the table.

"Better save that blood," Dr. Metcalfe said to Gunsby. "It may be all we've got." Gunsby had never participated in an autotransfusion, but she had heard of the procedure.

"Light, please," Dr. Church said. Atkins could tell from his tone that he was used to working under stress. His calmness was contagious and encouraged them all.

"It's right there at the splenic root," Metcalfe said identifying an arterial bleeder.

"Clamp," Church said. The instrument was placed in his hand and then snapped onto the bleeder.

"Who the hell tied off this stump, anyway?" Metcalfe said critically.

"Doctor Brownlea," Gunsby supplied.

"He doesn't know shit from shinola," Metcalfe said, inspecting the internal ties.

"He's an internist," Nurse Atkins said quickly.

"He's a what?" Church asked.

"He's a horse's ass, like the rest of them," Markham said. "But this time they're not going to get away with it. Like I told you on the phone, I'm going to turn the whole bunch of them in to the Board of Medical Examiners. I'll get their licenses yanked."

"I'll help you," Church said. "Surgery can't afford assholes like that."

Dr. Metcalfe had retied the vessels and had almost completed his methodical search of the abdomen for other injuries or bleeders. "She's dry," he announced.

"The pressure?" Dr. Church asked without looking at Gunsby.

"Coming up and holding," She said. "Ninety over seventy-four."

"Will you close, Jim?" Church asked. "Doctor Markham and I have a couple of errands to run."

"Yes, sir," Metcalfe said, assuming command. His five-year residency in surgery was almost completed. He welcomed every opportunity to prove that he was damned good. Especially in front of the Chief.

In the doctors' dressing room just across the hall from the OR Markham and Church found Dr. Kern sitting with his face in his hands.

"Where the hell were you?" Markham asked. "They tried to find you everywhere."

"I wasn't on call," Kern said weakly.

"We almost lost that girl in there," Markham said, grabbing Kern by the shoulder.

"She's not out of the woods yet," Dr. Church said, stepping between them. "But this won't help anything."

"I ought to kick the living shit out of him," Markham said through his teeth.

"We need him to help Metcalfe," Church said calmly. "Can you take a competent blood pressure?" he asked Kern.

Kern nodded his head compliantly, looking up at them for the first time. There was a small smudge of lipstick on his lower lip.

Markham shook his head sadly. "I hope the fuck she was worth it," he said. He relaxed his grasp on Kern's jacket.

Kern followed Markham's eye direction and slowly wiped his lip with the back of his index finger.

"Was Thatcher with you?" Markham asked.

"No," Kern said softly. "But his car is in front of his house. I saw it on the way in."

"That rotten, no good son-of-a-bitch," Markham said. "Come on, Walter. I want you to be present when I kick his face in."

When they got to Thatcher's house it looked like everybody's car was there. Even Yancey's truck. The door to the kitchen was unlocked and the only light on was in the den.

"There's something wrong here," Dr. Church said as they slowly crossed the kitchen. "It's too quiet."

"They're all drunk," Markham said.

Dr. Church gave him a shrug and a why-not expression with his mouth. Suddenly, his attention was captured by a low moan from the den. He looked at Markham for an instant before quickening his pace.

Neither of them were prepared for what they saw. Marilyn sat slumped in her chair, the middle of her throat and the tip of her chin blown away in a ragged shotgun wound. Her eyes were still open and she stared sightlessly ahead. In the middle of the floor, Bobby Lee, Jessup, and Brownlea lay in a tangled heap, their chests torn open by close-range shotgun blasts. Yancey was on the floor at the end of the bar. There was a gaping hole in his left upper-chest where it joined the armpit. The only difference in his wound was that it was still bleeding. Dr. Church spotted it immediately.

"This one's still alive," he said, stepping over Hamp Jessup to lay a finger on Yancey's neck. "He's lost a lot of blood, but he's still pumping. You know him?"

Markham nodded as he examined Brownlea and Jessup for pulses that were no longer there. "He's the lawyer. Name's Yancey Marshall."

"God," Dr. Church said. "I've never seen anything like this before. Have you?"

"Only in slides from the medical examiner's lectures in my residency."

"Must be a goddamned maniac loose," Church said. He tore Yancey's shirt from his chest and stuffed it along with his own handerchief into the wound. Then he slipped the lawyer's belt from its loops and pulled it tight around the makeshift bandage.

"It's Thatcher's house," Markham said. "If anybody's capable of all this, it's him." His words caused him to freeze and to stare at Dr. Church. They had suddenly realized that Dr. Thatcher was unaccounted for. Simultaneously, they looked over their shoulders but the room appeared empty.

"I'll call the sheriff," Markham said softly.

"And get an ambulance," Church whispered.

Markham nodded silently. He stood up and looked around the room again. The telephone was still in its cradle on the bar above Yancey. He stepped over Jessup's legs and reached for the phone. Brownlea's blood was still on his hands and it smeared the white phone. He put it to his ear slowly, half expecting Thatcher on another extension. The sound of the dial tone brought him a sigh of relief. As he dialed the operator, a flash of reflected light from the floor behind the bar caught his eye. He leaned over the bar for a better view.

"Tell them to crank up the OR again," Dr. Church said at his feet. "And tell them we've got three dead ones up here."

"Four," Markham said, looking at the body behind the bar.

Dr. Church looked up at the pathologist without releasing his pressure hold on Yancey's left subclavian artery.

"I found Thatcher," Markham said. "Or what's left of him. He must have put the muzzle in his mouth. The left side of his face is gone.

"Is he alive?" Dr. Church asked.

"Not with half of his brain splattered all over the bottles."

"Operator," a voice said in Markham's ear.

"Operator, this is an emergency. Give me the sheriff."

It was daybreak before Dr. Church and Dr. Metcalfe and Markham made it from the operating room to Donna's bedside. The nurse from the emergency room had teamed up with Kern and an LPN from obstetrics to watch her and to report her improvements to the men in the OR.

"If they both make it, it will be a miracle," Markham said.

"Hey," Dr. Metcalfe said, lightening the mood despite his own fatigue. "You've got the first team in up here. Dr.

Church and I don't lose them. We pull them through by their fingernails."

A weary frown from Walter Church cut the young man's enthusiasm to a more professional posture.

"You ought to save that clamp and frame it, Billy," Church said. "From what you told me in the OR, that's got to be the most dangerous instrument I've ever heard of."

"Only when left behind by crazy Joe Thatcher," Markham said.

"Only when skillfully recovered by Billy Markham," Metcalfe added.

Dr. Kern moved away from his sentry post at Donna's arm and relinquished the pulse to Dr. Church. "She's holding her own, I think," Kern said.

"She's doing better than that," Church said after a moment's evaluation. "Sometime later today we'll transfer them both to Atlanta. I can do more for them at Grady than I can up here."

"It's not much of a hospital," Dr. Kern admitted.

Dr. Church stood up and looked at the local physician with a curiosity that bordered on contempt. "There's nothing wrong with this hospital, Dr. Kern." He glanced at Atkins and Gunsby. "These women are as dedicated and as skilled as you'll find anywhere. And this is as good a hospital as you'll find in any small town. What makes the difference, *Dr.* Kern, is the staff. When the doctors are willing to serve the people the size of the hospital doesn't matter. If they're willing to bust their asses it'll all work, no matter how small the town is. That's what makes the difference."

"We used to do that," Kern said, "in the early days."

"But what happened?" Church asked. "Did you begin to feel left out? Did you think that all the smart guys practiced in Atlanta?"

"Something like that," Kern said softly. "And then that damned lawyer came around."

"Yancey was just doing his job, Charlie," Markham said. "If Thatcher had told Eula Pitts the truth, she might not have brought him in at all."

"They always cause trouble," Dr. Kern said.

"No they don't, Dr. Kern," Church said. "All the lawyers want is the truth. If the doctors level with them they're usually willing to work out a fair compromise for their clients."

"I guess none of us ever told Yancey the whole story," Markham said.

"You'll have your chance," Dr. Church said. "My bet is he'll be representing Mr. and Mrs. Pitts even before he gets out of Grady."

"We used to tell each other the truth," Kern said softly.

"And then you started to tell each other lies when nothing seemed to work out right?" Church asked. "You started to feel that the town was too small and the hospital was too inadequate for you to practice decent medicine? Is that what happened?"

"I don't know, Dr. Church," Kern said softly. "It all just started falling apart."

"But dammit, man that's what medicine is all about," Church continued. "It's not all ivory towers. We can't all practice at the Mayo Clinic. The real stuff is out here. In Pine Hill. In Dahlonega. In thousands of small towns. It's you guys. You and Billy Markham and Brownlea and, yes, goddammit, even the Joe Thatchers. You're the ones that sew it all together. You're the ones that have got to force each other into keeping up with things and staying in there even when nothing seems to work."

"Somebody will take my place," Kern said, his voice cracking.

"Take your place?" Dr. Church bellowed. "Who the hell is going to take your place, Dr. Kern? If you cut out and run there'll be nobody left."

There was a long moment of silence while everyone watched Kern study his shoes.

"We need you, Dr. Kern," Mary Atkins said.

Kern lifted his head to look across the room at Nurse Atkins. There were tears on his cheeks.

"Others will come to help," Gunsby said. "I'm sure of that."

"As a matter of fact," Dr. Church said, offering a little

smile, "one of my smartest surgical residents is finishing up in a couple of months. He's probably looking for a place where he can walk in and be the chief of surgery. Right, Dr. Metcalfe?"

Metcalfe looked at Walter Church and winked confidently. "I've always liked the mountains," he said, turning to Kern and extending his hand. "You know of any good property for sale?"

Epilogue

AT large teaching hospitals surgical patients feel lucky if their doctor's junior resident drops in on their day of discharge. The excitement of the surgery long past and the cold calculations of postoperative care now a humdrum of daily orders, the team in green finds other things to do when the patient finally leaves the floor, whether he goes home or to the morgue. Like the cavalry, they are not trained to look back.

Yancey Marshall was one of the lucky ones. Walter Church had saved his arm. The torn artery to the left upper extremity had been expertly repaired with Teflon and pieces of vein from the thigh, and exercises had been devised to show him how to use the minor, undamaged muscles to the shoulder. With a little practice, Metcalfe had told him, he'd be ready to pitch for the Red Sox, underhand, of course.

It had come as a bit of a surprise to Yancey when Dr. Church had offered to drive him home to Pine Hill. Yancey was even more surprised when, on the last day at Grady Memorial, Church had shown up, not in his usual long white lab coat over greens, but in a green-and-black checkered shirt stuffed into tan courduroy pants, a black Emory windbreaker, and ankle-high boots with rawhide laces.

"Are we going quail hunting or is this just my ride home?" Yancey had asked him as he gathered his few things from the tiny closet in his room.

"There's snow on the ground up there," Dr. Church said flatly. There was a floor nurse in the room and he felt a little out of uniform in front of her.

"Must be expecting a blizzard," Yancey said. He adjusted the sling on his left arm and threw a slightly annoyed look at his surgeon.

"Donna says it made two inches and stopped," Church said. "You've got the knot too high." He stepped closer to the lawyer and made a minor adjustment on the sling like a parent sending a child off to school.

"Don't expect me to get out and push when your Cadillac slides into the ditch on the way up my mountain," Yancey said.

"It's a Jaguar and if it gets stuck I'll sell it where it lies and move in with Metcalfe."

"How's he doing?" Yancey asked. "I miss him on rounds."

"He should be here, studying for his boards, but I think he fell in love with Pine Hill."

"Mountains and quiet beaches can do that to a man," Yancey said, slipping his good arm into his jacket.

"We'll see soon enough," Dr. Church said. "I'm staying the weekend at your place."

Yancey seemed delighted. "Donna again?"

Church nodded his head. "It's supposed to be a surprise so play along when we get there. Some kind of a welcome home party. Mostly people from the hospital and the town."

"Is she strong enough for that?" Yancey asked, picking up his canvas overnight bag.

"She's recovered like nothing ever happened. But for Christ's sake don't say anything about her scars when she gets into your bed. She's sensitive about that. I told her I'd help a good plastic man fix that problem for her in a couple of months."

"Who caused the scars? Thatcher or Brownlea?" Yancey asked. His jaw clenched despite his repeated intentions to forget the whole affair.

"Both of them, I guess," Dr. Church said, glancing at the nurse. "We'll talk about it on the way up there, if you want."

Donna was wrong about the two inches of snow. It was

closer to four by the time Church's Jag wound through Pine Hill and started up the potholed switchbacks to Yancey's A-frame. The snow had stopped falling, but the road had not been plowed. Apparently, several cars had driven up or down the mountain, and with Yancey pointing out the hidden potholes, Walter Church had no trouble running the road, gunning the switchbacks like an expert.

"This road ought to put a damper on the party," Dr. Church said as he made the last turn and skidded into Yancey's yard. He came to a stop next to Yancey's pickup. From the tire tracks it was obvious it had been recently used.

"Are you kidding?" Yancey said. "People up here live with the weather, not in fear of it. This is four-wheel country." He struggled out of the car and ignored the snow that fell into his low shoes. There were lights on in the A-frame and smoke curled from the chimney. To Yancey it had never looked so good.

He was only halfway up the clean-swept steps when the door opened and Donna rushed out to throw her arms around him. Instantly, she remembered his shoulder and released her grip.

"God, Yancey, did I hurt you?" she asked.

"Not yet," he said sensuously. He put his arm around her and kissed her on the mouth. After a moment, he stopped, looked at her, and kissed her again.

"I'm glad you're home," she whispered, laying her face next to his and closing her eyes.

Yancey's eyes suddenly filled with tears and he clamped his back molars together to hold himself together. "Yeah, baby," he said softly.

Walter Church had taken as much time as he could with the bags in the trunk of the car. He now came across the yard like a boy home from college, one bag in each hand, scuffing snow with every step. "Did you think we got lost?" he called to Donna.

"Not you two," she said, letting go of Yancey to take the smaller bag and offer a simultaneous handshake. Dr. Church accepted her hand but leaned in for a small kiss as well. "Thank you for bringing him home, doctor," she said as her voice choked.

"Up here," he said, brushing off the compliment, "it's Walter."

Donna put her arms around the surgeon and held him tightly for a moment.

Yancey put his good arm around the two of them. "I think we've got a fire and some good whiskey wastin' inside," he said.

"And that's not all," Donna said, breaking away from Dr. Church. She put her arms around the two men as they each picked up a bag and walked with her toward the door.

"Whatever it is, it smells real good," Yancey said loudly for whoever else might be in the house. He knew that Donna's kitchen talents didn't extend to those kind of down-home aromas.

"Mr. Yancey!" Eula shrieked. "God almighty, you *is* here."

"And here to stay, Eula," he said, matching her excited tone as the big black woman hugged him, sling and all. Tears ran happily down her cheeks as she kept him to herself for just a moment.

"Things are going to be good again, Eula," he said gently. He could feel her head nodding against his chest as he let his canvas bag slip to the floor.

CHAPTER ONE OF NOT A STRANGER

BY JOHN R. FEEGEL

An original hardcover novel from NAL BOOKS

NAL BOOKS
NEW AMERICAN LIBRARY
TIMES MIRROR
NEW YORK AND SCARBOROUGH, ONTARIO

CHAPTER 1

IT WAS LATE ON A gray Saturday afternoon, in November, and for Birmington, a large city in the South, it was cold. Tyrone Lewis was tired, and his feet hurt from standing on chilled concrete with only thin sneakers and worn tube socks to cover his feet. His feet wouldn't have complained if he had played pickup basketball behind the school with the rest of his friends. But here, at the Crossdale Shopping Center, the impending sunset was almost cruel. The sun was not big and yellow and warm, but hesitated reluctantly at the edge of the earth and brightened only the center of the gray shroud that covered the rest of the sky.

"Mind you don't eat none of them chocolate bars," his mother had told him that morning as he left the house. "Them's fo' the church. And you has to get a dollar for every one of them. Yo' hear?"

"Yas, Mama." There was no hope of escaping his assigned duty with more protests. He had voiced them all when she had announced that she had volunteered his services to the Lord. The Clara Diggs Memorial Society of the African Methodist Episcopal Church, a scant three blocks away from Tyrone's house, had decreed that several hundred dollars would be raised before Easter to repair the organ. To accomplish this economic miracle, the ladies had purchased an appropriate quantity of chocolate bars from a wholesale house that specialized in charitable causes. Their product was distinctively shaped, packed ten to the box, and bore the name of the church, school, or cause it allegedly supported. In fact, it was three or four times more profitable for the candy repackager than it was for the anonymous chocolate maker or for the laborers in the Lord's vineyard. But the salesman had not explained that to the ladies at the AME. In fact, he had not only sold them several cases of chocolate, but a lifetime supply of embossed car deodorizers that could be dangled from the mirror.

Tyrone was twelve and the fifth child of nine born to Bessie and Tom Lewis. He was a soft-spoken boy because Tom would not abide children's noises around the house. All of them had learned to do as he was told, ask for nothing, eat what was put in front of him, and move out the minute he was old enough. As a result, Tyrone was the next to the oldest still at home. His seventeen-year-old sister, Chanelle, was restless and ready to leave, but determined to be the first in the family to finish high school.

Tyrone's stomach growled and he looked longingly at the remaining chocolate bars in his box. He had sold five and the money was burning a hole in his pocket. Bessie had given him a quarter for lunch and other necessities, but it was gone by ten in the morning. At two he had carefully swiped two apples from the vegetable display of a large grocery chain store. But all of that was long gone as well.

He knew no one had seen him lift the apples, but the unmarked police car across the parking lot bothered him just the same. There was a man in it, and it had been there, on and off, since noon. Tyrone and all the other little black boys could spot an unmarked car from two blocks away. The city was too cheap to buy convincing decoys and too regimented to let these stripped-down Fords become dirty or dented. They might as well have painted them blue and white like the rest of the cruisers.

Tyrone walked to the end of the sidewalk outside Eckerd's Drug Store and stooped down to read the clock inside. Sale or no sale, he had agreed with his mama, a deal is a deal. At quarter of six he could close up and head home, confident that he had made God happy and that he would not be asked to sacrifice another Saturday for at least two months. (He didn't know about the car deodorizers scheduled to go on sale immediately after the new year.) The time on the clock made him smile. It was close enough. He was sure God did not measure eternal rewards in ten-minute intervals. He squatted down on the sidewalk in front of the drug store and carefully refolded the flaps of the box. It would be passed on to his brother James, who at age ten had been assigned to three hours' sale duty in front of a white Baptist church on the other side of town. James had bargained for the Sunday duty because it was short and got him the use of the bike. He also knew that white Baptists bought candy from little black boys if you caught them in front of their church, in full view of their well-dressed friends. In fact, Tyrone had James had sold some items over there when Bessie and her AME friends had no drive at all going on. (Calendars stolen from funeral homes were always good for a quarter.)

Tyrone did not see the unmarked car slide up behind him, amber parking lights only, as he reached the far side of the shopping complex. The macadam beneath his feet was a little warmer than the concrete had been and he was headed home. Why should he care about the soft hum of a Ford on his heels? The parking lot was half filled with cars anyway. If the cop wanted to talk about apples, Tyrone knew he could duck between the cars and escape. The trick, his older brother had told him, was not to run too slow. You had to wait until the cop had stopped and was busy with his paperwork.

The unmarked car rolled up next to Tyrone, keeping pace with him as the driver rolled down the window.

"Where you goin', boy?" the stranger behind the wheel said.

"Home," Tyrone replied. He kept walking.

"Hold up a second. I needs to talk with you." The man's inflection was a fair imitation of a Negro dialect.

The boy clutched his box of chocolate bars a little tighter to his chest as he stopped. " 'bout what?" Nobody seen me take them apples, he thought to himself.

" 'bout some of them missing children," the man said. "You know about that?"

"Uh-huh."

"There's been eleven boys 'bout your age that ain't never showed up again. You know that?"

Tyrone nodded. He'd heard. Everyone had heard. From the church to the newspapers to special lectures in class to the nightly news on TV, everyone had heard: young black boys missing, some found dead; no clues, no leads.

"Don't it scare you none to be out here all alone knowin' about them boys? We got cars staked out all *over* the place, and look at you. Walkin' along like it was a Sunday promenade." The man leaned out of the car slightly and gave Tyrone a closer inspection. "What you got in that box?"

"Candy. For my mama's church." He clutched the box a little tighter. He had placed the five-dollar bill inside.

"Your mama's church?" the man said incredulously. "What kind of a church prays with candy?"

"They *sells* it," Tyrone said firmly. "To fix the organ by Easter."

The man nodded slowly. "What's your mama's name, boy?"

"Bessie. Bessie Lewis."

"I knows Bessie Lewis. I knows 'bout everybody in this part of town."

"You does?"

"Sure do. The police chief made that part of my job. He says, 'Sam, if you is goin' to do *any* good at all lookin' out for them boys on the street, you've got to know their mamas and even where they live.'"

"You know where I lives?" Tyrone whined, his head cocked to one side.

"Yep. And it's not far from the church, neither. Get in, I'll ride you home."

Tyrone hesitated for a moment. He didn't know this man. He wasn't in uniform, although the car looked authentic enough. It even had a tiny aerial sticking out of the crack in the trunk door.

"Here," the man said. "take a look at this." He took a small imitation leather folder out of his shirt pocket and flipped it open. The badge was silver and said Birmington

Police Department. The identification card on the opposite side bore a picture of a man looking about the same, but a few years younger.

Tyrone squinted at the badge and nodded.

"That good enough?" the man asked. He was in his late thirties, clean-shaven, close haircut, good teeth. He wore a well-pressed blue suit and a starched white shirt open at the neck. His thick glasses slipped slightly on his large, thin nose.

"I guess so," Tyrone said, "but I don't live very far off."

"That don't make no never mind, boy. It's part of my job. I'm just doin' what the chief told me to." He leaned across the seat and opened the passenger side door. "C'mon," he said.

In the light of the open door, Tyrone could see the man's face better. He looked like all the rest of them cops, Tyrone thought.

"I'll even buy one of them candy bars," the man said.

Tyrone's eyes doubled in size. Six dollars! His mama would be *real* proud. "You will?" he asked, crossing in front of the car to come around to the passenger side.

"Sure will. Maybe two." The man leaned across the boy to help him pull the door closed. He smelled of some kind of aftershave Tyrone wasn't familiar with. It was the kind of smell you smell in big department stores where they have all those sample bottles open on the counter with little pumps sticking out of them just waiting to be squirted just once before the saleslady caught you. He and James had tried that at Rich's. James smelled funny for three whole days.

"This car don't have no radio," Tyrone said, adjusting himself to the passenger seat.

"Special unit," the man said almost secretively. "That way the bad guys don't know who we are."

"Oh," Tyrone said, unconvinced.

"You may have to tell me which block to turn," the man said, speeding across the parking lot. "I can't remember every single street down here."

Tyrone said "uh-huh" as he fumbled with the flaps on

the cardboard box in anticipation of his double sale. The man said nothing more.

After two or three fast miles and several turns that screeched tires, Tyrone looked out of the window more intently. The neighborhood was sort of strange to him. It was not his usual route home.

It was not his route home at all.

On Monday, they would find his body.

ABOUT THE AUTHOR

JOHN R. FEEGEL, like Michael Crichton and Robin Cook, holds an M.D. degree. In addition, he has a degree in law, and couples both areas of knowledge in his work as Associate Chief Medical Examiner in Atlanta. He is the author of three previous novels, one of which, *Autopsy,* was awarded an "Edgar" in 1976. His next novel, *Not a Stranger,* will be coming from NAL BOOKS in the Spring.

Ø

Recommended Reading from SIGNET